**Praise for Maggie McConnon's first
Bel McGrath mystery, *Wedding Bel Blues***

"McConnon has a surefire winner in Bel: a saucy, funny, flawed protagonist that readers are guaranteed to fall in love with."

—Susan McBride, *USA Today* bestselling
author of *Say Yes to the Death*

"Don't wait until St. Patrick's Day to read this delicious mystery! McConnon creates fetching characters drawn with warm humor and an authentic Irish voice. Bel McGrath will leave you smiling."

—Nancy Martin, *New York Times* bestselling
author of the Blackbird Sisters mysteries

"McConnon blends humor and intrigue like no other."
—Laura Bradford, author of *A Churn for the Worse*

"Spirited, fun, and as Irish as a shamrock, *Wedding Bel Blues* sparkles. A rollicking read."

—Carolyn Hart, *New York Times* bestselling
author of the Death on Demand mysteries
and the Bailey Ruth Ghost mysteries

"With dark family secrets, old flames, mysterious strangers and the odd dead body or two, McConnon has delivered a perfect blend of villainy and intrigue with laugh-out-loud witty one-liners and lashings of Irish bonhomie. A jolly good summer read."

—Hannah Dennison

# *Bel* OF THE BRAWL

## Maggie McConnon

St. Martin's Paperbacks

This is a work of fiction. All of the characters, organizations, and events portrayed in this novel are either products of the author's imagination or are used fictitiously.

BEL OF THE BRAWL

Copyright © 2017 by Maggie McConnon.
Excerpt from *XXXX* copyright © 2017 by Maggie McConnon.

All rights reserved.

For information address St. Martin's Press, 175 Fifth Avenue, New York, NY 10010.

ISBN: 978-1-250-07729-5

Our books may be purchased in bulk for promotional, educational, or business use. Please contact your local bookseller or the Macmillan Corporate and Premium Sales Department at 1-800-221-7945, ext. 5442, or by e-mail at MacmillanSpecialMarkets@macmillan.com.

Printed in the United States of America

St. Martin's Paperbacks edition / March 2017

St. Martin's Paperbacks are published by St. Martin's Press, 175 Fifth Avenue, New York, NY 10010.

10  9  8  7  6  5  4  3  2  1

*Dedication TK.*

# ACKNOWLEDGMENTS

TK

# CHAPTER *One*

When we were kids, we used to say that if heaven did indeed exist on earth, it had taken the form of Eden Island.

Set in the middle of the Foster's Landing River, a little tributary that flowed into the mighty Hudson, it was lush and green with spongy ground cover that protected the ecosystem below its surface. My friends and I knew the island well, had walked every inch of its pristine landscape, taking great care to remove the dead cigarette butts and empty cans from overnight expeditions that the local police department turned a blind eye to, mostly because they themselves—homegrown all—had spent a night or two there looking up at the stars, a little buzzed, marveling at both the good luck and the horrible misfortune they had to be growing up in a river town like Foster's Landing with everything and nothing to offer.

It had rained a lot the year I graduated from high school, so much so that Eden Island was the only one in the little cluster of islands still aboveground that year, but even there the water was creeping over the island's banks, closing over the edges of the little land mass, making its way toward the trees that sat in the center like a copse of sentries protecting their territory.

That early summer morning years ago, not long after our high school graduation, followed a night fuzzily remembered at best, when I was still a teen who forgot to wear sunscreen (much to my mother's chagrin), was always covered in bug bites, and wore a bathing suit under my clothes most of the time. That morning I woke up and turned onto my side, surprised to find myself outside and exposed to the elements. I could hear a little rumble of thunder in the distance and feel a light rain falling between the hanging leaves, the ones so low I could almost touch them. The moss beneath my cheek was cold and damp and provided a soft cushion for my throbbing head. My sweatshirt—FOSTER'S LANDING HIGH SCHOOL SWIM TEAM—was soaked through. I sat up, feeling the back of my head for a wound that I was sure was there but found nothing; this pain was just a result of having slept outside and having had maybe a go or two at the keg that some older kid had brought. This time, my usual go-to, a plate of greasy diner eggs and sausage, wouldn't allay the queasiness that the briny smell of the small river brought to my nose, nor the shakiness in my legs.

I looked around, alone in familiar surroundings but with a feeling of dread spreading icy tendrils through my limbs. "Hello!" I called out, wondering about the whereabouts of the rest of the usual quartet that accompanied me everywhere—Amy, Kevin, Cargan. The island wasn't big, maybe six hundred feet across, an eighth of a mile long, and a quick check of the perimeter on all sides told me that I was alone.

In those days, I wore Keds that were always threadbare, having been white and clean for about a week before my pinkie toe started to peek out from first the right one, then the left. They were beside me, soggy and soiled. I searched the pockets of my cutoffs and found a damp dollar bill and the key to my house but nothing else. I looked out across the northern edge of the island and stuck a tentative toe into the water: high tide. The water barely came up to my knees when I waded in, and determined to get home before the real rain came, the thunder rolling and rumbling closer to the spot where I stood, I strode across the expanse toward the other shore.

From the trees behind me, I imagined a rebuke. "Where you going, Bel?" they seemed to ask as they swayed and rocked in the wind, getting increasingly violent as the thunder reverberated, this time a little closer. I waded in deeper, my sneakers skidding and slipping on the rocks below. "Where you going, Bel?" the trees seemed to ask again, their cadence not unlike Kevin's when he'd asked me the same question the night before, the one that was buried in the deep recesses of my brain. Where I was, why he had asked, and where I had been going were all questions I couldn't answer. A thought went through my clogged brain, the synapses firing slowly but, in this case, deliberately.

I have to say I'm sorry, I thought, for the first, but not last, time.

The water was cold, colder than it should have been for June. It was all that rain making it chilly, bracing. Up to my thighs now, the water rushed from Sperry's Pond to the north, where rapids had stranded more than one overly brave kayaker out for a relaxing paddle on a gorgeous summer day, the kind of summer days that normally I lived for. I waded closer to the shore, turning back once to make sure I really had been alone on the island. My addled mind was playing tricks on me, and a place I loved was quickly turning into somewhere sinister and foreboding, a place that I needed to escape.

Finally, because it was easier, I began to swim, short strokes while bent at the waist, the current getting stronger, the wind picking up. The shore, which always seemed so close when I was on the island with my friends, seemed far away now that I was alone. Unreachable. I pushed through the water, my legs—short but swimmer's legs nonetheless—doing the work, my arms splashing at the water but really not helping my progress across the expanse. I pulled off my sweatshirt, noticing a purple handprint around my right bicep and Kevin's words as he caught me as I stumbled out of my kayak yesterday—"That'll leave a mark!"—ringing in my ears.

Where was everyone? Most importantly, where was Amy? I had left my best friend on the shore the night before, telling her she would be sorry and that I would never speak to her again, but a night on the beach, alone and wet, had convinced me that I had overreacted, that it hadn't been as bad as I thought. Maybe she hadn't looked at me the way I thought she had after kissing Kevin—my boyfriend—right in front of me. But the truth was that she had. I held on to the hope that Amy never would have ended the night without finding me first. We were a team. A duo. We were never apart.

Until now.

When I finally reached the shore, out of breath and soaked to the skin, a clap of thunder exploded directly overhead and the spot where I had lain just moments earlier was struck by a bolt of lightning so thick and sustained that I knew I would have been killed had I not awoken when I had. Something had roused me; I had no internal clock. Anyone who had seen the number of tardy markings on my report would know that I was never on time, ever. I looked back across at Eden Island, squeezing the water out of my sweatshirt and putting it back over my head.

Where *am* I going? I wondered.

I decided I didn't know.

I lay on the shore, looking at the murky sky overhead. It would be raining steadily soon but it didn't matter; I was already wet. Behind me, footsteps approached but I was too tired to be wary. The person crouched by my head and held out a hand.

"Ready to go home, Bel?" my brother asked, the sight of him bringing tears to my eyes.

"I had a horrible night, Cargan."

He had, too; he had been up all night. It was written on his face.

"I know," he said. "Let's go. Mom and Dad are worried sick. We've been looking for you for hours."

"I was right there," I said. "I was right where you left me."

He shook his head, his dark hair wet and flopping onto his forehead. "No. You weren't." He leaned over and hugged me, and the sound of a great sob—his or mine, I wasn't sure—disappeared in the latest clap of thunder. Over his shoulder, I spotted my other brothers—Arney, Derry, and Feeney—clamoring down the hill behind the Caseys' house toward the river, their voices loud and raucous, excited. I had been found.

In the distance, there were sirens and voices, coming together in a panic-filled cacophony. I looked at my brothers for the answer to the unspoken question, the worry on Cargan's face in particular still there in spite of the fact that I had been found.

Only Cargan spoke. "We found you."

There was something more, something ominous. It was written on his face.

One tear slid down his face. "But Amy Mitchell never came home."

It was a long time ago and I was a lot younger. Today, I sat at the edge of the water by Shamrock Manor, my parents' catering hall, and looked out, hoping that I would see her again. I knew I wouldn't; in my heart of hearts, I knew she was dead.

But still, all these years later, she was my sister from another mother, my confidante, my best friend. She was Amy Mitchell, the girl who never came home.

# CHAPTER *Two*

"Beets?" Gerard Mason, the groom-to-be, asked, sniffing the air as if just the mention of the root vegetable could produce an odor.

"No beets?" I asked, looking down at the handwritten menu that I had labored over for the past several days, a beet salad part of my entrée, adding a bit of color to an otherwise colorless meal—in my opinion anyway—of filet mignon and scalloped potatoes. It was a meal I could make in my sleep, even if for one hundred and fifty. Behind me, I could almost feel my mother's eyes boring into the back of my head, her words ringing in my ears: *We left the old country so that we wouldn't have to eat beets, Belfast. No beets!*

"I'm not a huge fan, but it's not a deal breaker," he said, smiling.

The bride looked at me expectantly. "And goat cheese? Will it have goat cheese?"

"It can," I said. "And candied walnuts, if you'd like."

The bride, Pegeen Casey, looked at her fiancé. "It sounds delicious, Gerry. I think we should do it."

I heard a door slam in another part of Shamrock Manor, whether by chance or on purpose, I wasn't sure.

Mom really had a thing against beets. And outdoor weddings. And off-the-shoulder dresses on brides. Something about the way the cake was cut. And a host of other things that I couldn't remember but which came to me every once in a while, in a rush, making my head spin.

Gerry looked at his bride-to-be. "Whatever you want, baby."

Good answer, Gerry, I thought. "Do you have any other special requests?" I asked, scanning my list. We had covered the cocktail hour and the main meal and that left the bar and the cake. "Any special requests for the bar? A specialty cocktail?" I asked, holding my breath. Seamus, our longtime bartender, was pretty one-note, that note being he could pull a pint like no one's business but everything else was up for grabs. He didn't know the difference between Chardonnay and Sauvignon Blanc and thought Merlot was something you got from a tick bite.

Pegeen Casey shook her head. "It's a pretty standard crowd, Belfast. Your bartender can handle pouring pints and a few hundred glasses of Chardonnay, can't he?" she asked, smiling. I loved a bride with a sense of humor; it made everything easier. Pegeen was as far from a "bridezilla" as one could get and I appreciated that.

"He can handle those two things," I said. "And the cake? Will we be making that for you?"

"I've ordered a cake from La Belle Gateau in Monroeville," she said. "Are you familiar with them?"

"Yes," I said. "Many of our couples use them for their cakes."

"Please tell me that they're good," Pegeen said.

"The best," I lied. Their icing was too dense and their

fondant flowers often required some emergency surgery after delivery. But Pegeen Casey didn't need to know that. Her wedding was in a week and I didn't want to add to her stress about the big day. I made some adjustments to the order sheet, signed it and handed her the original. "We're all set," I said. "If you think of anything in the meantime, please let me know and we'll do our best to make sure that everything is just the way you want it."

She smiled. "Thank you so much, Belfast. I was a little reluctant—"

Gerry interrupted her. "Yeah, who wants to have their wedding where a murder took place?"

She put her hand on her fiancé's arm. "You understand, don't you?" she asked. "It's nothing personal. Nothing against Shamrock Manor."

"I do," I said. "But that was a few months ago and it was really all just a tragic misunderstanding. I promise you that you'll be perfectly safe here and that your wedding day will go off without a hitch." I should have left well enough alone, but couldn't. "It's not like there is some crazed murderer running around Shamrock Manor."

Pegeen wrinkled her nose.

Shut up, Bel, I thought.

Gerry reached into his jacket pocket. "Well, if anything ever happens again, here's my card."

I looked at the card: "Gerard Mason, Private Investigator."

"I can't imagine that the Foster's Landing Police Department has the manpower to handle those types of investigations," he said.

I looked at him blankly, the idea that a private

investigator had fallen into my lap, just when I needed one, muddling my thoughts.

"A murder," he said. "Too much for the locals. Trust me on that one."

"Right. Yes," I said.

The local PD doesn't have the manpower or the investigative skills; he was right about that but the murder had been solved anyway.

"Love is all around at the Manor, huh?" Gerry asked, pointing out the window to the lawn where my brother Cargan was in an embrace with one of the banquet waitresses, a gorgeous girl named Pauline, an Irish girl just like her two coworkers. They exchanged a quick kiss, a peck on the lips really, but it was clear that there was something between them.

I laughed it off even though the sight of them came as a surprise. "Yes, the Manor has that effect on people."

"We're looking forward to the wedding so much," Pegeen said. "We've heard great things, murder notwithstanding," she said, trying to laugh it off even though it was no laughing matter.

"Well, thank you," I said. "But we won't be in need of a private investigator any time soon," I said, knocking on the molding surrounding the entrance to the dining room.

I led them into the foyer where a bust of Bobby Sands, Irish martyr and rebel for the cause, stood in the center. His poor, misshapen head not really resembling a head at all, he had become a "talking piece" as my father, the artist in question, described it. I hadn't met too many brides or grooms who wanted to talk about Bobby Sands or his distorted visage. "See you in a week," I said, holding the big front door open for them and watching them drive away.

Private investigator. That was a new one. Maybe I was lying just a bit when I said that I wouldn't be in need of a private investigator any time soon.

Maybe this was exactly the right time to be in need of one.

Too bad Gerard Mason ended up not being able to help me, his own wedding day being the last day he lived to see.

# CHAPTER *Three*

If you could judge the success of a wedding by how drunk the guests were, this one was our best ever at Shamrock Manor.

I went into the dining room and made my way toward the bar where Seamus, our longtime bartender, was doing his best to keep up with demand. "Seamus," I said. "Do you need help? I could pull Fernando, my de facto sous chef, from the kitchen and have him work back here for a bit."

The wedding, which I thought would be a rather staid affair even as Pegeen wagered that a lot of wine would be drunk, was looking more like a rager in a subterranean basement in hipster Brooklyn.

"I would love some help, Bel," Seamus said.

I started for the kitchen, stopping at the stage where my brothers played, pulling Cargan to the side. "Maybe it's time for some background music?" I said. "Take a break from the Latin beats?" I recognized the song that the band played as a Tito Puente song, more appropriate for a salsa dance than an Irish wedding.

"Good idea," Cargan said, and passed the word among the others, the members of the McGrath Brothers, Shamrock Manor's one and only house band. Before I hit the kitchen doors, a droopy-sounding Barbra Streisand tune was coming out in Feeney's tenor, disappointed murmurs coming from the emptying dance floor. I recognized it as a duet she had once done with the Bee Gees and wondered who was going to assume the falsetto role in this one. It didn't sound like there were any takers among the other song stylists in the band and Feeney made a go of it alone, singing his heart out about how he had nothing to be guilty of, that his love could climb any mountain.

On the dance floor, a man wearing a fedora indoors danced with the bride, while my mom stood in the corner of the room, her arms crossed, her face telegraphing what she thought of a guy wearing a hat in the dining room. The dancing couple was deep in conversation, and at one point Pegeen threw her head back and let out a raucous laugh, having fun at her own event, enjoying every minute.

The event that originally boasted one hundred and-fifty raucous guests was now quickly becoming a sight to behold if you were one of those people who enjoyed watching car wrecks happen in slow motion. If the reports coming in fast and furious from the dining room were true, if I didn't get the dinner service finished and follow it up quickly with the cake cutting, we were going to have a brawl on our hands.

I was a little off my game.

My father came into the kitchen, all piss and vinegar today, and snapped at the pretty Irish waitress standing by the expediting area.

"Colleen!"

"That's Pauline, Dad," I said, taking a damp dish

towel and wiping the edge of one of the plates to be served. "They have been here a long time. You need to get it straight. Pauline has dark hair, and Colleen is a blonde." And Pauline kisses Cargan when she thinks no one is looking.

"I'm Eileen," the girl said, and when I looked up, I saw that it was indeed Eileen and not Pauline or Colleen, the trio of servers at Shamrock Manor. "By the way, Mr. McGrath, the best man grabbed my ass."

"Language!" Dad said. "This is a wedding, not a rodeo."

"The best man grabbed my posterior, too, Mr. Mc-Grath," Pauline said, flicking her long ponytail over her shoulder; her look was definitely Irish Katy Perry. She looked as if she spent more time in my mother's Pilates studio than she did waiting tables, her legs long and lithe, her stomach taut and flat. Gracefully muscled arms hoisted a tray of plates with ease, despite the fact that she probably weighed only a buck twenty soaking wet, and it was not lost on me that even my married brothers—Arney and Derry—blushed a bit when she breezed by the stage as they were playing.

"Now, that's better," Dad said, not as concerned with the infraction at hand as he was with what he perceived as foul language. "Clearly, he is not the *best* man with that kind of behavior."

"Filet mignon all day, Bel," Pauline said, realizing she wasn't going to get anywhere with my dad. And what could he do exactly? Ask the best man in the middle of the wedding to unhand our serving girls? Dad was never good at handling conflict.

I kept it moving until there was no moving left to do. Everyone was fed; the girls had told me so. I leaned back against the counter and studied my hands, nicked from one knife that needed sharpening, an oily patch staining one of my palms. It wasn't fifteen minutes later that the boys—as my grown brothers were still called—started playing the song they always played when the bride and groom cut the cake, sensibly titled "The Bride Cuts the Cake and Then the Groom Cuts the Cake." Cargan had written it in the early days and they had never learned anything new to replace it.

As the bride and groom looked at each other adoringly, feeding each other cake with as much class and decorum as they could, their fingers covered with icing, Pauline came into the kitchen with another tray of dirty plates. "Pauline, where did this mushroom come from?"

She was flustered; it was the busiest time of the wedding, the clearing of plates, the serving of cake. "Who knows, Bel? Probably some rogue vegan out there brought their own food. Couldn't tolerate the thought of eating something prepared with butter or stock." She led me to the kitchen door to look out the window, pointing to a woman dressed in head-to-toe hemp or some other natural fiber, fair-trade sandals on her feet, her hair a mess of dreadlocks cascading down her back. "My money is on her."

The woman was twirling on the dance floor in a way to give Stevie Nicks a run for her money. She seemed to be enjoying another Barbra Streisand song immensely.

"I've seen it all, Bel. And spend a few more months here, and you will, too," Pauline said, pushing through the kitchen door and back into the dining room.

I followed her into the dining room to see how things were going in general. Every table appeared to be eating cake—the girls who worked for us were pros after all—and coffee was being poured at every seat, regardless of whether the guest wanted it or not. I was on my way to the restroom when the groom stopped me at the back of the dining room.

"Just wanted to tell you that this has been fantastic, Belfast," Gerry Mason said, putting a hand on my shoulder.

Gerry's card was in my pants pocket and I had been looking at it since we last met. Was I ready to take this step, take matters into my own hands? "Gerry," I said, "when this is over, I'd like to discuss something with you. If you don't mind?"

"Anything, Bel," he said. He wasn't as drunk as some of his guests but he was getting there, a high flush in his smooth, pale cheeks. "Whatever I can do for you. You have made me and Pegeen so happy today." He looked down at me, the picture of wedded bliss. "Why don't you tell me now? Then we can talk more when I get back from our honeymoon."

I looked around. Things were fairly under control if you didn't count the frenzy on the dance floor and the dozens of empty bottles of Chardonnay that were rolling around behind Seamus the bartender's feet. "I had a friend. My whole life. She disappeared when we were teenagers."

I knew this was a bad idea. Gerry's face clouded over and the previously happy groom was now concerned for me, someone who would say something like this on the happiest day of his life. I shook my head. "I'm sorry," I said. "This is the wrong time to be discussing this."

"I can help you, Belfast, but you're right, not now," he said, smiling sadly. "When I come back, okay?" He did a little jig to the music my brothers were playing. "I love a good case, though. What was your friend's name?"

"Amy Mitchell," I said.

It could have been my imagination—surely it was— but I thought I saw his face cloud over.

I waved a hand, trying to dispel the bad energy that I had brought to the conversation. "Forget it," I said. "Later. Enjoy your wedding." I winked. "And of course, your honeymoon."

I looked at him, a kind man with a happy wife, a woman who appeared to be having the time of her life at her own wedding, something we at Shamrock Manor always tried to achieve but rarely did. The food was cold. The beer was warm. The music was too loud. The speeches couldn't be heard. It had rained. But today, for the first time in a long time, people were drinking and laughing and dancing and having a ball.

I stood at the edge of the dance floor and watched Gerry Mason find his new wife, the center of his universe it would seem, kiss her heartily as people clinked the knives against the glassware, and spin her around the dance floor as my brothers started to play a disco number. Whatever we had done today was what we needed to do every time, the thought of murders past and my missing friend gone from my mind as I entered the center of my universe, my kitchen.

The walk-in was open and I mentally slapped myself; a few more minutes and the warm seeping into the cold would become a real problem. I headed over to it, starting to push the heavy door closed when I heard a happy groan, a giggle. The sound of my brother's name, Cargan, being whispered into the frosty air, the lilt of an

Irish brogue wrapping the word around the tongue of
its female owner.

I stepped back, leaving the door ajar, hoping that
whatever was going on in there didn't defrost my shrimp.
Behind me, Eileen and Colleen entered, leaving the
identity of the girl in the walk-in to be none other than
Pauline. I hurried the girls out of the kitchen with some
loud orders, letting my brother and his paramour know
that it was all clear, that it was safe to come out. When
I returned to the kitchen a few minutes later, Pauline
was leaning against the counter studying her manicure
and Cargan, an escape artist if there ever was one, was
back on the stage, his violin under his chin, beautiful
music coming from his instrument.

Like nothing ever happened. I would remember that
later when things started to fall apart.

The wedding winding down, Dad came into the
kitchen. "Good job, people," he said to the two of us.
"Mr. Casey was very happy with the event." He slapped
a fat envelope against his palm. "Time to divide the tip."

"Hold up, Dad," I said. "I need to visit the ladies
room."

The dining hall still held a smattering of guests, and
Eileen and Colleen were clustered together by one of the
big windows, deep in conversation. I put my fingers to
my mouth and whistled. "Big tip, ladies. Meet Mal in
the office."

I ducked into the first stall of the ladies' room and
fumbled with my chef's pants, the drawstring knotted
at my waist and bunching up beneath my fingers. "Damn
it to hell," I said as my bladder made its uncomfortable
presence known. I pulled my pants down forcefully, rip-
ping one side at the hip, and sat down. I thrust my hand

into the toilet-paper dispenser only to find that the Caseys and Masons, raucous and randy and a bunch of drunkards, had also used every square inch of toilet paper in this stall, which had been stocked to the rafters with tissue prior to the wedding. In the stall beside me, I heard a noise not unlike the air being let out of a balloon, but the stalls were so close together that I couldn't get a gander at the person's feet.

"Hey, a little help here?" I said "Could you pass me some toilet paper?" I asked, the request met by silence. I banged on the shared wall between the stalls. "Hello? Toilet paper?"

Nothing.

I rooted around in my pants pocket and found an old napkin that would do just fine. "Thanks for nothing." I said to the person in the next stall, landing on the thought that maybe they were one of the drunk Caseys, left behind to sleep off the liter of beer or wine they had consumed at the wedding. They weren't responding because they couldn't. That had to be the answer.

I went to the sink and washed my hands, studying my face in the mirror. Was I the kind of person who left a person, passed out cold, in a bathroom stall in a catering hall? I went back and forth in my mind and decided, ultimately, that I wasn't. I dried my hands and knocked on the door to the stall. "Hello? Do you need help?"

But whatever I had heard before, a little passing of air from someone's lungs, had ceased and all that was left was me listening to the hum of the air conditioner as it whirred to life above me, cold air rustling the hair that had fallen out of my head scarf. I pulled at the stall door, convinced it would be locked, surprised to find it wasn't. The door swung open, almost hitting the sink—another example of the architectural issues that existed at Shamrock Manor–and I took in the sight of our groom, his pants around his ankles, his face turning blue as he took what would be his last breath.

# CHAPTER *Four*

"It's like déjà vu all over again," Kevin Hanson said, rubbing his hand over the bust of Bobby Sands as if for good luck. He would need it. He wasn't the best detective I had ever met, but then again, the only detectives I knew were on TV, and most of them were mind readers, geniuses, and prognosticators. They would be a collective tough act to follow.

I had run screaming from the ladies' room, finding Cargan first. It was my favorite brother who called 911 and then constructed a story to keep the remaining wedding guests, along with the bride, from entering the back of the Manor and mucking up the bathroom, somewhere that Kevin would want to investigate, if only to figure out why a man was in the ladies' room.

I sat on the fourth step of the grand staircase in the foyer, holding my pants together. The rip that had occurred when I had forcefully pulled them off earlier had left me one false move away from being naked from the waist down, the underwear I had thrown on that morning not the kind you wanted other people to see.

Mom emerged from the office, a sewing kit in her

hand, which she shoved into my chest. "Here. There are safety pins in there," she said. "Stand up."

While I didn't want to do this in front of the entire Foster's Landing Police Department, it seemed I didn't have a choice. Mom hoisted me to my feet and pulled up my chef's coat, pulling my pants tight and pinning the two ragged edges of the waistband together after riffling through the sewing kit. "Thanks, Mom," I said, sitting back down on the step.

Dad raced through the foyer, passing Kevin, who grabbed his arm. "Mr. McGrath, and Mrs. McGrath, for that matter, this is potentially a crime scene," he said, asking Dad to take his place beside me. I think he was overstating that but since we had had a murder at the Manor not a few months before, I guess he was covering all of his bases. "All McGraths and McGrath employees. Stay where you are," he said, acting as if he were herding cats and not talking to a group of adults who could follow directions. Well, maybe he was right. We were the McGraths and following directions may not have been our area of expertise.

"It was a heart attack," Cargan called after Kevin. When Kevin ignored him, Cargan dropped his voice to a whisper. "Or an aneurysm."

That's what it looked like. Cargan had dragged Gerry Mason's body out of the stall and done CPR and mouth-to-mouth but it was too late. The guy was gone, his face going pale quickly, the light that had been in his eyes, just minutes earlier, starting to fade.

On the staircase with the rest of my family, I tried not to think about it. I looked around, hoping to find something else to take my mind off what I had seen. The boys were here, Feeney still wearing his guitar, and the waitresses and busboys were there, too, or so I thought. I looked behind me and saw Colleen and Eileen but no Pauline. I had seen her earlier when we assembled and now she was gone. I mouthed the question to Eileen. "Where's Pauline?" but she only shrugged in reply, her mouth set in a grim line, her arms crossed over her chest.

Something about her stance and Colleen's tear-filled eyes told me all I needed to know: they were nervous about the cops being here and not because there was a scintilla of suspicion on anyone's part that they had anything to do with Gerard Mason's situation. He had had a heart attack; that was clear. Or an aneurysm. Something that had happened quickly and without warning while he was in the ladies' room, a place he wasn't supposed to be. The girls had other secrets that they didn't want to share, namely of the immigration sort. I had always suspected, but now I knew.

The dining room doors swung open and a stretcher with the body of the dead groom in peaceful slumber atop it made its way through the foyer, pushed by an EMT.

Mom leaned over. "Is that EMT the McNulty boy?" she asked. "The one that punched Cargan during the CYO basketball championship in the fifth grade? For missing that foul shot?"

"I don't know," I hissed back. "Does it matter?"

"It does," she said in her stage whisper.

"That was thirty years ago, Mom," I said. "People change."

"Not that much," she said. "Little bastard."

But he was a big bastard now, and pretty adept at hoisting a stretcher into an ambulance.

When it was my turn to go into the office and give
the police a statement, I was glad that my mother had
pinned my pants so that I didn't have to manually hold
them up, but not delighted by how tight they were. My
muffin top was more of a soufflé hanging over my waistband and I asked if I could stand instead of sit, the
thought of folding myself into a chair in front of Mom's
desk, the desk at which Lieutenant D'Amato now sat,
making me light-headed.

"This is awful," I said. "How is the family doing?"

Kevin nodded. "We sent them to the station. Taking
it about as well as you'd expect."

"A crime scene? He had a heart attack or something.
I saw it with my own eyes." I looked at Kevin. "I don't
think this has anything to do with crime."

Kevin nodded. "Leave it to us, Bel. Given the history
of the Manor, we need to cover all of our bases."

"Our history is that there was one murder," I reminded him. "That's not much of a history."

"You don't think one murder is one more than necessary?" Kevin asked. "Now, anything else to tell us?"

I leaned against the wall and folded my arms. "I've
told you everything I know," I said, and I had. I left out
the part about no toilet paper but that was it. The rest had
all been revealed. The bathroom, the little breath of air
that had been released, the silence on the other side of
the stall otherwise.

Kevin was beside the lieutenant, sitting on the edge
of the desk. "Not that, Bel," he said.

"Then what?" I asked. "I've told you everything."

They looked at me expectantly and my mind flashed
on the events of a few days earlier, of Eden Island and
my missing friend, of the discovery, all these years later,

of some of her personal belongings. My mind went to the backpack that had been found, the sneakers alongside it, both coming to the surface when the current drought depleted the river of most of its water. It was different now than it was then; whereas that spring had brought us torrential rain, something that had hidden Amy's belongings, dragging them down into the depths, this summer had brought drought and, with it, the opening of a case long closed.

I also thought of Brendan Joyce, the guy who had pulled me out of my funk upon my return to the Landing. Everything was going so well, and then that afternoon, one minute he had been beside me and the next he was gone. I hadn't heard from him since but I kept that inside, not wanting Kevin to see the disappointment on my face, the fact that I realized that when the going got tough, Brendan Joyce got going.

It had been such a gorgeous day, Brendan and I sitting by the river, enjoying each other's company, when our reverie was interrupted by the police, some firefighters, and what turned into a massive investigation.

"I told you," I said. "Everything I told the cops all those years ago still applies. We had a party on Eden Island. Amy and Kevin," I said, not looking at Detective Kevin Hanson, now a man, "kissed." The lieutenant and Kevin looked at the ceiling, the ground, anywhere but at me. Each other. Kevin was in a long-term relationship with the lieutenant's daughter and even though what had happened had been a long, long time ago, it was still uncomfortable. I left out the part where my best friend had looked at me like she had finally done the one thing she had been waiting her whole life to do. "We were teenagers. I got mad. Amy and I had words.

I don't remember much after that except that I woke up, alone, on the island, and had to practically swim to shore because there had been so much rain and the river was so full."

Lieutenant D'Amato, Kevin's boss and, with any luck for Mary Ann D'Amato, his future father-in-law, looked at me sadly. "There must be something else, Bel," he said. "Anything." He rubbed his hands over his five-o'clock-shadowed cheeks. "Maybe you remember something else?"

I shook my head. "I wish I could help you, but I can't." I studied my hands, the scars from the little nicks that I had sustained over the years, the faded burns dotting my knuckles, the price paid for doing what I loved. Inside, there were scars, too, of the emotional variety, but I didn't let anyone see those. "What's next?"

Kevin spoke for the first time since we had entered the office. "We'll send people out there to see if they can find something else. Canvass the area again. Ask more questions."

It all made sense. But it wouldn't help. "She's dead" I wanted to say but didn't. "You'll never find her" I wanted to add. Instead, I asked, "Are we done here?" When neither of them answered, I added, "I don't have anything else to say."

Lieutenant D'Amato stood and looked at me, his hands shoved deep into his pockets. "Okay, Belfast," he said. "We may need a statement. You may want to bring your brother."

I laughed. "Which one?" Did he mean Derry, who was still angry over Cargan doing a quick segue into a reel instead of a jig during the wedding, or Feeney, who was dating a manager at Old Navy who wrote songs

called "My Love Is Deeper than a Bad Paper Cut"?
Surely he didn't mean Cargan, who up until a few months
prior I had assumed was a professional musician, not
an undercover cop. Using my powers of deduction, I
finally figured it out. "You mean Arney? The divorce
attorney?" I didn't add that he wasn't a very good one
at that.

"Well, yes," the lieutenant said, dead serious. "You
know, just for support."

"No, thank you." I started for the back door, holding
it open. "I don't need support."

But that night, when they were gone, and I was all
alone in my apartment next to Shamrock Manor, I realized I did need support, the walls closing in, the thoughts
of my best friend and her whereabouts only one of the
things I could think of when I closed my eyes, the other
being the sight of a newly married man, happier than
he had ever been it seemed the life in him draining out
on the floor, falling onto my feet.

# CHAPTER *Five*

Ah, Sundays. The Day of Our Lord. A day of rest. A day for a drive up the river to a quaint little town where brunch is on the menu, Bloody Marys flowing. In my family, though, it was a day that was different, a day in which none of the things I would like to do with my Sunday were done. It was a day for the weekly McGrath family dinner, which was neither a day of rest nor reminiscent of our Lord; it was when my entire family got together to talk about the wedding the day before and ruminate on past hurts, recriminations coming to the fore of every conversation.

Over Mom's lamb, everyone was subdued, tired of hearing of death at the Manor, wearied of seeing Kevin Hanson in his sport coat, writing little notes in a notepad that he probably hashed over when he was back at the station house.

My mother's sister, Aunt Helen, was there, as was her daughter and my first cousin, Caleigh, a bride herself only a few months before, a guest having been accidentally murdered by Aunt Helen's boyfriend, Frank, during the reception. It was still a bit uncomfortable for all of us, particularly me. As I watched Dad assess Caleigh's growing belly, a mosquito bite of a bump really, a "honeymoon baby" gestating inside, all I could think about was Caleigh having slept with the murdered guest two nights before the wedding and wondering just what the little tyke would look like when it emerged from her womb.

We sat around the table, everyone picking disconsolately at their lamb and roasted potatoes. Aunt Helen, in her inimitable way, broke the tension with a question.

"So, Oona, another death at the Manor," she said, delicately patting the sides of her mouth with her napkin. "How will you continue booking events?"

"Give them away for free, obviously," Feeney said, looking at my father. Dad was the king of the discount and that usually meant that the band, first and foremost, got stiffed. They were family after all and Dad felt as if they could be the first to take the financial hit.

"Now, Feeney, that is not true," Mom said, putting her own napkin atop her plate of unfinished food, her appetite gone. "We only cut the Casey wedding by ten percent."

"It is true and it's not good," Feeney said. "Do you know how hard we work?"

It was an old, familiar rant. The boys had worked hard but at this point in their long collective career, they were kind of mailing it in, Cargan's reinvention of old classics taking predictable turns, the other brothers reluctant to learn anything new.

"And didn't we get a huge tip?" Derry asked.

"Yes. Ten grand," Dad said, the only family member unaffected, at least appetitewise, by the previous day's

tragedy. He shoveled a forkful of food into his mouth
and we waited while he chewed and swallowed. "We'll
settle that up this week."

"That's the biggest tip we've ever gotten, Dad," I said.
"Mr. Casey is that wealthy?"

"He is," Dad said, helping himself to another glass
of Malbec, this one brought by Caleigh, who smiled de-
murely when Dad said how much he was enjoying it.
"Import/export."

"What does that even mean?" I asked. "What does
he import?"

"Yeah, and even more, what does he export?" Derry
asked, fancying himself the business brain in the group.

"I don't know," Dad said, already tiring of the conversation. "And I don't care. All I know is that up until
that poor lad had a heart attack or whatever it was, the
family was happy with everything at the Manor. And
that's what's most important to me."

Cargan pulled a phone from his pocket and started
poking at it. "No phones at the table, Cargan," Mom
said as if she were talking to a teenager and not a adult
male.

Cargan held the phone in front of my face and there
it was: Casey Import/Export. A very unoriginal name
for what was apparently a very unoriginal business.
They imported Irish food—tea, butter, blood pudding
and the like—and exported New York City trinkets, the
I LOVE NEW YORK T-shirt being most popular, it would
seem. Pegeen Casey and James Casey were featured
prominently on their Web site, the toothsome pair standing beside a large ship on the water in an East Coast
port, looking tanned and responsible.

"Well, I would definitely import or export with them,"

I said, making my serious brother break out into a smile. "They look very capable of importing and exporting."

"Cargan. Phone," Mom said, motioning with her hand. "Put it away."

"Casey?" Caleigh asked. "Import/Export?"

We all turned and looked at her. "Yes," I said. "Did they import something for you?"

"No," she said. "I know Pegeen Casey. We are in the same chapter of the Junior League."

"Of course you are," Feeney said. "And did you fund-raise for the same animal shelter?" he asked, sarcastic as usual.

"As a matter of fact, we did!" Caleigh said, brightening at the thought of her well-heeled friend. "She's lovely. But I haven't seen her images. She's missed several meetings."

"And the husband?" I asked. "Gerry? Did you ever meet him?"

"I did," Caleigh said. "Lovely man. Gerard? He's the one who died?"

"God rest his soul," Dad said.

"Afraid so," I said.

"Oh, I feel so bad," Caleigh said. "He adored Pegeen. As he should. Should have, I mean. She's wonderful." She looked down at her belly as if to confirm Pegeen's wonderfulness. "She'll be snatched up in a second," she said.

"As if that's what she's thinking about, Caleigh," Feeney said. "Getting married a few days after losing her own husband at her wedding."

He rarely makes a good point, but I had to give him that.

While the family talked among themselves about

Gerard Mason and his unfortunate demise, I turned to Cargan, whispering in his ear. "The girls say that James Casey is Irish mafia."

Cargan turned toward me. "Really?" He went back to his food. "That's interesting," he said, forking some lamb into his mouth. "But probably not true."

We went back to eating in silence for a few minutes until Mom spoke again. "So, Caleigh. The subway tile in the guest bathroom. How is that coming along?"

Caleigh was thrilled that someone was asking about her suburban home renovation. "It's fabulous, Aunt Oona. Just like you would see in a 1920s home."

"You always have had such wonderful style, Caleigh," Mom said, giving me a pointed glance. I lived in an apartment over my dad's art studio that was in serious need of renovation but I didn't know how that was my fault.

At the other end of the table, Derry groaned. Caleigh's status as best family member ever was a bone of contention and the one thing that bound my brothers and me together.

"Well, thank you, Aunt Oona," Caleigh said. "Your opinion means so much to me." She looked around the table. "I can't wait to have you all down for dinner."

"Yes, Oona," Helen said. "We were thinking . . ."

"Uh-oh," Derry said around a mouthful of potatoes.

Helen shot him a look. "Yes, we were thinking that maybe we would shake things up? Move Sunday dinner around the family? Have it at different homes?"

My brothers and I turned to stone, Arney's fork halfway to his mouth when he became paralyzed. Move Sunday dinner? That was sacrilege. We sat in terrified silence as we waited for Mom's answer.

"Well, Helen, you know . . ." Mom started, losing

steam and falling silent. She wasn't going to do this in front of everyone, but if I were Aunt Helen, and thank the Lord Jesus that I'm not, I'd be scared. Mom was simmering, her blood slowly coming to a boil. She was the grande dame, not Helen. And Helen had best not forget that.

Helen continued. "It's just that Frank . . ."

Frank. The guy who had shoved one of Caleigh's wedding guests over the balcony at the Manor a few months earlier. It always came back to "poor Frank" and "everything he had been through." I liked Frank well enough but I really wasn't jonesing to spend any more time with him than necessary. He had killed a guy in a ham-fisted attempt at chivalry but, ultimately, in cold blood. I really didn't think we needed to spend more time together than absolutely necessary.

Mom put her fork down. "Yes, Helen, I understand. He's under house arrest, he wears an ankle monitor, he can't leave. I get all of that." Frank had had a great attorney, one not named Arney McGrath. Mom looked at her sister; the case was closed. "Sunday dinner will remain here. We'll see Frank when he is no longer incarcerated."

"He's not incarcerated," Helen said.

"Well, he kind of is," Derry said. "And he kind of killed someone."

Helen threw her napkin down on her plate and stood. "Well, I'll let him know how terribly concerned you all are about his well-being. Caleigh, let's go." She started for the door.

Caleigh looked at all of us, an apology almost making its way from her brain to her lips before her mother shut her down. "Caleigh. Now."

Dad stood, the soft touch among the more hard-hearted. "Helen, please. Don't leave like this."

"Mal, this is between my sister and I," Helen said.

Together, my brothers and I shouted, "Me!", all having been taught by nuns who believed that diagramming sentences was the only way to learn good grammar. Mom shot us daggers as she stood, going into the foyer of our family home to talk to her sister, try to smooth things over. It was only moments later that we heard the front door slam.

Feeney looked across the table at me. "Import/export. We import family and export hard feelings."

# CHAPTER *Six*

Brendan Joyce finally surfaced and I had mixed emotions. I hadn't seen him since the day at the river, a little over a week ago now. My heart fluttered still at the sight of him but, at the same time, his physical absence had me perplexed. Sure, there had been texts but it wasn't the same.

Monday morning, while I prepped in the kitchen, the one place that had not been designated a "crime scene" (it was a heart attack, I wanted to scream . . . or something) and open for my use, he made an appearance, his curly hair wet and plastered against his head. His navy oxford brought out the blue in his eyes and his tie looked as if it had been hastily done, the narrow part sticking out from under the fatter top piece.

I didn't look up from the pasta I was hand rolling. "Shouldn't you be at school?" I asked. His texts to me indicated that he was spending so much time at the high school, getting ready for the Fall Art Show, that he was "knee-deep in alligators," an expression he had picked up from me.

"I should," he said, his voice still tinged with a hint of the old country, the place he had lived until he was a teen and had landed in Foster's Landing. It was one of the things that had first attracted me to him; that and that he wasn't my ex-fiancé. He was quiet and kind and small-town, all of the things that Ben Dykstra hadn't been; that appealed to me after my life in the city and its downward spiral. "I wanted to see you."

"Bad timing." I cut the pasta into gnocchi pillows. "Another bad stretch here at the Manor."

"I heard something about that. What happened?"

"Groom didn't make it to the end."

"Dead?"

"Yep," I said. "He was carried out by the EMTs on a stretcher. If he was having second thoughts about getting married, that was a pretty dramatic way to handle it."

The blood drained from his face. "That's awful. Where did it happen? Not in the middle of the reception, I hope."

"No, ladies' room. I found him," I said. "Not sure why he was there."

"What happened?"

"Heart attack, they think." Jeez, you have one murder at a wedding and suddenly you're the Hall of Death.

He chewed on that for a minute. "Nice guy, the groom?"

I thought back to my few interactions with Gerry Mason and decided that yes, he was. I thought, too, of Pegeen's face when Cargan shepherded her to the ambulance, still in her wedding gown and climbing up with my brother's help into the back of the vehicle. "Yes, he was," I said. "Where've you been, Joyce?"

"I told you, Bel. School." He ran a hand through his wet hair. "Start of school is busy."

"Where'd you go? That day?" I asked. "You left me . . ." What? Alone? Hanging? Without a friend? There was no end to that sentence that didn't sound pathetic so I let it go. The last time we had been together had been that day Amy's things had been found, me wading into the river to see what the police had found beneath its now-shallow depths and him leaving without letting me know he was gone. I didn't know, for the past days, whether he was gone for good or gone for just a little while, but it didn't matter: he had left and taken with him any trust that we had built up over the course of our short, but intense, relationship. Whereas we had been spending nearly part of every day together in the summer and leading up to the new school year, we hadn't seen each other in what for me—for us—was a long time.

"I'm sorry," he said. "It was wrong of me."

"It was," I said. "I thought that maybe we were done."

He looked stricken at the thought. "Done? You and me?"

"What else would I have thought?"

He chewed on that for a minute, decided I was right. "I'm sorry. That's all I can say. I was scared."

"Scared?"

He looked as if he were choosing his words carefully, wondering how to put it. He finally decided just to blurt it out. "I didn't like it, Bel. I didn't like it one bit," he said.

"What? Didn't like what?" I asked.

"The river. The stuff they found. What it made me remember."

I put down my knife and looked up. "What did you remember?"

He shook his head. I noticed that the water from his freshly shampooed head had soaked the collar of his ironed oxford. I grabbed a clean dish towel from the rack by the sink and put it around his neck, soaking up as much wet as I could. I resisted the urge to wrap my arms around his waist, lay my head against his back, and feel the warmth coming from him. To drink in the scent of a guy I had fallen for, hard.

"Remember what?" I asked again.

"Nothing," he said, shaking his head again. "Everything."

"What does that even mean?" I asked, wringing the towel out in the sink. "Nothing? Everything?"

"I don't expect you to understand, Bel," he said. "I know you were there. I know you saw her last."

"Did you also know that I woke up on that island alone that day and that all of my friends had left me? If you knew that, you never would have left me there last week. You never would have left and not called me to let me know you were okay." I thought of the text messages and the voice mails I had left him and wondered why I had only heard about school, the Fall Art Show. "Or what you were thinking."

He was silent. Contrite even. He looked down at his shoes, nice tie-up shoes for work, shined to a high gloss. "You don't know because you left here when it happened. It changed everything. It changed this town."

"I was here long enough to know that, Brendan. I know how everything changed. I know how everyone was sad and nervous and wondering just where she had gone. That wasn't lost on me before I left." I started cutting up some carrots, leaving the pasta to the side of the prep table. Lots to do before the following Saturday's wedding and not a lot of time. I was doing a carrot soup as an appetizer, little shooters in Shamrock Manor shot glasses, and for at least a hundred and fifty guests, that was a lot of carrots. "I also remember how everyone treated me and sometimes it wasn't nice. So, you can forgive me if I'm not sympathetic to how you felt after everything that happened."

He stayed silent for a minute while I chopped carrots. "You're right," he said finally. "You're right to feel that way."

I didn't need his validation of my feelings. I changed the subject. "Now, you can either stay and help me cut these carrots or you can go to school," I said. It sounded harsh. "Obviously, I'd prefer if you'd stay and help me cut these carrots but I would understand if you wanted to leave."

He smiled. "I do have a job to go to."

I wanted to believe him. I had fallen hard for him just a few months ago and had already spent nights wondering if he was Rebound Man, Mr. Right, or Mr. Right Now, all categories in some ridiculous women's magazine that Mom had left in the office and that I had purloined for bedtime reading. I didn't have any female friends in Foster's Landing to ask whether or not I had become so crazy about him because of my bad choice in attaching myself to my former fiancé, Ben, a choice that had led to a called-off wedding and a lost job. I finally decided after taking as many quizzes as I could find on the topic that I was truly, deeply in love with this guy, only to get let down again. This all went through my head as I stood in the kitchen, a pile of chopped carrots under my hand, my eyes trained on his face.

"Can we get past this?" he asked, moving toward me, his arms outstretched.

"We can," I said. "Just never do that again." I stared up at him. "I was scared, too, Brendan."

He stopped just before taking me in his arms, not because of what I had said but because of the appearance of Mom, who waltzed into the kitchen, fresh from one of her Pilates classes, wearing leggings and a form-fitting shirt with some kind of Indian Sanskrit on it. It was hard having a mother who made the boys blush but, then again, I'm just lucky that way. Brendan didn't seem to know where to look, so he studied the ceiling. It was a lot to take in, a woman Mom's age with a body like that. A woman any age, really.

"Oh, Brendan," Mom said. "Lovely to see you, lad. How's your mom?"

"Grand, thank you, Mrs. McGrath."

"Call me Oona," she said for at least the fiftieth time. But we all knew he wouldn't. "Please give her my best." She looked him up and down, taking in the wet collar. "Is it raining?"

"No, just in a rush," he said, touching his hair instinctively.

"Oh. So I guess you heard about the unpleasantness here at the Manor over the weekend?" she asked, all brisk efficiency, bustling around the kitchen, putting a fork away here, replacing a knife to the block here. "Horrible, I tell you. We're going to have to do a lot of damage control after this one. And I don't know how we're going to use the ladies' room on Saturday if the police still don't want us to use it."

I guess "unpleasantness" was one way to describe it. Mom studied the prep table. "And what's happening here?" she asked, picking up a can of coconut milk, one of the ingredients for my soup. "And this? Coconuts?"

"Coconut milk, Mom," I said. "Trust me. It will be delicious."

"Trust me," Mom repeated. "I hear that at least once a week. Mr. McByrne is still calling about the caviar that he inadvertently ate."

"What did he think he was eating?" I asked. "Caviar is generally pretty identifiable. And I'm sure the girls described the dish while serving it." That last part was unclear; as many times as I had instructed Eileen, Pauline, and Colleen about the finer points of serving a banquet meal, including the passed hors d'oeuvres at the cocktail hour, they had their own way of doing things, some of which included making things up as they went along. I had recently discovered that when serving my lovingly prepared Manchego squares with fig jam, they had called the bite-sized appetizers "cherries jubilee."

Sometimes I wondered how long I'd last here.

Mom was on a tear. "Capers, Belfast. He thought he was eating tiny green capers. That were, for some reason, black. Rotten, perhaps."

I shut my mouth before I could ask "Who eats rotten capers?" but Brendan Joyce wasn't as smart as I was. He asked for me.

Mom glared at him but didn't respond, putting the can of coconut milk down on the table. "And that was exotic enough for him. Caviar? Not what he bargained for."

"But he loved it," I reminded her. I remember seeing the old guy shoving them into his mouth as if he were eating his last meal.

"I'd like to taste this soup before we go forward," she said, exiting the kitchen.

I looked at Brendan. "See what I have to put up with?"

"Will you make me carrot soup sometime?" he asked.

I considered that. Would I? I was still smarting from his retreat the other day, his silence the next. I had sworn to myself that I wouldn't be a pushover anymore when it came to men—this man—but before I could think about it further, I blurted out, "Sure. You'll love it."

"I'm sorry, Belfast," he said. "There's not much more I can say, no way I can really explain myself."

As I watched him walk away, I wondered about that. I think there was plenty more for him to say, but did I want to hear it?

When I was alone in the kitchen again, Mom working on the computer in the adjacent office the only sound I could hear, I dug my phone out of my pocket and dialed Pauline's cell. I had texted her several times but had gotten no response and I hadn't seen her since before I had discovered Gerry Mason collapsed. Kevin had seemed mildly concerned with her absence during our group interrogation after the wedding but I didn't know if he had found her in the interim. I hadn't yet brought up my concern to Cargan, and the look on his face, as always, was inscrutable when it was clear yesterday that she had vanished after the wedding. But the girls' faces, coupled with Pauline's unceremonious departure, had me concerned.

I listened to the phone ring and ring but when it was clear that no one would answer, I hung up.

She was in the wind. I was sure of that. I just didn't know why.

# CHAPTER *Seven*

My father had decided that a midweek check-in on the preparation for the upcoming wedding was necessary to make Shamrock Manor "run like a clock." Heck, even a broken clock is right twice a day, right? We all came from different parts of the Manor, our tasks relegated to specific areas in the big mansion. The waitresses did other jobs at the hall during the week, mostly cleaning and ironing so everyone was present and accounted for. I grabbed Eileen as we walked toward the dining room, asking her if she had seen Pauline.

"No," she said. "And neither has Colleen. And they're roommates."

I didn't know that. "Really? How long?"

"Long time," she said. "Colleen says she hasn't seen her since the Casey wedding and she's worried, Bel." She grabbed my arm. "Do you think . . . ?" she asked, trailing off.

"That she was picked up? Deported?" I asked.

Eileen clapped a hand over my mouth. "Don't say it."

"Well, that's what you're worried about, right?" I asked. "Deportation?"

Her look told me everything, wild and panicked.

"Deportation is the best thing that could happen. She might be in a detention center. Awful places," she said, shuddering.

"But why?" I asked. "How? If she was picked up, then certainly you might have been, too, right?" Around us, everyone was assembling in the dining room and Dad was gearing up for his talk. We didn't have much time to talk further about the situation.

"I don't know, Bel." She started for one of the banquet tables, stripped of its soiled tablecloth, the top scarred after years of use. "All I know is that she had a lot going on here and wouldn't just leave." She turned back and looked at me. "Unless she had to. Was made to."

Dad took his place on the stage where the boys normally played, actually using the microphone even though his voice at its normal timbre was as close to a foghorn as one could get. He could be heard for miles.

The mic whistled an ugly feedback in response to Dad's welcome to the crew.

"You've got a hot mic there, Dad!" Feeney shouted out, despite the fact that he was sitting not ten feet from the stage.

Dad fiddled with the mic for a few minutes before giving up and placing it on top of one of the unplugged amps. "Can you hear me now?" he asked.

Montreal could hear him. And maybe St. Petersburg. The one in Russia, not Florida.

He clapped his hands together. "Well, we've had some unpleasantness here at the Manor."

"Again," Arney said.

"Yes, Arney, again," Dad said. Suffice it to say that it seemed that no good came from having your wedding at my parents' historical mansion. And when all was said and done, the first deceased party guest a few months earlier turned out not to have had a good heart or soul and made trouble for just about everyone with whom he had come in contact.

"And the families this weekend," I said, looking at the information sheet in front of me to refresh my memory of the happy couple. "The O'Connells and the Smiths are still on board to have their wedding here?" I asked the obvious question, the one no one ever seemed to want to ask.

"Well, yes," Dad said, nodding vigorously. "They are delighted to have their special event here at Shamrock Manor."

"And what did you discount them, Dad?" Cargan asked.

Dad blustered a moment or two before spilling it. He chose not to say it into the mic, hoping we would miss it. "Forty percent."

The boys went crazy. Cutting the price forty percent impacted their bottom line significantly. Me? Well, I wasn't getting paid that much to begin with so it was all the same to me. I was happy not to lose the business. One more deceased patron here and we'd be shutting our doors for good.

Dad ignored the chaos in the room and continued, his voice carrying over the cacophony of disappointed and outraged staff members. "As a result of the events last weekend, the ladies room is not usable for the time being so we're going to have to come up with a plan to make sure our one hundred and fifty upcoming guests have proper facilities to use, particularly our female guests."

We looked at each other. This wouldn't be an easy fix.

"So, Belfast," Dad said, looking at me. "We'll need to give them access to your apartment."

My mind went to the pile of laundry on the floor, the hole in the ceiling that had never been fixed. The ring around the tub. Housekeeping, it should be said, was not my strong suit, and Mom had just given up, having not made her usual clandestine visits to my abode in several weeks. Cargan looked at me and mouthed "I'll help you."

"And girls," Dad said, looking at Eileen and Colleen. Pauline, of course, had failed to show for the meeting. "We'll need to devise some kind of system for allocating two stalls in the men's room for the ladies. Put your thinking caps on."

The two girls looked at each other and then back at my dad.

"Where's the other one?" Dad asked.

"The other who?" Derry asked.

"The other girl. The dark-haired one."

We all looked at each other; I, for one, was surprised that Dad had noticed. When no one responded, he went back to the matter at hand: toilets. He looked at all of us, impatient. "You're creative!" he bellowed. "Make it happen."

Cargan spoke up. "Um, Dad. May I make a suggestion?"

"I'm all ears, lad. What is it?"

"Why don't we turn the men's room into the ladies' room just for this one day? Until everything is sorted out?" he said. "There are usually more women than men who need to use the restroom, generally, so it might be a good idea." Before his brothers could protest, Cargan held up a hand. "And you all can use my bedroom en suite."

"What the hell is an en suite?" Feeney asked.

"An attached bathroom," Cargan said.

"Better than what I have," Feeney said. "I have a shoilet."

"A shoilet?" Mom asked.

"A shower and toilet combination," he said. Feeney lived in a converted sugar factory in the middle of town, one that promised to include high-end features like a gym and a spa when completed but whose developers had run out of money prior to the last phase of construction. As a result, my brother had bought his condo for a song but had few of the promised amenities beyond the one parking space for the boys' band tour bus.

Mom turned away, repulsed. "I don't even want to know."

Dad considered Cargan's idea and finally pronounced it brilliant. "Yes. We'll have the men use Belfast's apartment and the women use the restroom. The lot of you," he said, waving a hand toward the rest of the staff, "will use Cargan's . . . en suite." He consulted a piece of paper in his hand. "Belfast. Your turn. What's on the menu?"

I cleared my throat, the list in my hand. This wasn't going to go well; I could feel it. "Well, for the cocktail hour, we'll do pigs in a blanket," I said, looking at Dad who nodded positively, "scallops wrapped in bacon, a cheese platter, chicken satay . . ."

"Chicken satan?" Derry asked. "What in God's name is that?"

"Satay," I said. "Satay. It's chicken on a skewer with a peanut dipping sauce."

Feeney gagged audibly. "Sounds atrocious."

I ignored them, continuing. "And carrot and coconut

soup shooters." I caught Mom, out of the corner of my
eye, rolling her eyes to the ceiling. "It's new. It's different. And it uses some of our tried-and-true ingredients
in a new way. Like carrots." I looked at the rest of the
staff hopefully. Only Colleen, the most positive of our
serving staff, nodded agreeably. "And for dinner," I continued, "prime rib of beef, au jus, scalloped potatoes, and
a beet salad with goat cheese."

"No goat cheese, Belfast," Mom said. "And no beets."

"It's a major component of the dish," I said, and before
she could protest further, added, "and the bride requested
it. The Caseys and the Masons loved it!"

Mom was unconvinced but the subject was tabled by
the arrival of Kevin Hanson. He stood in the doorway
and listened to my father expound on the finer points of
cocktail service, directed at our longtime bartender,
Seamus O'Dea, who had a hard enough time finding
Shamrock Manor after thirty years behind the bar, never
mind trying to figure out how to make some of the newer
drinks that people requested such as Cosmopolitans—
so out that they were back in again—and any number
of the things one could do with a small-batch bourbon.
Seamus poured pints and glasses of wine and made a
mean Manhattan but when it came to anything else, he
was a bit adrift.

"Belfast!" Dad bellowed. "You'll help Seamus, girl,
won't you?"

"I'm a chef, Dad, not a bartender." I looked over at
Kevin, a smile playing on his lips. We had been friends
since childhood; none of the histrionics that my family
displayed were news to him. He was used to Dad's bluster and Mom's tough-girl routine and my brothers' inability to find their collective way out of a paper bag. I

held up a finger and motioned that I would need a minute.

"And Arney," Dad said. "What new tunes do we have for the wedding?"

Arney punted to Derry and Cargan. "Yeah, what new tunes do we have?"

Cargan straightened. "I wrote a new reel and we have a jig that segues nicely from 'Celebration' by Kool and the Gang."

"Very good, lads," Dad said. He consulted a list he had written and stuffed into his pants pocket. We covered serving etiquette, length of the cocktail hour, length of the meal, and how to handle an unruly cake-cutting, as we had witnessed at the previous wedding. We didn't discuss what to do when you found someone slumped over in the toilet. That was not on the agenda. "Do not engage if they start smashing cake into each other's faces!" Dad cautioned. "Keep your distance!"

"Unless the police need to be called, and then we can make that decision as needed," Mom said. She looked toward the door. "Detective Hanson, would you agree with Malachy's and my assessment of what to do when the cutting of the cake goes awry?"

Kevin hadn't been expecting to be part of the conversation regarding proper behavior at Shamrock Manor but he rose to the challenge. "Well, yes, Mrs. McGrath, by all means please call us if you feel the situation is getting out of control. That's why we're here."

"Our tax dollars at work," Feeney said, though I was pretty sure he hadn't paid a village tax in over three years. "What are you doing here anyway, Hanson?" There was no love lost between my brothers and Kevin Hanson. Our tumultuous relationship and subsequent breakup had seen to that. Ever hear of Irish Alzheimer's? You forget everything except the grudges. My brothers made that old joke the truth.

"Good question," Derry said. "Didn't we answer every question you had for us the other day?"

"You did," Kevin said, walking into the ballroom. He was still dressed for work, though his tie was stuffed into the pocket of his sport coat. Clearly he had stopped by on his way home but why was still the question. "By the way, you can use the ladies' room this weekend. I think our work there is done. It's no longer a crime scene. Just wanted to let you know."

"Well, thank the Lord," Dad said, making a sign of the cross. "So we don't have to use anyone's bathroom, en suite or . . ." he said, stopping and searching for the correct word, "*shoilet*. Thank you, Detective. I feel much better."

Next to me, Colleen and Eileen looked around, trying to affect airs of nonchalance without success. They hurried off, not making eye contact with anyone before leaving.

I grabbed Cargan before he left the room. "Have you seen Pauline?" I asked, getting a sad head shake in response and a quickened step to get away from me. He wasn't talking but that wasn't odd behavior for him. But he was blushing and that was some kind of sign; I didn't know what that meant but I could guess.

A man was dead, a waitress was missing, and I seemed to be one of a trio of people—the girls included—who was concerned about her disappearance. Kevin didn't seem to notice and no one else at the Manor was particularly up in arms about it.

I had been working with the girls for a few months

now and I had gotten to know them pretty well. I had seen them happy when a big tip came their way, stressed when a party was proving challenging, exhausted when we had finished service.

But I had never seen them scared.

# CHAPTER *Eight*

Kevin wanted to talk to Seamus, and while he did that, I found the girls downstairs by their lockers and asked them to come into the kitchen.

"What gives?" I asked Eileen, who tried to pretend that nothing was wrong. "Where's Pauline?"

She clearly didn't have the stomach for acting and gave up the whole thing. Thank God I was the one who had started with her instead of the police; she folded like a cheap suitcase. "She's gone, Belfast."

"What do you mean 'gone'?" I asked. "Where did she go?"

Colleen was a little more blasé about the whole thing, not quite as concerned as her friend was. "I'm hoping she took off with the lad but I'm not sure."

"What lad?" I asked. "Help me out, girls. We have our second incident here in as many months and now one of our employees is missing. We need a little more to go on than she's away with her boyfriend." When they didn't answer, I went further. "She left rather abruptly, don't you think?" I looked at Colleen. "You're her room-mate, right? Doesn't it seem odd that she wouldn't tell you where she was going?"

"Was," Colleen said, her blue eyes flashing angrily. "Till she met the boy. Then everything changed. Technically, she still lived there but she was hardly ever home. Now, I'm left holding the bag on the rent."

I dropped my voice to a whisper. "Do you think she was picked up by INS?" I asked Colleen, and at the mention of the immigration organization, her face turned pale.

Colleen gasped. "Don't say that out loud!" she said. She thought about it for less than a second before coming to the same conclusion that I had. "Yes."

I chewed on that for a minute. If that was the case, I didn't know how we'd track her down, what the process might be for springing her from a detention center.

Colleen wept into her hands. "I can't pay the rent without her."

Eileen sat atop one of the counter stools studying her fingernails. "That big tip from the wedding should help then."

Colleen nodded. "Sure, it should." She frowned, her sadness turning to consternation. "If we ever get it."

She was right; in all of the fuss, Dad had never distributed the tip that Mr. Casey had left. Colleen looked around wildly, her missing roommate and her lack of funds making her attention wander.

I snapped my fingers in Colleen's face. "Focus, you. Where do you think she's gone?"

Eileen yawned. "Maybe she's just tired of working here, decided to try something else."

"Yes, maybe, Eileen," I said. "Right. She worked here for years, seemed happy, loved my family, and then took off without telling anyone because she 'decided to try something else.' That makes the least sense of all," I said, rolling my eyes. "You were the one who was so worried about her being in a detention center. Why the change of heart?"

The girls exchanged a look. I wasn't that far removed from being a millennial myself, but compared to these two, I was positively a middle-aged baby boomer, driving a sensible, albeit almost dead car and saving for retirement. Colleen seemed concerned, and while I had thought I had seen fear on Eileen's face when Hanson entered the dining room, I could see now that I had been wrong. It had been boredom. "Who's her boyfriend?" I asked.

"Some guy named Connolly. She calls him 'babe' all the time so I don't even know his first name. Moonlights at his pub occasionally."

That wasn't a lot to go on but I wondered if he was related to the Connolly boys I had gone to high school with. "What's the name of the pub?" I asked.

"I dunno," Colleen said. "We didn't talk much."

"Why not?"

"She's secretive. Private. Perfect roommate, but we were never friends."

I tried a different tack. "Did you check her room in your apartment?" I asked.

Colleen shook her head. "She has a lock on the door. I don't have the key."

"That's strange," I said.

"Is it?" Colleen asked.

"Do you have a lock on your bedroom door?" I asked.

"I don't," she said. "She put it on there right after we moved in. One of the boyfriends handled it."

" 'One of the boyfriends'?" I asked. "How many have there been?"

Colleen shrugged. "I don't know." She looked at Eileen. "Three? What do you think?"

"At least three."

I pulled a pad off the shelf over the sink and pushed it toward Colleen. "Names. Give me names."

"What are you going to do, Bel?" Colleen asked. "We need to find her. What if she didn't go with Connolly? What if it's something worse?"

"Worse?" I asked. "LIke what? What could have happened to her?"

The girls exchanged a glance. Colleen finally voiced their fear. "Kidnapped. Dead."

"Kidnapped?" I asked. "Dead? Now what would make you go to those two scenarios?"

"She was mysterious. Stayed out all night. Locked her bedroom door when she wasn't around. You know. Stuff like that," Colleen said. "It's not normal, Bel."

I worked at Shamrock Manor with a bunch of insane people. I wasn't sure I was the one to be judging what was "normal."

Eileen came back to life. "What if she's been kidnapped? Then what?"

The girls had hit on a narrative that they liked better than the deportation one. I held a hand up. "Stop. Not another word about that."

Eileen looked at me as if I had the answers. I didn't want to tell her that I didn't have a clue as to what to do, where to start. "What are you going to do, Bel?"

Why was this my problem now? Oh, right. Everything that happened at the Manor was my problem. That had become clear since I had arrived home.

"I'm not sure," I said. "Just give me the names of the boyfriends and let me see what I can find out."

Kevin stuck his head into the kitchen. "Just wanted to say good-bye, Bel."

At the sight of him, the girls made excuses as to why they couldn't stay in the kitchen—linens to be folded, silverware to be polished—and exited, leaving me alone with the guy, who at seventeen, I thought I'd spend the rest of my life with. I pocketed the list of names they had given me.

"Get what you need, Kevin?" I asked.

"I did," he said. "Except I still wanted to talk to . . ." he said, looking down at his little notepad. "Pauline Darvey. Any idea where she might be?"

I shook my head. "Sorry. No. I'm sure she'll come back to get her tip," I said. "When she does, I'll tell her to call you, okay?"

"Sounds good. Just covering all of the bases. Feeling a little exposed since you basically solved our last case," he said. "You know, the dead guy at the wedding? The first one?"

"Seems a little excessive for a guy who had a heart attack or something but I'll leave it to you how you spend your time," I said, smiling.

He looked around the kitchen. "Well, this place looks so much better than before."

"Thanks," I said.

He picked up a melon baller and tapped his palm with it before putting it down. Stalling. "How's everything going?"

"Everything is good. You?"

"Busy," he said. "Really busy."

"How's Mary Ann?" I asked.

"She's busy, too."

Just when things had become normal between us,

Amy's belongings had surfaced and with them years of hurt and sadness. We were back to being strangers and it didn't feel good.

"Anything on Gerry Mason? I asked. "It seems like it was a heart attack, right?"

"Maybe so," he said. "We'll see. I'll follow up with his doctor and see what it was specifically, but you're probably right. We're a little gun-shy, you know." He had already explained himself on that one so I let it go.

"Did you know he was a private investigator?" I asked. "I thought that was just a TV job. *The Rockford Files. Magnum P.I.*"

He smiled. "Remember when we used to come home from school and watch those shows on reruns?"

"I remember," I said. I also remember Amy sitting between us, a package of cookies being passed back and forth, all of us trying to figure out the perpetrator of the crime before Rockford or Magnum did.

He changed the subject. "Hey, I heard you're making carrot-coconut shooters for the wedding on Saturday."

"Who told you that?"

"Seamus," he said, smiling. "It's the talk of the Manor, apparently." He looked down at his shoes, fiddled with the tie in his jacket pocket. "Will you make those when I get married?"

"When you get married?" I said, laughing. "You'd have to get engaged first, Hanson."

He blushed a deep red. "Well, I did."

"Did what?" I asked.

"Get engaged." He pulled the tie out of his pocket and wound it around his hand. "Last week."

It took all I had to not let the shock show on my face. He and Mary Ann D'Amato, a saint of a woman if there ever was one, had been dating for longer than any two adults had the right to. She had her own house and he rented a condo, propriety being her middle name, apparently. I had always wondered why they weren't married; after all, everyone's biological clock was ticking, not just mine. I chalked up their unmarried status to my own former boyfriend's inability to grow up and commit to anything or anyone.

Apparently, I had been wrong.

"Um, congratulations?" I said. He didn't seem like someone who was overjoyed at the prospect and, as a result, I wasn't sure how to respond.

"So, yeah. That's happening," he said, looking around the kitchen. "You'll do the honors?"

"Of cooking?" I asked. "Of course. When's the wedding?"

"Halloween."

"What year?"

He looked confused. "This year."

"We've got work to do, then," I said. "Have you talked to Mom and Dad about confirming the date? Making sure it's available?"

"I have," he said.

Curious. Neither of them had mentioned to me that the Hanson–D'Amato wedding was in the offing. We'd definitely be having a conversation about that.

"Great. When you're ready, we should talk about the menu," I said.

"That's why I was talking to Seamus," he said. "Mary Ann wants a specialty cocktail."

"Good luck with that!" I said. "Oh, sorry," I said, seeing his reaction to my disloyalty to Seamus. "What did he say?"

"He was noncommittal," Kevin said as diplomatically as he could. "We'll talk soon about it?"

"Yes, talk soon," I said, my heart feeling a wee bit broken, a feeling I wasn't entitled to have.

With nothing else to say, he left the kitchen, me standing there and looking around. In the office next to the kitchen, I heard my mother and father whispering furiously, probably figuring out what to do now that I knew that Kevin Hanson was getting married and I knew that they knew before I did. I went into the office, ready to talk about the Hanson/D'Amato wedding but Dad was in high dudgeon, more so than usual.

He looked at me, red in the face. "Ten grand, out the door," he said.

"I'm not following, Dad."

Mom filled in the blanks. "The tip from the Casey wedding. It's gone."

# CHAPTER *Nine*

Dad undertook the questioning of the entire staff, called back to the Manor yet again, like a dog with a bone. There was no one on staff that we didn't trust, all long-time employees devoted to my parents in a way that was almost unnatural. I gave Feeney a look as he passed in the foyer, asking him silently if he had taken the money, and he had glared back in a defiant yet disappointed way, making me immediately sorry that I had suspected him. Feeney always needed money, his earnings from weddings and the odd jobs he took to support himself not really doing the trick. There was only one person Dad couldn't question and that was Pauline Darvey, a woman employed by my parents, who I now knew had overstayed her welcome in the U.S. and who seemed to be the likely culprit.

There were hardly any other suspects as most of the people who worked at the Manor were either blood relations or family by default. The missing money coupled with the missing server pointed to her guilt.

I couldn't think of a better reason to look for her, if at least to throttle her for putting my parents in a very sticky predicament. I heard Mom and Dad discussing fronting the money themselves, but I told them to sit tight and wait it out; we'd get the money back, one way or another if I had anything to say about it.

When my day was over, I decided that I really didn't want to spend any time in my apartment alone. On my way out of the kitchen, I found Cargan walking across the empty dining room toward the back of the big hall; I followed him, my professional chef's clogs making just the barest squeak on the highly polished floor. He stopped under the giant chandelier in the middle of the room and turned.

"Following me?" he asked.

"You always were a hard one to fool," I said. "Where are you going?"

"Ladies' room," he said. "I want to get rid of the police tape."

"That was a little excessive, don't you think?" I asked. "It wasn't a crime, just . . ."

"Or something, as Dad likes to say?" Cargan said.

I told him about my conversation with the girls. "I think Pauline took the Casey tip, Cargan," I said. "That's the only explanation."

"Well, that's not very nice," he said in his usual understated way.

"Did you have plans for the money?" I asked.

"Saving for a new kayak," he said. "Fancy cleats. A few odds and ends."

We got to the bathroom and stared at the door.

After he pulled all of the police tape off the doorjamb, he entered the bathroom. "I just want to take a quick look."

I put a hand on his arm, my mind still on Pauline. "Car . . ." I looked around the dining room to make sure we were alone.

"I can go in," he said, pulling the police tape down, letting it hang. "I'm a professional. Remember?"

"No, not that." I had learned, just recently, that the brother I had no secrets from had kept a huge secret from me for years. That he was a cop and had been a cop all along, not a professional musician. So, I had to find out about Pauline, about their relationship. "Cargan, what was going on with Pauline?"

"I don't know," he said. "Seems like she's gone."

"No. Not that. With you. And her."

He looked up at the ceiling. "Ah, that."

I waited. Having a conversation with Cargan is difficult in general, but touch on a topic that he didn't want to talk about? That was the worst.

"Well, we had a little attraction to each other."

"I heard you in the walk-in."

He looked at me and smiled. "Just a little attraction, Bel. Nothing else."

"She's a lot younger than you," I reminded him.

"And that's why it stayed where it did. It was just a little kiss, Bel. Nothing more."

But in his eyes, his manner, I saw something else, something that led me to believe that it had been more than a little kiss. He had a thing for her, and if the girls were to be believed, he wasn't the only one.

When we got to the stall door, he pushed it open, and I brought up the one thing besides the death at the wedding that was concerning me. "Car, Pauline hasn't been seen since the wedding. The girls are really worried. Like something has happened to her."

If he was concerned, he didn't let it show. Things like this—how he could subvert even the tiniest reaction, the smallest expression of emotion—was how he had been so successful at pretending to be someone else for so many years, how he managed to stay deep undercover. I knew the truth now, though. "Huh," he said. "Now why would they think that? Something sinister?"

"They've gone from deportation to kidnapping to murder," I said. "They alternately are really upset and then seem not to care. But there's nothing to support any one of their theories."

"They have any other ideas? Anything to go on?"

"Maybe off with her boyfriend?"

"And who's that?" he asked. If he was jealous, it didn't show.

"No first name. Just 'Connolly.'"

Cargan raised an eyebrow. "As in the local Connollys?"

"Don't know. Does one of them own a pub nearby? Pauline moonlighted at a pub, according to the girls," I said. "They didn't give me a lot to go on. I'd say yes, but who knows?"

"Rough group, that family. Remember them from high school?"

I did. I had a vague recollection of a quiet boy in my class with a bunch of older brothers who were trouble, the kind of trouble that ended up in the local newspaper with their names attached to general mischief and one or two garden-variety DUIs where no one had been hurt, but a mailbox or two had been sacrificed. Mrs. Connolly was a churchgoing, God-fearing lady who served with Mom on the Ladies' Guild and I didn't remember a Mr. Connolly on the scene, which may have contributed to the unruliness of the bunch but only partially. A bad seed ran through the Connolly crowd and at the mention of the family name and Cargan's vaguely concerned face, it all started to come back to me. "Jamie Connolly was in my class," I said. "Nice kid. Quiet."

"The older ones were the problem."

"Would there be one old enough to have a son dating Pauline?" I asked. "Just how old was the oldest Connolly boy?"

"Not sure," Cargan said. "But I should ask around." He continued to look around, thinking. "What about the one in your class? He wouldn't be that much older. Maybe ten years?"

"Good point," I said. "Where do we start?"

"*Why* do we start? That's the question," he said. "She's a big girl. She can do what she wants."

"I don't know, Car. The girls seemed scared."

"That she left?"

"I guess it's how she left. That's all I can come up with." I picked up the police tape on the floor and pushed it into the garbage can. "And the money. She's got our money."

He thought about it for a minute. "We can poke around a bit. I, for one, would like our money back."

"So where do we start?"

"With the Connollys? Let me see what I can find out about the pub that one of them supposedly owns," he said. He turned to face me. "But not you. Stay out of it. I'll handle it."

"I'm already in it, Cargan," I said. I pulled the piece of paper from my pocket with the names of Pauline's three former flames, the ones that I had asked the girls to give me when we had chatted in the kitchen. "And here are a few more people to track down," I said, glancing at the list before handing it to Cargan. Before it reached his hand, I pulled it back. "Now that's interesting," I said, looking at the list more closely.

"What's that?"

I looked at Cargan. "Want to know one of the other names on the list?" Cargan looked at the list in my hand. "Jed Mitchell."

Cargan didn't react. Jed Mitchell, Amy's brother, was a cop in Foster's Landing and very much married. Or so we thought. If the girls knew about him and his relationship with Pauline, maybe things had taken a bad turn with Cassie Montreaux, a girl that we had all gone to high school with and who Jed married not too long after graduating from the local police academy.

"Where do the girls live?" I asked Cargan, figuring he knew better than I did. I had a vague idea of where Colleen and Pauline had an apartment but not an exact address.

Cargan took one last look around the bathroom, getting a visual of the whole thing that I was sure would stay in his head, a clear and accurate picture that could be recalled days, weeks, and even months from now. I'm not sure why he needed it, but it was clear that he did. "Let's find out," he said.

# CHAPTER Ten

The waitresses' addresses were in a book that Mom kept in the office, a list that went back years and detailed every employee that the Manor had ever had with notations in Mom's swirly script providing their positive attributes as well as their faults. But mostly their faults. Doreen Hogan had been "messy with unkempt hair; not a very hospitable server" while Fidelma Doherty had "a scowl that had clearly been placed there by the Devil." Whatever that meant. Cargan quickly found what he was looking for and the two of us set off for the middle of our little village in my old Volvo wagon, the one that Dad had procured for me when I had arrived home. Cargan, curiously, had a Vespa that he rode around the little village, an odd sight among the pickup trucks at one end of the socioeconomic spectrum and the fancy luxury cars at the other. But clearly the Volvo was better for this errand.

Colleen and Pauline lived on the top floor of a tidy two-family house that I recognized as the childhood home of one of my old school friends, Veronica Mulroney. A check of the mailbox indicated that the

Mulroneys were no longer in residence, their place on the ground floor having been taken by the Martinez family.

Colleen appeared to have just woken from a nap when we arrived. She was surprised to see us when she answered the door after running down the long flight of stairs that led to her apartment. "Bel. Cargan? What are you doing here?" she asked, pulling her hair back into a messy ponytail.

"We were hoping to take a look around Pauline's room," Cargan said. "You haven't heard from her, have you?"

Colleen led us up the stairs and into a tiny but immaculately kept apartment. The furniture was second-hand, or maybe third, the cushions on the couch sagging but clean. A handmade throw was draped over the back to hide what was likely a little wear and tear on the fabric. The kitchen was spotless; I could see why Colleen and Pauline had been employees for so long at the Manor and why next to their name in the employee book, there had been stars only, no negative comments from Mom. They were neat and fastidious about their surroundings, something that Mom valued in her employees.

"I haven't heard from her and I don't know what you think you'd find in her room," Colleen said. "I don't know how I feel about you looking in there, either."

"Just a quick look around," Cargan said.

"Well, you know it's locked," she said.

Cargan smiled. "Not a problem."

I could tell that Colleen considered Cargan someone in authority, her boss. "Do I have a choice?" she asked, stepping aside and motioning toward a door. "Don't make a mess," she cautioned, flopping onto the couch and examining her nails.

Cargan approached the door and, with some kind of sleight of hand, was in the bedroom in no time. I whistled. "Nice work, brother. The old credit card trick?"

"If I told you . . ."

"You'd have to kill me?" I asked. "There's a joke that never gets old."

We stood in the doorway of Pauline's room, taking it all in. Pauline's tips must have been better than I thought because her room was beautifully appointed. As a matter of fact, I had ogled the entire bed ensemble in the Pottery Barn catalog just the week before, noticing that if I bought everything for my old queen bed, it would have cost close to a thousand bucks, about nine hundred and eighty bucks I didn't have. "Is that a Waterford lamp?" I asked, touching the linen shade lightly.

Cargan poked around the room. "There's a lot of nice stuff in here. Could she afford all of this on a waitress salary?" he asked.

"Banquet server!" Colleen called from the living room.

"My apologies," Cargan whispered, pulling a pair of rubber gloves from his pocket and donning them. He opened drawers slowly and poked around while I wandered around the room, which rivaled some of the best hotels in which I had ever stayed.

I touched a framed picture of Barack Obama that hung on the wall across from the bed. "This is an interesting design choice," I said. "Obama?"

"His mother's people are from Tipperary," Cargan said. "Irish-born love him. Like Kennedy before him."

"Offaly!" Colleen called from the other room. "Not Tipperary. It's on the border, but it's not Tipperary."

"Again, my apologies." Cargan peeked into one of the drawers in the beautiful antique dresser.

Colleen appeared in the doorway of the bedroom. "There's a Barack Obama Plaza in Ireland. Best roast beef sandwich you'll ever have."

That got my attention. "Really?"

"Would melt in your mouth," she said, leaning on the doorjamb.

"How do they make it?" I asked, thinking that a mini roast-beef sandwich might find its way onto the cocktail-hour menu.

"Not a clue," she said. "Marinate it in buttermilk maybe?"

"Maybe," I said. That was a real old-school method but one I had never tried.

Cargan shot me a look and in that look was the declarative statement: focus.

"What do you think you're going to find?" Colleen asked.

"Don't know," I said, getting a side-eye from Cargan that meant I should distract her. "You know what would be great now?" I asked.

"A glass of wine?" she said, looking at the clock. "It's five o'clock somewhere."

"A cup of tea," I said. Two in the afternoon was early even for me to start imbibing.

"Grand," she said. "I'll put on the kettle."

I walked through the living room and spied a large bouquet of freshly cut flowers sitting on a side table. If they weren't from Mom's garden, they were from someone who had the exact same flowers that Mom had planted in the spring. I looked up and saw Cargan in the doorway of the bedroom.

"Mom's?" I asked.

He nodded. "Just a little something to take home from work," he said, turning, the blush on his face giving him away again.

I followed Colleen into the kitchen. "I'm worried about Pauline, Colleen."

She turned from the stove and looked at me. "Me, too."

"You've overstayed your work visas, haven't you?" I asked as gently as I could.

The words came out in a steady gush. "We have but your dad pays us in cash and we make good money. I send some home for my little sister who wants to come to college here in the States." She looked down. "It just happened. I always intended to go back but there was never the right time. I met a fellow. I broke up with the fellow. I met another one." Her eyes were shiny with tears. "You know how it goes."

I did. "So you don't want to go to the police?"

"If we do, they'll find her for sure and send her back."

"And you, right?" I said. "They'll send you back, too, right?"

"She would never betray us," Collen said, defiant.

"If that's the case and you really believe it, what would be so bad about that?" I asked. Better than being in the weeds, wandering around looking for a safe place to land. "What would be so horrible about her getting sent back to Ireland, provided that she didn't spill the beans on you and Eileen?"

Her answer was swift. "If she goes back, her husband will kill her."

# CHAPTER *Eleven*

Pegeen Casey's tearstained face was one of the first things I saw the next morning when I entered Shamrock Manor. I was thinking about husbands killing wives and how Pauline was on the run, probably, from an abusive relationship so was already distracted; I couldn't imagine what our formerly blushing bride could want with us again. Colleen couldn't tell us much about Pauline's husband, but she knew that they had married young, been together for two years, unhappy most of that time. Pauline had split and come over here, her dad an old acquaintance of my dad and all that, so there was a job waiting for her.

Cargan's ears had turned red at the thought of the girl being abused by her husband and it was in that physical clue that I saw what was really going on here: he had a crush on the girl, if not more.

Pegeen stood in the lobby of the mansion with a man, staring disconsolately at the door to the dining room where just days earlier she had danced with her new husband.

"Pegeen?" I said, putting my hand on her shoulder, interrupting her depressed reverie.

"Oh, Belfast. Hi," she said. "Is there somewhere we

could go to talk?" She turned to the man standing next to her; I recognized him from the wedding. "You remember my brother, James?"

He held out a hand. "James Casey. I don't think we officially met at the wedding. We apologize for dropping in on you unexpectedly but hope you can help us." Like his sister, he was dressed pretty formally for morning; his suit had an impeccable cut and his tie was knotted expertly. Pegeen wore a pencil skirt and a crisp white blouse, a strand of pearls around her neck. He noticed my taking in their attire. "Pegeen left here in such a hurry that she may have left a few things behind," he said.

"Of course," I said. I took a furtive second look at him; why hadn't I noticed him at the wedding? He and his sister resembled each other but not their parents; the siblings were tall and lean with fair skin and dark hair. The parents were short, stout, and with ruddy complexions. Whatever genes had missed a generation had been kind to Pegeen and James; their poise, looks, and bearing spoke to being related to another Casey family, not the one who dabbled in importing and exporting and who the girls had whispered had connections to the Irish underworld, if there was such a thing.

I had never known the Irish to be that organized but what did I know?

We went into Mom and Dad's office; it was early and Mom was teaching a Pilates class in her studio and Dad was who knows where. My guess is that he was foraging for items to use in his latest installation, rocks, sticks, old pieces of metal, and other discarded artifacts that were his stock-in-trade. I took a seat at Mom's desk, noticing happily that the old-fashioned register that she used for bookkeeping looked healthy and robust. More black than red, literally and figuratively. We were making money. All we needed was for more bad press to upend what we had carefully created over the last several months, my food being an integral part of our newfound success.

Pegeen sat across from me, holding a very expensive purse in her lap, her hands worrying the thick leather strap. James sat beside her, their legs almost touching. I couldn't decide if it was weird or a close bond. I decided to go with the latter. Better that way.

"I can't believe this, Bel," she said. "That just a few days ago I was the happiest person on the planet and now I feel as though I'll never laugh again."

James reached over and patted her hand. No ring. I don't know why I noticed, why I cared. I blushed red at the thought that I was thinking about that in this setting, on this occasion. You are an awful person, Belfast McGrath, I thought as I drew a circle with my finger on the desk.

I didn't know what to say and I knew this wasn't the right time to bring up our mutual acquaintance, my cousin and her friend, Caleigh. Sure, I had had a broken engagement at the beginning of the year but my sadness didn't approach Pegeen's. Although I would have loved to see Ben have a massive heart attack in front of me, I tamped down the memory of my revenge when I saw just what a toll this death had taken on this woman's life. I poked around the desk but didn't see anything with Pegeen's name on it. Mom and Dad hadn't mentioned coming up with anything belonging to the bride so it was hard to know what she might have left behind.

James spoke finally, holding his sister close while he did, trying to comfort her. "Gerry had been fine. A little under the weather right before the wedding but we thought it was just nerves."

"Nerves!" Pegeed said, crying even louder.

"It was just so sudden," James said. "And on their wedding day."

"My wedding day!" his sister said.

James looked around uncomfortably. If his family was as Irish as my family, Pegeen's display was making him uncomfortable. We keep everything inside, for the most part, stoicism being lauded in our culture.

I didn't know what to say so I did what I did best: I babbled. "Well, his job as a private investigator must be very stressful. It's stressful, right? Doing that kind of work?"

"And Gerry was retired from the NYPD," Pegeen added. "He probably had a lot of pent-up stress that I didn't even know about." She wiped her eyes with a dainty hankie procured from her expensive purse. When she saw my face, though, the question about how such a young man could have retired so young, she clarified. "He was injured in the line of duty."

My mind went to Cargan, his own affiliation with the NYPD, how his work had scarred him so much that he had taken a leave of absence from "the Job," as he referred to it, resting in his room in the Manor, playing his music, trying to get his mental equilibrium back. I don't know what he had seen or what he had had to do, but clearly it had left him slightly broken.

"Your husband was a very nice man," I said.

She bristled. "He was. A nice man, that is. He was the nicest," she said, her tone defensive.

I let it go. She was in pain and I had been there myself not that long ago. Words were misconstrued, feelings heightened. Sensitivity and defensiveness become your armor and make communication difficult at times. "I'll speak to my parents and see if they found anything after the wedding. What is it that you lost?"

"It's a purse. Do you have a lost-and-found department?" Pegeen asked. "Somewhere I could look to see if it's there?"

"Maybe?" I said. I actually had no idea. I opened a closet in the office and, sure enough, a box on the floor contained a bunch of odds and ends that looked like they had been compiled from a variety of weddings. There were some extra favors from "Doreen and Jake's" nuptials the October before, a couple of little bottles of wine, the liquid now discolored and probably undrinkable; weirdly, a shoe that had been dyed purple to match some unfortunate bridesmaid gown; two pairs of socks; and a little bag that had been designated to hold wedding gifts, most likely. "Well, here's something," I said, pulling out the box. "Doesn't look like a purse is in here, though," I said. "What did it look like?"

"Large. Black." Pegeen looked at the box's contents and then up at me quickly. "No."

"Was there anything else that you're missing?" I asked. "I can ask Mom and Dad when they get back," I said, thinking that if this is how they ran their business, disappearing in the middle of the day, it was no wonder the Manor was going under before I had returned home.

James jumped in, breaking the uncomfortable silence. "Thank you, Bel. We appreciate it. It's just Pegeen's purse, the one she brought that day. If you find it, please let us know. It was worth a bit of money."

Import/export must have been a lucrative business because the bag in her lap was also worth a small fortune.

I led them out of the office and into the foyer where Dad
was hanging a new painting, this one almost indescrib-
able, a postmodern take on . . . the sun? Who knew?
It was a big splash of yellow paint strewn across an
otherwise blank canvas, and larger than any of his other
paintings. He was hammering a nail into the gorgeous
wainscot that lined the grand staircase, eyeballing its
placement. Never a good idea but Dad wasn't one for
convention. Or levelness.

"Oh, Pegeen!" he said, running down the stairs, the
scent of turpentine and paint thinner all around him,
like a cloud. "You poor girl! How are you holding up?"
he asked.

Seeing my father, she let loose the tearful floodgate
she had been holding back. With customers, Dad showed
a warmth he had never displayed to his progeny and with
this girl, someone he had met only a few times and knew
only in a business sense, he opened his arms and let her
in, holding her while she cried.

James and I stood by the Bobby Sands bust, looking
around uncomfortably. While Dad comforted Pegeen,
James turned to me. "The waitress, Pauline. I didn't see
her at the end of the wedding. Did she leave early?"

Now that was an interesting question. I looked at him
to see what his intention was with regard to our way-
ward server. "Yes, she wasn't feeling well," I lied. Why?"

"I never did get a chance to tell her how much her service meant to our guests."

"I wouldn't worry about that, James," I said. "She's no
longer in our employ." And she's run off with the tip
money your father gave us so save it.

When Pegeen had stopped crying, she broke the embrace with my father. "Mr. McGrath, I'm afraid I left my purse here the day of the wedding. Did you find it?"

"A purse?" Dad said. "What bride carries a purse the day of the wedding?" he said, asking a question that only someone who had seen a lot of brides would ask. It was out of his mouth before he realized he had even said it, a hallmark of Dad's conversational style. "Oh, excuse me, Pegeen. It's just that . . ."

"I had some personal items in there," she said.

"Ah, yes, personal items," he said, his face flushing as if he were having a hot flash. "Uh, no, we didn't find anything. So sorry. We'll keep looking. I'll get Cargan and the other lads on the case."

James reached into his pocket and pulled out a card. "Here. My business number is on the front and my home number is on the back. In case you have any additional questions," he said.

I took the card and stuck it in my pocket. "We'll do everything we can to find your purse, Pegeen."

Dad hugged the forlorn newlywed again. "Saying a prayer for the lad," he said. "A terrible, terrible thing."

We watched them leave. Dad threw an arm around my shoulders and I hugged him around the waist. "I'm getting a whole new view of you from working here, Dad. You done good," I said. "Nice recovery on the whole 'brides don't carry purses' thing."

"Now what kind of language is that? 'Done good?'" he asked. "You're smarter than that, Belfast. I know you are."

"It's an expression, Dad. Never mind," I said, when I saw his confusion. "Let me know if you find that purse."

He shook his head. "No purse here. Didn't have the

heart to tell her." He patted my head. "Found a tie, though. And a weird necklace that looks like a finger on a string."

I grimaced. "That's a weird fashion choice," I said, not really giving it much thought. Dad sees the world in a different way than most people. It was probably a gemstone set in a long oval for all I knew. "Where were you, Dad?" I asked.

"Having a full physical," he said. "Can't take any chances. Seeing that young guy have a heart attack or something really put the fear of God into me."

"Good for you, Dad," I said. "Taking charge of your health is a good thing."

"Well, if I didn't," he said, a twinkle in his eye, "your mother would kill me."

# CHAPTER *Twelve*

I had only been in the basement of the Manor once since returning home and that visit hadn't turned out well. I had discovered that Cargan had a secret hiding place down there, one where he lay on an old mattress, read fine literature, and listened in on everything going on in the Manor. But thinking about Pauline, how she might be on the run from an abusive husband who may have discovered her whereabouts, if the girls were to be believed, brought me down there early the next morning to go through the gym lockers that Dad had installed when I was in high school. They stood up against a back wall, next to the door that led to the great lawn of Shamrock Manor and afforded the employees a safe place to stow their belongings during their shifts. I opened them, one by one, trying to ascertain each locker's owner, which wasn't terribly hard to do. Fernando's had a photo of his car, which I had seen parked in the lot behind the Manor; Eileen's had a photo of Gerard Butler with her initials and his surrounded by a heart; and Colleen's had a photo of her and a very hot guy standing on a beach somewhere. I went down the line and finally arrived at what could only be Pauline's locker, pulling open the door.

It was empty.

I stood there and pondered that. She had fled but had taken the time to empty her locker so the move wasn't entirely unpremeditated. I couldn't imagine what she might have kept in there that was so important to take with her; most everyone else had a change of shoes or an extra apron or pair of pants, things you wouldn't think you'd need if you were trying to go missing.

People were strange, I decided. The only proof I needed were the individuals who were toiling above me, my mother, father, and brother, all head cases in their own right.

I had told Cargan what Colleen had said about Pauline and I saw the wheels turning in his head. How would the husband know if she returned to Ireland? How would he find her? Colleen didn't have a lot of answers but we did get a name out of her—Domnall Kinneally, a man with a plethora of *l*s in his name— and Cargan was going to poke around to find out what he could about a guy who sounded like he needed a swift kick in the arse. Or three.

Before we parted, I asked Cargan if he knew Gerry Mason from the PD but he had shaken his head. "I was undercover so long, Bel, that if the guy wasn't undercover with me, I wouldn't know him."

Later that afternoon, I wanted to get off the grounds of Shamrock Manor desperately, so when Brendan Joyce showed up at the end of the day looking less contrite but just contrite enough, I told him that we were going to my new favorite restaurant, an expensive place a few miles up the Taconic. I thought I deserved a little pampering after his disappearing act, and just to remind him how hurt I was, while I went to change my clothes, I left him in the Manor with Mom and Dad, who peppered him with questions about what he did, where he did it, and how he did it, even though they knew all of the answers. They were special that way. They liked to see if the story had changed at all, if this man who was courting their only daughter could be trusted.

"But I thought you said you taught art and painting?" I heard Dad saying as I headed to my apartment. I couldn't think of a more suitable punishment. "Not art and drawing. Which is it, lad? There's a big difference!"

That'll learn you, I thought, as I closed the big double door behind me. When I came back down ten minutes later, Mom was doing something that no one's mother should be doing to their daughter's boyfriend.

"Mom, two questions," I said after taking a deep breath. "Why do you have a scale in your office and why are you weighing Brendan?"

Mom looked up. "Two-oh-five. On a strapping boy like yourself. You could be a good two-ten and look the same by turning some of that flab into muscle," she said, grabbing a hold of a little piece of flesh above Brendan's right hip. He jumped off the scale, knocking into a photo of the five of us kids that had been taken outside the Manor a long time ago, the trees in the front of the building much smaller than they were now.

"Thank you, Mrs. McGrath," Brendan said, deftly catching the large framed photo before it fell to the ground. "I'll keep that in mind."

"I'm running a special this month at the Pilates studio," she said. "Ten percent off your first visit and a bigger discount for five sessions. We can do private or in a group." She looked at Brendan expectantly, and it was all there on his face: the thought of my mother in a leotard, him surrounded by a cadre of yoga-panted, middle-aged women, everyone commenting on his physique, which up until now, he probably thought was just fine. It was. I knew from experience. His face made a few approximations of an appropriate response until he finally fell upon the one that was the least acceptable.

He started laughing.

Mom turned to Dad who stood in rapt attention in the corner. "Well, I guess I have your answer," she said, turning on her heel and exiting the office while Brendan laughed uproariously at the thought of taking one of Oona McGrath's Pilates classes, clad in a giant, leggy leotard himself, my mother touching his "core" and expounding on the length and tone of his muscles. At least that's what it looked like in my own fertile imagination.

Dad looked at Brendan first and then at me. "That might not have been the best response, son," he said, and shaking his head sadly, followed Mom, no doubt getting into her leotard to let off some stress in the studio. I didn't want to think about what that entailed.

When we were alone in the office, I gently smacked Brendan in the head. "What is wrong with you?" I asked.

But that just made him laugh harder, so hard that he could barely breathe. Tears streamed from his eyes and down his cheeks and I wondered if those tears were real. Or if they were born of giddiness or sadness.

When he took me in his arms and buried his head in my hair, I had my answer. "I am so, so sorry, Belfast McGrath." He pulled away, his hands on either side of my face. "Can you forgive me?"

I wasn't sure for what, but seeing his face, the pure

penance that he surely had done, I knew that I could. So I let him kiss me to see if it was still there, that electricity that existed between us, and I was happy to find that it did.

And later that night, as we crept up the stairs as quietly as we could to my apartment after a delicious dinner where we reconnected fully—two adults who should have been able to freely come and go—and he told me he was sorry again and again and again, I forgot it all: the day at the river, his leaving, the void he had left when he stayed away.

His cowardice.

# CHAPTER Thirteen

"What's a nice girl like you doing in a place like this?"

Cargan and I had hit every gin joint in Foster's Landing and its surrounding environs the next evening, hoping to catch a glimpse of at least one of the Connolly brothers. Cargan was looking into Domnall Kinneally and his whereabouts but nothing had come through yet. We had had an early-afternoon wedding, a brunch really, and while we were tired after working all afternoon, we were more interested in what had happened to Pauline and even more concerned with her affiliation with the men on the list the girls had given me.

Oh, and there was the not insignificant fact that she had taken our tip, most likely, and I, for one, wanted that money back. The Volvo was on its last legs, and if that went, I would have to find a new car, or a Vespa, if that was all I could afford.

"We should start a private investigation agency," I said to my brother as we drove along the darkening streets of Foster's Landing, streetlights starting to light in the oncoming gloom. "We could be called the 'Accidental Sleuths.'"

He wasn't impressed. "Now why we would do that?

We have jobs," he said. "Plus, we didn't do such a great job of finding out which Connolly owned which bar in the area. I don't know why that was so hard to do. And I don't want to be an accidental sleuth. I want to be a prepared, on-his-game sleuth."

"Just a flight of fancy, Car," I said, pulling into our third bar. "It's exciting, this mystery stuff."

"It's really not," he said. "You know what we say in the PD? Being a cop, or even an 'accidental sleuth,' is ninety percent being bored and ten percent being terrified. Remember that," he said, holding the door open for me at the Grand Mill, the first place I had ever gone with Brendan Joyce and the place, if I was being completely honest with myself, where I had fallen hopelessly in love with him, far sooner than I should have, given my recent broken engagement.

Cargan and I sat at the bar and ordered some beers. "Now, why are we doing this again? Why are we looking for the Connollys?" I said, dropping my voice to a whisper while looking over my shoulder. The crowd tonight was mostly women, the Grand Mill running its weekly "Ladies Night" where drinks for the female clientele were half price. If I had any female friends, this would be the place we would meet up, a warm, woody, cozy place that served decent food. The bar was alive with young-to-middle-aged women, toasting each other and getting progressively louder with each round.

"Making our way through our list of guys," he said, as if that were a perfectly reasonable response.

"Well, Jed Mitchell would probably be the easiest to find," I said. "He works right in town."

"We'll get to him," he said. "I have to figure out a way to handle that one."

I didn't, I thought. "If I see him, I'm going to ask him why he's cheating on his wife and if he knows where Pauline is."

"That's a terrible idea, Bel."

"Why?"

"I don't think I have time to run you through an entire course on interrogation, so let's just leave the sleuthing to me, okay?" he said.

I didn't answer him but I definitely was not going to leave the sleuthing to him. He was slow and deliberate and a girl was out there, running possibly from any number of problems and with a pocket full of our cash. I was going to find her. I was sure of that.

Later that evening, after drinking one too many crappy beers and after giving the keys to a sober Cargan, we hit O'Halligan's, a bar in the next town that Cargan discovered Angus Connolly owned after calling in a favor and getting the word from an old colleague. Cargan's friend added, just so we would know, that the Health Department was no friend to Angus and his establishment.

I was tired; the late night with Brendan followed by a long day in the kitchen had sapped my energy and now, despite being someone who could hold her liquor usually, I was half in the bag. But this was the most fun I had had in a long time, the night before notwithstanding.

"How perfect is that, Bel?" Cargan asked, and by the way he breathlessly recited the address, I could see a little life coming back to my brother, a guy who had spent the better part of the last year hanging out at Shamrock Manor and, even worse, with my parents.

"Can I go with?" I asked, putting my hands together in prayer. "Please? Pretty please?" I slurred.

"I think I should bring you home before I go," he said. "Besides, what are you going to do? You haven't been a heck of a lot of help up until this point and your instincts are for shite," he said as we traversed the parking lot to our car, me tripping over an invisible curb. He considered his options. "But Mom is going to kill me if I bring you home like this."

"What am I going to do, you ask? Just sit there. Look pretty," I said, batting my eyes at him to show him just how pretty I could look.

"You look like an eejit," he said, mimicking our father and his heavy brogue. He had thought it over and decided it wasn't a terrible idea, the wrath of Mom a far more daunting prospect than dragging my butt around the Hudson Valley. "No more drinks. And don't blow our cover."

"What's our cover?" I asked, but it was clear he hadn't gotten that far in his thinking so he stayed silent, staring straight ahead at the road.

At the bar, a glass of club soda in front of me, Angus Connolly sidled up to me and held out his hand. "I'm Angus," he said.

It was all coming back to me: the stocky build, the long eyeeteeth that made him look vaguely wolflike, the slicked-back hair. He was the spitting image of his younger brother, Jamie, the kid that had been in my class and who didn't utter a word hardly until he got his diploma and said "thank God," making the entire audience at the FLHS graduation burst out laughing. Angus hadn't changed a bit since I was a kid when he worked at McGillicuddy's Pub in town and Dad used to take me there for a hamburger every now and again. Our town is full of Irish but not too many guys named Angus so seeing this one jogged my memory.

He threw out an arm, proud of his accomplishments. "I own this place."

"And what a place it is," I gushed. In reality, my opinion of the place was changing as I really took it in; it was a caricature of an authentic Irish pub, all green and dark wood with leprechaun "art," if you could call it that, adorning the walls. It also featured some terrible musicians—a fiddler, a button accordionist, and a mandolin player—playing in the corner. When they launched into a jig that was beyond their musical capabilities, I saw Cargan cringe. There was a lot he could tolerate but badly played Irish music wasn't one of those things.

We were at the bar and a waitress delivered Cargan's order, a pasty-looking potato soup and a roll that he picked up and bounced off the bar, its staleness making it a weapon as well as a side dish. Why he was eating at a time like this was beyond me, but he had a cast-iron stomach and didn't let much stop him from filling it up. Any wedding leftovers at the Manor mysteriously disappeared not long after going into the refrigerator.

"I haven't seen you around here," Angus said, leaning up against the bar.

"New in town," I said.

Beside me, Cargan coughed loudly. In addition to not blowing our nonexistent cover, I wasn't supposed to "engage with the subject," something I had been advised of before we had gotten out of the car. This was supposed to be "reconnaissance," but I wasn't the type to sit idly by while a man, clearly interested, wanted to talk to me. This guy may have been one of Pauline's paramours, even if he was fifty if he was a day, but if he could provide any information as to her whereabouts, I would play along.

"New from where?" he asked.

I figured I'd go for broke. "Canada."

"Ah, I thought I detected an accent," he said. "And your boyfriend there?" he asked, pointing at Cargan. "Is he Canadian, too?"

"Him?" I said. "Yes. Canadian. But my brother, not my boyfriend. And unfortunately, a mute." I smiled at Cargan. "Actually, he would make the perfect boyfriend, the muteness and all." That'll teach him to boss me around, I thought. I was getting farther with Angus Connolly than my brother ever would have on his own.

"I had a Canadian girlfriend once," he said. "A gem."

"I prefer the Irish lads myself," I said.

"I had an Irish girlfriend once," he said.

Well, that was easy.

"Gorgeous gal, I bet," I said. "Fair with blue eyes? A true Irish rose?"

He shook his head. "Dark as night," he said. "Black hair. Like the devil, that one," he said, shuddering. "But you. You're attached, are you?" he asked. "Or does your mute brother scare everyone off?" He looked pointedly at Cargan who, for all intents and purposes, really was a mute. He said little and contributed almost nothing to most conversations.

"Not everyone," I said. Who was the eejit now? "So tell me about this Irish gal. What broke you up?" Next to me, Cargan was noisily slurping up potato soup, playing the role of my mute brother very well. I didn't want to hear from him in a few hours when food poisoning set in.

He waved a hand. "I don't want to talk about her. She

broke my heart, that one," he said. A waitress who bore more than a passing resemblance to Pauline sidled up next to Angus and whispered in his ear. His hand lingered on her shoulder as he instructed her to give table five a round of drinks on the house. She gave me a sidelong glance as if to say "hands off." No worries, my friend. There would be no hands of mine anywhere near Angus Connolly.

"What did she do?"

"Dropped a soup in someone's lap," he said.

Stay with me, Angus. "Not the waitress," I said. "This Irish gal."

"Cheated on me," he said, motioning to the bartender for a drink, his usual, it would seem as no words were exchanged before a short glass of amber-colored liquid showed up on the bar in front of Angus. He downed it in one swallow. "With a cop, no less."

"A cop, huh?" I said, not following why that was a problem specifically.

"Yeah, a cop. He turned me in to the Health Department."

I looked over at Cargan. "How's your soup, brother?"

He gave me a thumbs-up with a grimace.

"How did that happen? The Health Department stuff?" I asked.

"She worked here. Told the other chap that she thought that maybe the kitchen wasn't sanitary and should be shut down." He grimaced. "You see one mouse and all of a sudden they want to throw you into Sing Sing. Show me a restaurant that doesn't have stray vermin and I'll show you a restaurant that's paying off the Health Department."

"Ah, I get it. So she betrayed you, this dame," I said. I don't know why I was starting to talk like a character in a forties noir movie; it must have had something to do with the beers I had been consuming. I resisted the urge to belch out loud, belching loudly being one of the many talents I had learned over the years from my four older brothers.

"She did," he said. "And I'll never forgive her."

I arched an eyebrow in response.

"I loved that girl. Would have married her," he said.

If she hadn't already been married, I thought.

He straightened up, pulled his vest flat against his protruding stomach. "But why are we talking about that? You never answered me. Are you attached to anyone?"

With my family, I was attached to *everyone* but that wasn't a suitable response. "Oh, I get around," I said, the wrong answer because it piqued Angus's already heightened interest. "But there is one fellow I spend most of my time with."

"Back in Canada?" he asked.

"Back in Canada," I said. "A lovely lad. Very talkative. Not like this one here."

My brother lifted a hand in greeting.

"That's not a nice thing to say about a mute," Angus said.

He was right, if a true mute had been in our presence. "So have you seen your old girlfriend?" I asked. "Ever hear from her again? Or too much bad blood?"

"Funny you should ask," he said. Around us, the dining room was filling up and I knew I wouldn't have Angus for much longer. That and the fact that I had a fictitious Canadian boyfriend was sure to make him lose interest in our conversation. I waited for him to tell me more but something had caught his eye across the room.

"Why?" I asked. "Why is it funny that I asked?"

"She was here two days ago. Looking for money. Said she needed to leave town in a hurry."

# CHAPTER *Fourteen*

The next day, a pounding headache reminding me why I had stopped drinking beer a long time ago, I went into the kitchen at the Manor where a note had been left for me, taped to the refrigerator.

*D'Amato/Hanson wedding planning. 9:00!*

The left-slanting handwriting and exclamation point let me know that Dad had written the note as did the admonishment "Don't be late!" as if a professional, like me, would be late to a meeting.

Yes, when I was growing up, punctuality was a problem. Now, as an adult, I was punctual to a fault. Working in a kitchen, I couldn't afford to be late and needed to time everything to the second. But Dad couldn't know that; in his mind, I was still a little girl who needed reminding. That said, it did me no favors when I skidded into the dining room, ten minutes late for the meeting with Kevin and Mary Ann, my chef's coat unbuttoned and billowing around me, a deep dive into a new recipe having thrown my timing off. My parents looked at me in reproachful unison, my hangover telegraphed by the bags under my eyes and my sallow complexion. And was I technically late for a meeting I hadn't even known about?

I was coming in momentarily anyway to take stock after yesterday's event and to put together a carbonara; Mom had requested pasta for dinner tonight, Sunday dinner, something she rarely did. Helen didn't like pasta but it seemed that Helen wasn't coming to dinner. So, pasta was on the menu and I, for one, couldn't have been happier. Nothing better to soothe a raging hangover than a big bowl of carbs.

"Hi!" I said breathlessly as I skidded into the room. "How are you?"

Mary Ann smiled warmly at me, always the lady to my disheveled broad. "Belfast," she said, leaning in and giving me a hug. "Can you believe it?" She pulled away and presented her left hand, the ring finger holding the largest diamond I had ever seen.

"What are they paying you, Hanson?" I asked, an indelicate response that was out of my mouth before I could think; I was turning into Dad. "I mean, wow. It's gorgeous. Great job, Kevin."

"Thanks," he mumbled, looking around the dining room. I guess he had a hard time imagining it as a wedding venue, since the last two times he had been here in a professional capacity.

My father clapped his hands together, hands that were splattered with paint, just like the rest of his outfit. "Let's talk wedding!"

"Working on a new piece, Dad?" I asked as we made our way to a table that Mom and Dad had set as they would for an event. I hadn't known about this meeting prior to this morning so I hadn't prepared any of my cocktail-hour offerings, but I geared up to give Mary Ann and Kevin a vocal tour of what they could expect at their reception.

"I am, Belfast. I'm calling it *Love*."

"Just *Love*?"

"Love is all you need," he said, winking at me.

I sat between Mom and Dad, an expectant Mary Ann sitting across from me, Kevin beside her. "So, what were you thinking?" I asked.

"Thinking?" Mary Ann said, looking at Kevin. After all these years, she still looked at him as if he were the smartest, most handsome, loyal guy on the planet. And rather than feel any snark about it, anything approaching jealousy or envy, I admired it. I had once felt the same way about Kevin, a long time ago when we were much younger and a heck of a lot more innocent.

"Yes, thinking," I said. "Let's start with the cocktail hour." I outlined some of the things I had brought to the cocktail menu since coming back, things that went way beyond the pigs in a blanket and frozen canapés that Mom and Dad used to consider standard cocktail-hour bites. "And I'm going to do a mini roast-beef sandwich with homemade horseradish sauce on toasted baguette slices." It wasn't innovation and it wasn't new but I was determined to figure out how to make melt-in-your-mouth beef just like they served at Barack Obama Plaza in Ireland.

"All of those items sound wonderful, Belfast," Mary Ann said. "Kevin? What do you think?"

Kevin was looking out the window at the river that ran along the south side of the property, the same river where, a few weeks prior, he had unearthed the remnants of

Amy Mitchell's life. The backpack, the key chain, the sneakers. Amy's sneakers. "Huh?" he asked. "What?"

"Must be love, son, if you're that preoccupied," Dad said. "I remember meeting this one here," he said, hooking a thumb in Mom's direction, "and not being able to form a complete thought for a year!"

There was a reason Dad had kept this place running for all these years, despite the bad food: he, like Mom, was the consummate host. He could turn any situation into a party, any negative into a positive. Although their culinary experience was limited, I bet that no one had ever left Shamrock Manor hungry or not having had a good time.

Kevin looked away from the river and at Mary Ann. "Yes, beef," he said.

"That's all you have to say?" she said, not unkindly, the rapport between them evident. "Just beef?"

Kevin straightened in his chair and focused his attention on his fiancée. "Yes. Beef. And whatever else Bel thinks would be good for a crowd of hungry guests."

"My grandmother is coming from Italy," Mary Ann said. "So, do you have any Italian recipes in your repertoire, Bel?"

"I do," I said. "I can make minimeatballs. I did a summer in Rome and got the recipe from a chef's great-grandmother. I think they'll pass muster with your grandmother."

Mary Ann smiled, a woman who was as beautiful inside as out. "That would be wonderful."

"How about a caprese salad, too?" I asked. "I'll only do it if I can find good tomatoes. It will be late in the season for tomatoes but I'll try. If not, I'll do something else."

We went through the menu and settled on three choices: salmon, chicken, and beef. It would be a sit-down dinner for one hundred and I would do a wine pairing with each course and then each individual entrée. There would be a specialty cocktail that I would devise and show Seamus how to make. The boys would not be playing the entire event, something that raised Dad's hackles a bit, but the McGrath Brothers and their brand of crazy were being minimized in favor of a jazz trio who, in between sets, would allow my brothers to perform. But even Mary Ann realized that a jazz trio playing her and Kevin's song—the Righteous Brothers' version of "Unchained Melody"—would be a mistake, given that Feeney had an incomparable tenor and could hit the high notes with ease. He wasn't on good terms with Kevin, though, so I wondered how he would sing "I hunger for your touch" without completely losing it.

Mary Ann perused the menu and then looked up. "I have to admit, Bel, I feel somewhat guilty asking you to cook at our wedding."

"You do?" I asked. "Why?"

"Well, you should be a guest. An honored guest. We go way back and you would have been invited, obviously. Making you cook that day seems inappropriate but there is nowhere else we'd rather have our wedding than here at Shamrock Manor."

"Oh, Mary Ann, that's so nice," I said. "But cooking for you that day is my gift."

Mom and Dad looked at Mary Ann as if she were the reincarnation of the Blessed Mother and I guess that wasn't too far off.

"It's settled," I said, and rattled off the rest of the items on which we had decided.

When we were done, we pushed away from the table. "May I see the bridal suite, Mrs. McGrath?" Mary Ann asked. "I'm wearing two dresses, one for the ceremony and then something a little more fun for the reception. I'd love to be able to change here. Would that be possible?"

The bridal suite wasn't really used for newly married couples anymore, most newlyweds preferring something off the grounds of the place where they had had their receptions, so Mom rented it out for photos and for brides to take some time off between photos. With its sweeping views of the river and a three-season panorama—winter was kind of a bust unless there was snow—a lot of brides used it for their "before" photos, the ones they took while getting dressed or having their makeup done, their own homes not quite as grand or luxurious. My cousin Caleigh had used it the day she married and it hadn't been used since.

"Of course, dear," Mom said as she spirited Mary Ann away, asking if her dress for the ceremony would "cover her shoulders," shoulder covering being one of Mom's prerequisites for a church wedding. Mary Ann was discussing her first dress in hushed tones as the two of them made their way across the foyer.

Dad looked at Kevin. "Anything else, lad?" he asked. "Anything we here at the Manor can do to help you have a wonderful day?"

"I don't think so," Kevin said. "Thank you. I think it's going to be really nice."

"'Really nice'?" Dad exclaimed. "Amazing! Gorgeous! It is a Manor wedding after all." Dad straightened a painting on the stairs. "So start praying to Saint Medard, son."

Kevin looked at me.

"Patron saint of weather," I said.

Dad stood on the stairs, halfway up to the second floor, and turned, a pensive look on his face. "Saint Medard," he said.

I knew exactly what that meant. In weeks, or even days, we would have an installation of Saint Medard or, at the very least, a painting depicting him as a child, an eagle hovering over him, protecting him from the rain. Whatever it was, it would keep Dad busy and that was always a blessing.

Thanks, Saint Medard.

Once we were alone in the foyer, the light streaming in from the windows at the front of the mansion, I took a good look at Kevin. He looked terrible, like he, too, had a hangover. He had always looked vaguely like the boy I had fallen in love with a long time ago but now he looked like a beleagured man. "Kevin, what is it?" I asked, trying to keep it light. "Wedding plans keeping you up at night? I would say that you should have been engaged for a year or more but we're not getting any younger, am I right?" I said, giving him a little chuck to the shoulder.

He ran both hands over his face and I could see the calluses he still had from playing the standing bass on the tips of his fingers. He composed himself, straightening his tie, touching his belt, the gun on his hip. "Bel, there's something you need to know."

There was nothing I needed to know, particularly if it was coming from this person, clearly tortured by something. Is this where he told me it was all a mistake, that after all these years, he still had a thing for me? That the deep, passionate love we had for each other as teenagers had been a real, true thing? If so, his timing couldn't have been worse. I got that feeling in the pit of my stomach, both excited and sick at the same time. It was something I had always wanted, if I were being completely honest with myself, and also the one thing I thought I didn't want to hear.

Turns out I was wrong about one thing: what he said was something else, and *it* was the one thing I didn't want to hear.

"We found something else. That day," he said.

He didn't need to elaborate; I knew which day it was. Right now, there was only that one day, a day I didn't want to revisit. But I couldn't help myself. "What? What did you find?"

He blurted it out, having held it in for far too long. "The remains. Amy's remains."

# CHAPTER *Fifteen*

After all these years, all that water, it couldn't be a body. I knew that but I didn't want to know what it was that they found, how Kevin could be so sure that it was Amy.

Later that night in my apartment, preparing for a date with Brendan Joyce that I didn't really want to go on, I thought back to my conversation with Kevin and the look on his ashen face when he told me what they had found.

Not a body, really.

More like bones. And the remnants of clothes that I remember too well. Cutoff shorts, they thought. Rubber flips-flops. A bracelet that bore the initials AM, worn down over time and from the surging water. All of the things I remember about Amy, the physical reminders of my long-lost, long-dead, if anyone was really telling the truth, best friend.

"Where is she . . . where are they . . ." I had started to say to Kevin but couldn't continue, the air having come out of me like a balloon that had become unknotted. Mentally, I started to fold in on myself, the walls in my brain where I kept memories of her closing, one after another, like dominoes.

"Medical examiner," he said, his words clipped and professional. "Don't know what they'll find. If they'll find anything at all." He looked at me, his face contorted in a way that made me fear he would start crying. But he didn't, which was just as well, because if he had, I would have started and never stopped.

I looked in my bathroom mirror, playing the conversation over in my brain. I pulled my hair back into a messy ponytail and washed my face, dotting a little moisturizer around my eyes, under my chin, the way I had seen Mom do it. I put on some lip gloss. And I tried to smile at myself, knowing that what lay behind that smile was the knowledge that I had been right all along.

Amy was gone and my last words to her had been "You'll be sorry."

I would have to live with that and at that moment, I didn't know if I could.

A knock on the door forced me to put the closest facsimile to a real smile on my face. I went to the door at the back of the apartment, the only place to gain entrance, and saw Cargan standing on the elevated porch. "Hiya, Car," I said, opening the door and letting my brother in. "What brings you here?" I asked, affecting a breezy nonchalance that I didn't feel. "Did you like the carbonara?"

On his best days, Cargan looks sad, but today, he looked sadder than I had ever seen him look. He stepped into the apartment and stood in the back hallway. "I don't know. I thought there was a chance . . ."

"That she'd be alive?" I asked. Whatever I knew, he had known way before me. That's the way it always was and always would be.

He shrugged sadly. "Maybe? I knew it couldn't be but I always hoped."

"Me, too," I said, and it was with my brother, my closest ally, that I knew I could let my guard down. The moisturizer that I had applied to my face and that I hadn't rubbed in properly mixed with the salty tears that ran down my face, almost twenty years of pent-up hope and regret coming out in one sob-filled explosion.

"Ah, Bel," he said, letting me cry, something that just wasn't done in my family. Criers were "emotional" and "too sensitive" and we were taught to be tough. There were fisticuffs and brawls and rows but I never cried, not even that one time when Derry had sat on my stomach until I had nearly passed out. I hadn't cried then but he had when I punched him square in the nose upon rising, bloodying it and letting him know that his nine-year-old sister was tougher than any boy he knew. It was only later, when I was older, that I realized the ability to cry—something Dad did every time he heard "Danny Boy"—was a sign of strength and not something to be ridiculed. It wasn't weakness. It was strength.

I pulled away and grabbed a paper towel from the roll on the counter, blowing my nose loudly. Cargan sniffed the air. "You have a date?" he asked. "Smells like the cosmetics counter at Bloomingdale's in here."

I laughed, in spite of everything. "I do."

"With the Joyce kid?"

"Yes, the Joyce kid," I said. "All six feet five inches of him."

"He get his braces off?" Cargan asked, even though he had seen Brendan and knew that he had two straight lines of teeth.

"You know he did," I said.

"Does he wear his retainer when he sleeps over?"

"How did you—"

"Know that he sleeps over?" Cargan asked. He put a finger to his head. "I know everything," he said. "You should know that." He picked up a magazine on the coffee table, *Food and Wine*. "So, the retainer?"

"Get out of here," I said, pushing Cargan toward the door. "He'll be here any minute," I said.

Cargan stopped by the hooks that Dad had hung by the back door and on which the only thing hanging was my chef's coat, the one that Mom had bought me and on which she had had my name embroidered. All of it, even my confirmation name: Belfast Jane Mary Magdalene McGrath. It was a mouthful but thankfully I have an ample rack and could wear my name proudly and without a crease to obscure it. Cargan laid a hand on one of the hooks.

"You know, Bel, you need to let it go. Move on."

"I have moved on," I said, a little stridently and too quickly for it to be true. I would never let it go, that part of my brain, the one that remembered that night in vivid detail, the part that would always be eighteen years old, stunted and immature. "I have moved on," I whispered.

"For real. For good," he said. He touched my chef's coat. "We worry about you, sister."

"No need, brother."

"And by 'we,' I mean 'me,'" he said but it was unnecessary. The other boys were so wrapped up in their own lives that it was possible that until I had returned a few months previous, they had forgotten they even had a sister.

I could hear Brendan Joyce ascending the stairs to the apartment so I wiped a finger under each eye to catch any errant moisture. "How do I look?" I asked my brother.

"Rode hard and put up wet," he said, our old banter back. "Is that the look you were going for?" he asked. You can't have four older brothers and be too "emotional," "too sensitive." Or even too confident; they would make sure that I felt a little off-kilter, not very sure of myself. But not Cargan. His jokes were really jokes and nothing ever went too far, not like with the other boys. He reached out and touched my shoulder and I thought, If he gets serious or emotional, I'm going to lose it.

But instead, he poked my shoulder and said, "Got you last!", darting out the door and scrambling down the stairs before I could "get" him, too, leaving Brendan Joyce with a bewildered look on his face.

"'Got you last'?" Brendan asked. "Do I even want to know?"

"It's a game. That we played as kids," I said, leaning out the door and watching my grown brother running across the lawn of Shamrock Manor under a very full moon, the sight of him bringing me back to a much simpler time, a time when everyone was happy, and I had Amy and she had me. I reached up and dug my fingers into Brendan's curly mop, pulling his head closer so that we could kiss.

I looked at Brendan before planting a wet one on him. "Did you bring your retainer? I would love for you to sleep over."

# CHAPTER *Sixteen*

The next day, Brendan left early, before my parents or brother could see him, and I spent the day trying out some new things—much to my mother's chagrin—in the kitchen. Things with weird ingredients like walnuts and cheeses that weren't American and pastas with names she couldn't pronounce. I delighted in it all, wondering just what she would think about the new hors d'oeuvres, imagining that her head might actually explode at the thought of another caviar-based bite leaving the kitchen.

I found Dad on the lawn looking out at the Foster's Landing River, his hands on his hips around sunset. Although we weren't supposed to touch each other, or tell each other how much we loved one another, I came up behind him and put my arms around him from behind, something I had done as a little girl, and planted a kiss on his cheek.

He didn't turn around. "That Joyce boy good to you, Belfast?" he asked, his eyes still trained on the river below.

"He is, Dad," I said.

"Don't rush it," he said.

"I won't."

He continued, his back to me. "I don't want to see you get hurt again," he said, a little hitch in his voice, which he cleared with a throaty cough.

I laid my head on his back. "I won't, Dad. I promise."

But was that a promise I could keep? Would Brendan be the guy that would erase the years thinking about Kevin, the time with Ben? I didn't know.

Later that night, my feet up on my coffee table, a pad and pencil in my hand as I sketched out a new recipe—this one for a pâté—my phone pinged on the end table.

Colleen.

"Someone's been here and they've taken all of her stuff."

I didn't involve Cargan in this newest development because I wanted to handle it myself. The last thing I needed was him tailing me and putting in his two cents.

Being the youngest sibling, a girl no less with four older brothers, puts you at a disadvantage in the family. Although I had been a rough-and-tumble tomboy as a child, my brothers expected nothing from me in terms of brains or brawn. They thought I needed protection and help, even in spite of my bloodying Derry's nose and being able to take care of myself. That event, to them, was an aberration. Cargan, in particular, was protective, even though I was the one protecting him when we were small, my cousin Caleigh being a particularly imaginative tormentor of my poor, wee brother.

Cargan wanted his hand in this entire thing, Pauline's disappearance, the story of what had happened to her; I could tell. I also knew that if he got wind of my going this alone, he wouldn't be happy, but so be it. I didn't know where he was even though he was usually only at one or two places: home or soccer. It was too late for soccer so my guess was home. And God help him if Mom and Dad knew because he'd end up watching another episode of season three of *Downton Abbey,* which Dad still referred to as *Downtown Abbey* despite everyone screaming at him for several weeks running that that was not what the show was called.

When I got to the girls' apartment, Colleen was at the top of the long staircase, wringing her hands. "Oh, Bel," she said. "Come on up."

I started asking questions before I reached the landing. "Who has a key to this apartment, Colleen? What time did you get home? Did the downstairs neighbors see anything?"

"Only the landlord, five o'clock, and they don't speak English, only Spanish."

I ran back down the stairs. My Spanish was passable after having worked in kitchens for most of my adult life. I ran through some vocabulary in my head while I waited for someone to answer the door. A young woman with a baby on her hip answered, giving me a tentative smile that grew wider when I launched into my questions in Spanish.

"I speak English," she said, without a trace of an accent. "I'm from Foster's Landing."

"So sorry," I said. "Colleen said you didn't speak English."

The woman lowered her voice. "We can't understand a word she says. She talks funny. But we don't want her to know that so we just smile when she talks to us."

Ah, a great cultural divide at work. "Did you see anyone take anything from the upstairs apartment?" I asked.

"I didn't," she said. "My husband and I both leave the house by seven and I drop the baby off at day care in town. This house is empty most of the day."

As I stood there, a smell wafted out to me. "Sofrito?" I asked.

She smiled. "Yes. You like sofrito?"

"I do," I said, "but I've never been able to master it."

"Come on in," she said. "I'll teach you." The baby smiled at me before sticking a fat thumb into his mouth.

Colleen, still at the top of the stairs, cleared her throat.

"I'll come back if you don't mind," I said. "My name is Bel McGrath."

"I know who you are," the woman said, not unkindly. "I'm sorry. I followed your story closely when it was in the paper."

Well, then, she was the only one in Foster's Landing, most of its residents acting as if the world began and ended within its borders.

"I'm a bit of a foodie," she said. "I've been thinking of opening my own restaurant here in town."

I wanted to scream "Don't do it!" because of my experience in many a kitchen, but I could tell that her love of food was driving her, and one thing I knew well was that a culinary passion was a driving one.

"My name is May Sanchez," she said. "My husband is Efraim Martinez, which is why it says 'Martinez' on the mailbox." She smiled. "Old-school Puerto Rico."

"Nice to meet you. Listen," I said, leaning in close so Colleen couldn't hear us, "what goes on up there? What do you know about Pauline?"

"Nice girl," she said. "Loves Matthew here." She pulled the baby closer. "Even babysat for us a few times."

"Have you seen her? Spoken to her?"

She shook her head. "No. Come to think of it, I haven't seen her in a few days. Is something wrong?"

"We don't know," I said. "But she hasn't come to work and we're getting concerned."

"Did you go to the cops?"

My look told her everything.

"Got it," she said. "That's a problem I understand all too well."

I had a bent Shamrock Manor business card in my pants pocket which I handed to her. "If you hear anything or remember anything, anything at all, would you call me?" I asked.

"I will," she said. And as I started up the stairs, she stuck her head out of the apartment door. "And Bel, if you need help at Shamrock Manor, please call me. I would love to work under a chef like you. I'm currently at a restaurant in Morrisville and the commute is killing me." She smiled. "Really, I'd love to work with you."

I thought about Cargan, the waitresses, the busboys, the one sous I had hired who clearly found me annoying and bossy. "Well, you'd be the only one," I said, taking the stairs two at a time.

At the top of the stairs, Colleen was fuming. "We don't have time for you to make new friends, Bel," she said. "I'm getting really worried here."

I looked at the door and could see that whoever had entered had either had a key or was a professional. It was either Pauline who had come back when she knew no one would be around, or someone else, someone who had decided that cleaning out Pauline's room was a good idea. I thought back to my last visit here and Cargan slipping into Pauline's room with ease; the front door to the apartment didn't look any harder to break into using a paper clip or a credit card. Inside the tidy apartment, the door to Pauline's bedroom was open and, indeed, it was empty. The furniture was still there, as was the picture of President Obama, but everything else was gone: clothes, shoes, personal items.

I looked around a bit before turning to Colleen; to me, it looked pretty clear. "I think you're going to need to find a new roommate. Seems like Pauline has moved out for good."

"She would never do that, Bel. Never," Colleen said. "We weren't super close but she wouldn't leave without telling me."

It was clear that she had. "She wouldn't? She's been missing for days," I reminded her. "What makes you think that she wouldn't leave without telling you?"

"She wouldn't leave for good without telling me," she repeated. "Not unless she had to."

# CHAPTER *Seventeen*

"If I have to watch one more episode of *Downton Abbey* with Mom and Dad, I think I'm going to go crazy," Cargan said.

When I arrived home from Colleen's, he was sitting on my couch, his feet up on my coffee table drinking a glass of some luscious Cabernet that I had been saving for me and Brendan. "Make yourself at home," I said, flinging my purse onto the kitchen counter. "How's the wine?"

"A little dry for my taste," he said.

I held the bottle up. He had consumed more than a glass so I guess he had choked it down, martyr that he was.

"Where you been, Bel?"

I poured myself a glass and settled into the chair next to the couch. "Pauline's room is cleaned out. Colleen was freaking out so I went over there."

"Pauline clean it out? Or someone else?" he asked.

I shrugged. "Hard to tell. My guess would be yes, but stranger things have happened." I put my feet up on the coffee table and stretched out. "Colleen seems to think foul play."

"We need to go to the police."

"Aren't you the police?" I asked. "We've already gone to you."

"The real police. Not the semiretired police," he said, tugging at the neckline of his soccer jersey. "Well, as real as the Foster's Landing police are."

"If we do that, the girls will all be deported," I said. "They haven't said it outright but that seems to be the major concern here." I uttered the words that had been floating around in my brain like a gnat on the loose. "Mom and Dad. They will be in huge trouble if it gets out that they hire illegals."

He mulled that over, sipping his wine like a real connoisseur. "I get that. That doesn't show great judgment on his part, hiring illegals."

"So you see why I don't want to go to the police just yet, as you suggest."

He knew I was right but was too stubborn to admit it. "So what do we do?"

"Well, short of getting the girls green cards, we need to find Pauline." I recounted my conversation with James Casey when he and Pegeen had stopped by, looking for the missing purse. I wondered just what had been in that purse if Pauline had absconded with that as well. "He seemed to have taken notice of her as well. Don't know if there is more to that. He said something about tipping her. Maybe that's all it was." I shook my head. "She was a pretty gorgeous girl, now that I think of it. I guess I'm not surprised that she was noticed."

By the deep flush in Cargan's cheeks, I knew he had noticed as well. He didn't acknowledge my comment, focusing on a spot over my head, a neutral zone.

"Car, I already know. You were sweet on her. There's no shame in that," I said.

"I'm not ashamed," he said.

"Embarrassed?"

He didn't answer.

"Because she was younger?" I asked.

"Because I wasn't the only one," he said, admitting something that I hadn't banked on.

I decided to focus on the business at hand. "What's our next step?" I asked. "Where do we take this?"

"I'm not sure," he said, draining his wineglass. "Why don't you let me think about this for a while? Figure out where we go from here?"

"Sounds like a plan." I looked at my brother, an enigma wrapped in a conundrum but my best friend. "Car, when will we find out?"

"Find out what, Bel?"

"Who it is." I said. "About Amy. Whether it was her or not."

He pulled his lips together in a sad frown. "I think we know who it is, Bel." His voice was barely a whisper.

"You think so?" I asked. "For all these years, I was sure she was dead, but now I don't know."

"And why's that?" he asked.

"I don't know," I admitted.

"It's Amy, Bel. I'm pretty sure," he said.

"But what if it's not?" I asked, my gut the only thing that I had at that moment. Sure, it had to be her; I don't know why I was full of doubt suddenly. "But what if it's not?" I repeated, as if saying it again would make it true.

"I'll tell you as soon as I know something," he said. "Kevin promised me he'd let me know."

And implicit in that was that Cargan would be the one to tell me because Kevin wouldn't want to, whatever it happened to be. Good news or bad news, if the news could even be categorized that way. It was all bad news, whatever way you looked at it.

I walked him to the back door and watched him run down the stairs, back to the Manor, back to where we felt safe. Back to before any of this. And in my little apartment, by myself, I envied him just a bit, my brother the semiretired cop, the guy who got to come home and recharge his batteries before setting out on a new adventure at some point. That was what I was supposed to be doing, but now, with things moving at the speed of a runaway train, I had a feeling that I wouldn't leave. Or couldn't.

## CHAPTER *Eighteen*

Even the city papers had picked up on the story of what had been found in the Foster's Landing River, and one intrepid reporter had even had the temerity to visit our little town, hoping for the big scoop. She hadn't found me but had been seen in the Dugout according to the gossip chain that started the minute she arrived in town. Amy's disappearance had been news in the Hudson Valley all those years ago, but that was in the days before the Internet and the ability for anyone, at any time, to research any story they chose. Back then, the biggest thing that had happened was that the town had shot a segment for a show about missing kids and our little village had experienced a minute of fame, not unlike a shooting star that flashes across the sky and then disappears into the inky universe.

But after all this time, the discovery of Amy's belongings—her remains—things sort of frozen in time, as it were, was just too much to leave alone. It had all the hallmarks of a dramatic story: a gorgeous girl gone missing, a town that had never really recovered, a group of friends who had gone on with their lives (or had they?), a mystery that literally resurfaced when most everyone had decided that all hope of finding her was lost.

I was in the kitchen of the Manor the next day flipping through a copy of *Bon Appétit* that Mom had left behind when a woman, around my age but bearing the signs of New York City living—black pants and black turtleneck, expensive messenger bag, a nice layered shag that surrounded her face in frosty highlights—appeared, looking around the kitchen as if she had just been beamed up from earth to an alien spaceship. "You can really do over a hundred covers in this kitchen?" she asked.

So she was a foodie. Or had been in food service. One or the other. I closed the magazine and stood up.

She held out her hand. "Duffy Dreyer. *New York Times.* I'm working on a story for the Sunday magazine. About unsolved cases. Mysteries of the Hudson Valley."

Name sounded familiar. "Duffy Dreyer?"

She put the pieces of my puzzlement together. "Nope. No relation. He was Duffy Dyer," she said.

"I still don't know what you're talking about."

"Duffy Dyer? Catcher for the Mets? 'Ya Gotta Believe'? Nineteen seventy-three?" she said. "My dad loved the team through thick and thin. That's where I got my name."

Mom was a huge Mets fan. It was all starting to make sense. "Right. I knew it sounded familiar."

"I get that a lot," she said. She pulled out a notepad. "I'm doing a story on Amy Mitchell. Her disappearance. What was found in the river. You were the best friend, right?" she asked.

I felt a heat start in the bottom of my feet and start to climb through my body, alerting every nerve ending to trouble. I stayed silent. "The best friend"? I was "her best friend." Big difference in my book.

She pulled up a stool and sat down, placing her bag on the counter. "Can I ask you a few questions?" she asked.

I shook my head. "No. You cannot ask me a few questions."

"I ate at the Monkey's Paw once," she said, referencing my former place of employment. "Best meal I ever had."

"Flattery will get you nowhere," I said, but I couldn't help asking, "What did you have?" Mentally kicking myself for continuing the conversation.

"A hot foie gras. A piece of chicken that was absolutely sublime," she said, rhapsodic in her description of the food I used to cook. "Some kind of cocktail with muddled blackberries . . ."

"Queen of the Fairies."

"Pardon me?"

"It was called 'Queen of the Fairies.' Vodka, curaçao, simple syrup, muddled blackberries. It was named after my mother, Oona." Tart and never sweet. Just like Mom.

She closed her eyes, remembering it. "It was just the right amount of whimsy."

"Have you been back?"

She opened her eyes, which were the color and shape of a chocolate-covered almond. "Back where?"

"The Monkey's Paw."

She smiled. "Yep. It stinks now."

"Man, am I happy to hear that," I said to her delight, her reporter's spidey sense going off; there was a story here. "Off the record, of course."

She put her pen down. "Ben Dykstra is no Bel McGrath."

"That's what I tried to tell Francesco," I said. "But he wouldn't listen."

"You ever coming back to New York? The food scene?" she asked.

"And leave the culinary hub that is Foster's Landing?" I asked. "Never."

"No, really. You like it here?"

I thought about it for a moment. Like it? That was a stretch. What it had been, what it was now, was a safe place to land. And that was something I couldn't articulate to this snappily dressed beat reporter for the *Times* who had been named after a professional baseball catcher from long ago. "Why are you here, Duffy?" I asked, sitting back down on the stool. I pushed the *Bon Appétit* away and gave the reporter my full attention.

"To figure it out. To see what I can find about what happened to Amy Mitchell," she said.

"That was a long time ago. We've all moved on."

"But have you?" she asked. "I spoke to Detective Kevin Hanson and he seems as raw and beat up as he might have been when it happened."

"Really?"

"And his colleague, Jed Mitchell. Amy's brother."

"I know who Jed is."

"He thinks she's still alive," she said, looking closely at me, gauging my reaction.

"Well, she's not," I said. "If she was, we'd know. She would have contacted us."

I could tell that she agreed with me. "She's been gone a long time, chef. Couldn't have been easy for you to live with this."

I was going to cry but I couldn't let myself, not here, not in front of her. I turned and went to the sink, ran the water, used the sprayer, anything to give me a chance to compose myself. "I've got a lot of work to do. Can you excuse me?" I asked from under the cover of a steady stream of water. In the office, I could hear Dad rumbling around, banging into things, slamming drawers. "I have to help my father."

She dropped her card on the counter. "You'll call me if you want to talk?"

"I will," I said. But I wouldn't. Want to talk, that is. "Who else have you spoken with?"

"Hanson. Jed Mitchell." She flipped through her notebook. "Francie McGee at the police station. And Brendan Joyce." She looked up. "Know him?"

"Just a little bit," I said, before showing her the door. Not much of a reporter, are you? I thought as I watched her go.

# CHAPTER *Nineteen*

The next day, after I had finished my preparations for the upcoming Saturday wedding, I walked down the long gravel path toward the village, the autumn sun still high in the sky and bathing me in a golden warmth that felt good after several stints doing inventory in the walk-in. I had made this walk countless times during my academic career in Foster's Landing and knew the route by heart. There was the tree that Cargan had plowed into on his bike the day he decided he didn't need training wheels any longer, and there was the ditch, now deeper and filled with more weeds than years ago, where Feeney had pushed me after I beat him in a foot race down the hill, breaking my wrist in the process. And there was the little stone wall where Amy used to wait for me to finish my chores on otherwise lazy Saturday afternoons, the hill up to the Manor daunting on her old three-speed bicycle. It was all there, a history of my life as I trudged along, every tree, stream, and bump in the road bringing up a memory long suppressed and hopefully forgotten.

My phone vibrated in my pocket, the ring tone—a sassy Beyoncé song—scaring the bejesus out of me as

I trudged along. I looked at the screen. "Hey, Car," I said. "What's shaking?"

"I got a call from someone named Duffy Dreyer," he said. "No relation to the Met."

"Yeah, I know," I said. "I talked to her yesterday."

"I'm not talking to her," he said. "Just so you know."

"That's your decision." I passed a group of kids running down the hill in front of the high school, one missing me by inches.

"And I've talked Dad out, once again, of fronting the Casey tip money to me and the boys. He's hell-bent on giving the staff the money anyway but I told him that we have a motto and it's 'family hold back.' I hope you agree," he said.

"You know I do, Car. Mom and Dad need the cash flow, and if it kills me, I'm finding Pauline and getting that money back."

"You sound pretty sure."

"I am," I said. And I was. I was putting every ounce of my energy into finding this girl and I wasn't going to stop until I found her. There was too much at stake.

I arrived at the high school a few minutes later. The front door of the school was fitted with a fancy security system now and it wasn't like the old days when you could walk right up, let yourself in, and wander around at will. I took a place on a bench in a small garden that had been created in honor of an art teacher who had passed a few years previously, the information about it all on the plaque affixed to the brick wall. I texted Brendan to let him know I was outside. All around me, kids raced around the parking lot, the front lawn, and down the front steps, happy to be done with their school day, ready to go to extracurricular activities and after-school jobs and, finally, home.

A few teachers exited, two in particular chatting amiably. I recognized them from my time at FLHS as Troy Maloney, the phys ed teacher, and Sandy Parks, a guidance counselor and girls' volleyball coach. Maloney took a step back when he saw me; we had spent many a morning at the local indoor pool training for swim meets.

"Belfast? Belfast McGrath?" Maloney asked.

Ms. Parks waved and then hurried off to a waiting school bus, a bunch of girls banging on the windows and getting psyched up for a volleyball match.

"Hi, Mr. Maloney," I said. When I was in school, Troy Maloney was young, fit, and the focus of more than a few crushes. Now, he was approaching fifty, wearing a wedding ring that looked as if it were cutting all the blood off to the rest of his finger, and sporting a potbelly that strained against his FLHS striped polo. "Yep, I'm back in the Landing."

"I heard something about that," he said. "Back at Shamrock Manor? My wife and I got married there."

"And back at the Manor," I said. "How are you? You got married?"

"Yes," he said, looking at the blue sky and smiling. "Going on fourteen years now. We have two little ones."

"That's nice."

He looked back at me. "And you? What's new in your life?"

"Not too much. Was living in the city and am back now with my family," I said, trying to inject a little enthusiasm into my brief recitation of my history.

"You can go home again, right?" he said.

"I guess so," I said.

He patted my shoulder. "Good to see you, Bel. Hope to see you around," he said before walking off to the parking lot.

I waved as he drove by in his pickup truck, a different truck than the one he drove when we were in high school but the same style. He waved back, his eyes in the rearview, studying me, it seemed, as he drove down the driveway to the street below.

A voice whispered in my ear. "Bring back memories?"

"Brendan, hi," I said, getting up and giving him a hug. "I didn't hear you come up behind me." From across the parking lot, a group of kids let Mr. Joyce know that they were proud he had game, a girl.

"Tell your story walking, Sweeney!" Brendan called back, taking my hand.

"Can we take a walk?" I asked. "Somewhere away from the village?"

We walked down the driveway and headed in the opposite direction of the center of town, finding a trail that I had forgotten existed and that created a nice flat path behind the middle school and down to a small body of water. We sat beneath a shady tree that hadn't lost its leaves yet and I picked up some pine needles, letting them fall between my fingers.

"You're not here to break up with me, are ya, Bel?" he asked. "You know, taking me out to the woods like this. No one would hear my sobs of sorrow out here. Might be the perfect place for this to end." He went dramatic. "Or kill me? Is that what you have in mind?"

I laughed. "No, Brendan. I'm not. Why would you think that?" I asked.

"Well, I haven't been the best boyfriend," he said. "I

have lots of schoolwork and then I paint on the weekends . . ." He hesitated. "And then there was that day when I left you alone."

"I'm over that," I said. But even to my own ears, the protest sounded hollow. I wasn't over it completely and I wasn't sure I would ever get over it although I told myself that I would try really hard.

He smiled sadly. "You're not, Bel. That's clear to me." He gripped my hand tighter. "But I will make it up to you. I promise." He leaned over and kissed me. "Just tell me what to do."

"Never do it again," I said. "Never keep a secret from me."

He looked aghast. "Keep a secret from you? I would never do that."

"Then why didn't you tell me about Duffy Dreyer?"

"The catcher for the Mets?" he said.

"Stop it, Brendan. I already know. I met her."

He dropped my hand and ran his hands through his unruly curls. In the small pond, one that had once been much deeper before the drought and on which we used to skate as kids, a bird flew down and ducked in to see if there were any tasty morsels beneath the surface, coming up empty-billed and probably disappointed. Brendan lay back on the bed of pine needles and closed his eyes.

"Why you, Brendan? Why did she talk to you?"

"I don't know, Bel. Jaysus. It was as much a surprise to me as it was to you. I had nothing to do with you, Kevin, or Amy back then. I guess she just looked for people of our age, in our year at school. I'm not hard to find." He put his hands on his stomach.

"Where did she find you? How did she find you?"

"Craft fair at the castle in Grand Mill."

"She just walked up and started asking you questions?" I asked.

"Yep." He sat up again. "She bought a painting first. Said she loved my work."

So compliments were her stock-in-trade. God, Brendan was naïve but then again so was I. She had established rapport with me and I had fallen into her net, giving her more details than I should have.

"What did you tell her? About then? About me?" I asked.

"Nothing. Not a thing. There's nothing to tell, Bel. I don't have a lot of recollections to share. I just remember the sadness. The aftermath."

"Don't talk to her again, Brendan," I said. "Please. It's enough that I was there that night, that I was one of the last people to see her alive, that we had an argument. I don't want to be in this again." But I was and always would be, Belfast McGrath, the best friend. Her best friend.

He looked at me. "I don't generally like being told what to do, Bel, but in this case, I think I'll take your advice." He leaned over and held my face. "I do love you, Bel. More than anyone I have ever met."

"More than the last Rose of Tralee you went on a date with?" I asked.

"Much more than her," he said. "She talked with her mouth full anyway."

It was my turn to lie in the grass and look up at the sky. I guess I had been the naïve one thinking that the discovery of Amy's things beneath the water wouldn't bring at least one reporter out of the woodwork to get the true story of what had happened that night. As much as everyone asked me, I didn't know anything beyond that last ugly scene, the final words I ever spoke to her.

*You'll be sorry.*

I thought of my brothers, looking for me that whole night. Had anyone looked for Amy the way they had looked for me? I didn't know and it was too late to ask.

Brendan was waiting for something from me, my reciprocal declaration of love. But this wasn't the right time to say it so I left the words unspoken in the afternoon air, the idea that I might never say them again a thought that entered my mind as I watched the bird over the water looking for something she would never find.

## CHAPTER *Twenty*

"Where's Bel?"

Where was I ever? In the kitchen, I wanted to call out into the foyer, but Colleen had figured it out on her own before getting an answer to her question. She came in the next day, dropped her purse onto the counter and let out a dramatic sigh. "I heard from her."

"Pauline?" I asked.

"Yes," she said. "Said she's had enough of the States. She's moving back to Ireland."

"Really?" Based on everything I now knew and all of the things the girls had told me, Ireland was the last place that Pauline would want to be. "What brought that about? What about the abusive husband?" And most importantly, now that I knew she was safe, what about our money? The ten thousand she stole?

"Dunno," Colleen said. "But your da owes her money. A couple a weeks' pay. She wants me to meet her and drop it off," she said.

"When?" I asked.

"Why do you want to know?"

"Because I'm coming with you," I said, stripping off my chef's coat and going into the office, which fortunately was empty. I went through Mom's accounting folder and found the check, in an envelope with a little window indicating that it was addressed to Pauline. I went back into the kitchen. "Let's go."

We took my car. Colleen took a look around. "Good thing the Health Department doesn't check your domicile or your vehicle," she said, sniffing. "This car is a disgrace, Belfast."

"I know! I know," I said. "Do you see what I have to do during the week to get ready for a wedding?" I asked. "Oh, right, you don't because you don't help with prep."

"No need for the nastiness again, Bel. It was just an observation."

"Where are we going?" I asked at the bottom of the hill. "Left or right?"

"To the river. The place where people put in their boats."

"The kayak put-in?" I asked.

"She said to meet her by the picnic table. Is there more than one picnic table down there?" she asked as we sped through town. School was in session so the village was scantily populated, just a few people going in and out of the few stores that remained open after a recession had nearly decimated the place. It was starting to come back, though, and that made me happy.

We made it to the meeting spot in less than ten minutes, my old car groaning and protesting as we drove over the gravel that led to what used to be the water's edge, now so far out because of the drought that we could have driven halfway to Grand Mill. I pulled as close as I could to the picnic table and, not seeing any other car, got out and looked around, seeing if Pauline was in the vicinity. She was, parked near the kayak racks and a bank of lockers that Foster's Landing's municipal department rented to people in town for the year. You could stow your boat and any gear you had without taking up room in your own garage. If I still had a kayak, I would probably put my name on the list to rent the space, but alas, my kayaking days were over for the time being.

Pauline was still in her car, the likes of which it would have taken me close to a hundred years to save for. Francesco Francatelli, my former boss and a movie star in his own right, had had a similar car and I had ridden in it more than a few times; he was such a braggart that I knew how much a car like that cost. Pauline got out of the car and it was clear that she was there to collect her check and nothing more. No chitchat, no explanation for where she had been or why she had so unceremoniously left the employ of Shamrock Manor.

"Hey, can I see your car?" I asked. "Sweet ride." I ran my hands over the hood.

She looked at me. "Sure." She looked at Colleen. "But I'm in a rush. Do you have my check?"

"Yeah," I said, waving the envelope in the air. "Do you have my parents' tip from the Casey wedding?"

"I don't know what you're talking about," she said. That was her story and she was sticking to it.

"Yes you do," I said as I got into the car and found the ignitionless key fob. Gone were the days of putting a key into a slot and turning it for power; Pauline's car, like so many others now, required just the push of a button. I turned off the car, put the fob in my pants pocket and got out. "Do you have my parents' money?"

She put her hands on the roof of the car and screamed. When she had calmed down, she turned to me. "What money?"

"You know what money, Pauline," I said. When she didn't reply, I continued. "Okay. So now that you're not going anywhere," I said, "tell us what's happening."

She looked around. "Nothing going on. I'm going home. Want to be with my family again."

"I don't think that's true, Pauline," I said. "I think it's a little more complicated than that. Seems like you're leaving a trail of broken hearts behind you. Maybe that has something to do with it?" I asked.

"A girl can date, Bel. No law against that." She looked around nervously. "Now, can I get my keys back?"

"And there is something about Angus Connolly and the Health Department?"

The blare of a train horn, the train farther down the tracks, didn't spook anyone but Pauline, who jumped higher and moved faster than I had ever seen her jump or move during dinner service at the Manor. "Give me my check," she said. "And my keys."

We stood in a tense standoff for a few minutes, Colleen begging me to hand over the check and the keys when Pauline finally broke. "Bel, please. Just give me the check and the keys and I'll tell you where I'm going. And why."

I considered the options but, in the end, decided that there was no harm in giving her what she wanted. If it told me why she looked so scared, it would help solve at least part of the mystery. I handed them to her. "Now, what gives? Where are you going? And why are you going?" I asked.

She got into the car and I was afraid that I had trusted her only to be conned. But she rolled down the window and looked at me. "I'm going anywhere but here because I have to."

"Why?" I asked again. In the distance, a lone car made its way toward us. Pauline saw it too, her eyes going to the rearview mirror.

"I'm sorry, Bel, but I have to go." She started to roll up the window but I stuck my hand in it hoping she would stop before my fingers were crushed. "I saw the whole thing. Gerry Mason didn't have a heart attack. He was poisoned."

# CHAPTER *Twenty-one*

Pauline sped away, the big tires on her car spraying me and Colleen with pebbles and dirt. By the time we had rid ourselves of the dust and rock in our eyes and mouths, she was a half mile away. My old Volvo is good for a lot of things but a car chase isn't one of them. Colleen and I jumped into the car anyway, hoping that we could catch a glimpse of where she was headed. As we got closer, the car that had started toward us did a quick U-turn and started following her as well, putting a car length between us.

"Well, that solves one mystery," Colleen said.

"And what mystery is that?" I asked, driving as if I had been taught to be a Hollywood stunt driver.

"What happened to that poor groom," she said.

That seemed to raise more questions than it answered. For one? "Why didn't she call the police then?" I asked as I made a hard right down a small street that I knew only had one side street before it ended in a dead end.

"Bel, sometimes I think you're an eejit," Colleen said, holding on to the door handle as Pauline and the car behind her made the turn that I had anticipated.

"Thank you?" I said. "What's that supposed to mean?"

"It means that as smart as you think you are, you really don't think things through. She can't call the police. You know that."

"Have you ever heard of an anonymous tip?" I asked. "She could have called and left the tip anonymously."

"And they could have traced her phone or kept the recording or traced the call to her location even."

"You watch too much TV, Colleen. This is Kevin Hanson and Lieutenant D'Amato of the FLPD not Crockett and Tubbs on *Miami Vice*," I said.

"What's a Crockett and Tubbs?"

"Never mind." We headed up the street that appeared right before the dead end and my old car made a chugging noise, not used to going so fast up a hill. I could sympathize. I couldn't run up this hill if you paid me. In front of me, the distance between the Volvo and the cars I was following grew wider and I knew it was a matter of time before I lost them both.

"You don't understand, Bel, you with your American citizenship, your safety of living in this country legally. You don't know what it's like for us," she said, looking out the passenger-side window. "It's dangerous. Shamrock Manor keeps us safe from all of that."

"Fair enough," I said. "So now she's on the run." And we have another major problem at Shamrock Manor. Great. Dad was going to take to his bed for a week after he got that news. If Pauline was telling the truth, that is. And where was our money?

We finally hit the highway and that's when the distance became so great between me and the two cars that it was clear that the chase was over. I gave the gas one last push and got the Volvo up to seventy miles an hour but it wasn't enough for good, old German engineering and the BMW and the car in front of me, which I finally ascertained was a Mercedes and a fast one at that. I watched both cars speed down the left lane and into the encroaching sunset and took my foot off the gas just in time to see flashing lights behind me, the source of their consternation me and my Swedish behemoth of a car.

"Oh, great," Colleen said, sinking down in her seat.

"Just stay quiet," I said. "Chances are I know who-ever this is, and while I'll probably still wind up with a ticket, you'll be fine." I rolled down the window and looked at the cop, trying to place his adult face into that of a child's. "Is that you, Davie Egan?" I said to the stern-looking cop staring at me. "Well, I'll be."

"You'll be what, Belfast? A speeder?" he said. "Do you know how fast you were going?"

"Seventy?" I asked.

He put his thumb in the air and indicated that I should adjust my answer accordingly.

"Seventy-two?" I asked.

"Seventy-eight," he said.

"Wow," I said. "I didn't know the old girl had it in her. Good job, Phoebe!" Just that morning, I had won-dered how long I would be able to drive the car.

"Your car has a name?"

It does now, I thought. Anything to let him know that I was possibly the least threatening person he had ever pulled over and for that reason, and that reason alone, didn't deserve the ticket I truly did deserve.

"License and registration, Bel." He leaned in and looked at Colleen who was trying to make herself in-visible.

I hoped I had at least the registration. I had left the

Manor so quickly that I hadn't had time to grab my purse
in which my license resided. I opened the glove box and
came up with the registration, handing it to Davie with
a smile. "One out of two isn't bad, right?"

"Oh, no, it's bad, Bel. One out of two in this case is
bad. Wait here," he said, walking away from my car and
going to his.

I banged my head on the steering wheel. Colleen
opened the car door. "I'll be going now, Bel. Thank you
for this incredibly exciting afternoon," she said.

I reached over and grabbed her arm. "Stay here, Colleen. If you get out of the car and start walking away,
you'll make him suspicious."

"More suspicious than he already is?"

"I don't think he's suspicious. I think he is wondering why I'm driving without a license and how I got the
car to get above fifty. But I don't think he's suspicious."

He was back in five minutes with my registration and
a ticket. "Sorry, Bel. Driving without a license requires
that I give you a summons but I put you only ten miles
over the speeding limit on that infraction. All of the information is on the summons here. You'll probably pay
a fine and—"

"Jail time?" I asked.

He looked at me quizzically. "Well, I don't think
so . . ."

"I was kidding, Davie. I hope to God that there's no
jail time for a suspended license and a speed."

"Oh. Ha," he said, not amused. "You'll probably have
points on your license so take it easy, okay? No more
Daytona 500 for you on local roads."

"Got it," I said. "See you in court?"

He shook his head as he walked away, the humor in the situation lost on him.

As his car passed mine on the highway, Colleen breathed a sigh of relief. "Just bring me home, Bel. I think I've had enough for today."

I pulled up in front of her house a few minutes later and stopped the car; she had walked to the Manor that morning. "Does Pauline have a flair for the dramatic?" I asked Colleen. "I mean, this contention that Gerry was poisoned is a bit of a tall tale. I saw him myself. He had all of the hallmarks of a man having a heart attack."

"And you'd know that how, Bel? Now you're a doctor?" Colleen asked before getting out.

I thought about busting out the old joke about playing one on TV, but she didn't seem in the mood for humor. "You didn't answer my question, Colleen. Pauline. Dramatic. Prone to flights of fancy?"

Colleen looked at me. "Does that really matter, Bel? That Pauline was dramatic? Excitable? I don't think it does." She opened the door. "All I know now is that this is going to get more complicated and I'm going to end up in a heap of trouble. That's what I'm focused on now."

I watched her as she climbed the steps to the front door. I had felt trapped when I had first arrived home, but knowing what I knew now about these girls and their situation, I knew that I was as free as a bird.

# CHAPTER *Twenty-two*

I had gotten a plate number on the car that had been following Pauline and committed it to memory, using
mnemonics to help me. I wrote it down when I got home,
knowing now that in order to figure at least part of this
mystery out, I would need my brother's help. He had
connections and if anyone was going to be able to tell
us who the car belonged to, it was one of his guys or
gals in the PD or DMV.

He was kicking a soccer ball around on the lawn
when I arrived home, heading one into Mom's azaleas.
"Do you really think it's a good idea to use your head?" I
asked. "It's not like you have a ton of brain cells left. I
remember what you were like in the nineties."

"Hilarious, Bel," he said. He pointed to the summons
in my hand. "What now? Public indecency? Resisting
arrest?"

I walked across the lawn and picked up the soccer
ball, throwing it back to him. He headed it again.
"Speeding. No license."

"You don't have a license?" he asked.

"Well, I have a license, I just didn't have it on me
when I got pulled over by Davie Egan."

"He still a tool?" Cargan reminded me that it had been Davie Egan who had gotten us busted by our parents for toilet-papering the principal's house one Halloween night, an offense that was punishable by death in my house. Fortunately we were granted a stay of execution when the principal decided that we would join the janitorial staff at the high school for two weeks, our only chore to clean the toilets in the school bathrooms.

"Kind of. He wouldn't let me go on the missing license."

"Not sure I would have either, Bel. It's not a good idea to be driving around without a license."

"Don't tell Dad, okay?" I asked, the words coming out of my mouth belonging to someone much younger, much more attached to her family and their opinion of her. It was just that I couldn't take the old guy's histrionics. He was the guy you wanted in a foxhole with you, for sure, if something truly dramatic was happening, but the little stuff? That sent him over the edge.

"You've got it." Cargan kicked the ball to me. "Need any help in the kitchen? I have a few hours free. I know tomorrow's wedding is a small one. Got it covered?"

"Now that you ask," I said, giving him a quick-and-dirty summary of what had happened in the past hour. His eyes grew wide when I got to the part about Pauline's contention that Gerard Mason was poisoned. I rattled off the license-plate number. "Can you call someone and find out who that car belongs to?" I asked.

"What do you think I am, Bel?" he asked, but I could see that I had piqued his interest.

"I think you're someone with a ton of connections who can help me figure out why Pauline was running scared." Sure, there was the abusive husband but it seemed as if he were still in Ireland, somewhere she didn't want to go back to.

"What was it again?" he asked. "The plate number?"

I said it again and I could see he was doing his own mind tricks to remember it.

"Give me a few hours," he said, picking up the soccer ball and starting toward the Manor. Before he got up the hill, he turned to me. "And don't tell Hanson yet."

"Understood," I said. The last thing we needed was Kevin involved. Selfishly, and I wasn't proud of this, I was worried about what we would do if we lost the girls. With a ton of weddings on the books, it would be hard to find and train people in time. If Brendan Joyce, a college graduate and contributing member of society, found it difficult to execute some of the tasks associated with being a banquet server at Shamrock Manor, I shuddered to think of what we might find if we had to start filling positions left open by Eileen and Colleen. We were already one down with Pauline's disappearance; we didn't need any more vacancies on the service staff.

I was deep in thought when I entered the kitchen, not realizing that the two people I expressly didn't want to see were deep in conversation at the far end of the stainless-steel prep area. If I didn't know better, they were exchanging the nuclear codes, the tilt of their heads and their hushed tones suggesting something dangerous and dramatic was about to take place. Both Dad and Kevin looked up at the sound of my rubber-soled clogs squeaking on the tiled floor.

"Well, then ask her, son!" Dad bellowed.

"Ask me what?" I said, pulling an apron off the hook and pulling it over my head.

Kevin looked up at the ceiling.

"Spit it out, lad!" Dad said.

"Mary Ann wants a change to the menu we discussed," he said.

"Okay," I said, suspicious. "What kind of change?" If she wanted me to make Swedish meatballs for the cocktail hour—something one of my brides had requested over the summer—I would tell her no. The batch that I had made for that previous wedding had sat in a gelatinous pool of liquid, untouched and uneaten, and I had tossed all but the one I tried into the garbage. If Mary Ann D'Amato wanted Swedish meatballs, she could go to Ikea and eat in their cafeteria.

Kevin finally looked at me. "Duck ballotine."

"What?" I said. "Did I hear you say 'duck ballotine'?"

"Yes," he said. "She saw it on *Top Chef* the other night and thought it looked delicious."

"It *is* delicious," I said. "But it's not something you make for one hundred and fifty people."

"She wants it."

"Well, she can't have it."

Dad looked back and forth at the two of us, wondering who would win this verbal tennis match.

"But that's what she wants."

"You know what I want, Kevin?" I asked. "I want a new pony. And maybe a unicorn. And one chin, not two. But I can't have those things because they are completely impractical for the life I lead. And duck ballotine is just like that pony or unicorn. It's completely impractical for a wedding, particularly one held at Shamrock Manor." I continued unnecessarily with the details of making a very intricate dish while the two of them looked at me blankly. "So, you see why this is completely not in the cards for your wedding, as much as I would like to help you."

Dad interjected his thoughts. "The customer is always right. And here at Shamrock Manor—"

I put up a hand. "Save it, Dad. I know what I know and what I know is that duck ballotine is not something we can offer at banquet service." I looked at Kevin. "Do you know what that will do to your per-person cost? It will double it. No, it will triple it," I said, doing a little math in my head. "And the labor? Holy cripes. You start two days ahead with one duck. It will take a week to poach all that duck, make the forcemeat . . ." I trailed off, putting my head in my hands. Kevin looked at my dad and I knew instantly that that was what they had been discussing—the cost of all of this—when I had walked in. I looked at my father. "You didn't."

"Now, Belfast . . ."

"Dad, I understand Kevin is an old friend and all but we have to make a profit on our weddings. It just doesn't make sense to keep giving people discounts. Our rates are nonnegotiable. I'm tired of people nickel-and-diming you." I looked at Kevin. "With all due respect, of course. No offense."

"None taken," Kevin mumbled.

"There will no extra charge for the duck," Dad said. "And there will be duck ballotine. That's an order."

"Thank you, Mr. McGrath. Bel." Kevin was sheepish as he brushed past me and out of the kitchen, not making eye contact with me.

Dad went into the office and closed the door. Mom was in there and I could hear him recounting the story—Dad is a man incapable of whispering—as I tried to calculate in my head just how many ducks I would need to feed the D'Amato/Hanson crowd, two families that wouldn't know a duck ballotine from a meat loaf. It was not exactly "wine o'clock," as I liked to call it, but it was close enough. I took a bottle of Malbec from the stash I kept under the sink and opened it, pouring a healthy portion into a water glass. I was chugging it down when Cargan walked into the kitchen. "Want to hear this, Car?" I asked. "Dad wants me to make duck ballotine—"

"Shush," he said, holding up a piece of paper. On it was the license-plate number I had given him. "You want to know who the car belongs to?" he asked.

"Car?"

"The car that was chasing Pauline."

I put the water glass down. "Who?"

"James Casey."

# CHAPTER *Twenty-three*

The lie fell from my lips so effortlessly that it kind of scared me. "Yes, I'm trying to learn everything I can about the import/export business because I'm thinking of branding a line of soda breads and believe that they could have international appeal."

On the other end of the phone, James Casey cleared his throat. "Really? Soda breads?"

"Yes. My mother's mother's mother's recipe. Straight from the old sod. The Emerald Isle. The land of . . ." I couldn't think up another nickname for my parents' birthplace so I fell silent.

"That's interesting, Belfast. Soda bread. Huh."

"So can you tell me a little bit about the import/export business? What it would take to get something like this off the ground?" I asked. I knew that James Casey had seen me, most likely, tailing him tailing Pauline but he didn't know that I knew it was him. I was sure of that. The tone of his voice gave me no indication that he was suspicious of me beyond the fact that I had a lousy business idea that was never going to work. Shipping soda breads? Maybe it was just crazy enough to work. "We would put a photo of Shamrock Manor on the packaging. You know, a nice advertisement for the family business."

"I'm not sure it's the best idea I've ever heard, Bel, but let's get together to discuss it. Crazier ideas have worked," he said.

Well, that was the least confident vote of confidence I had ever heard. "How soon?"

"How soon what?" he asked.

"How soon can we get together?" I looked at the clock. It had been an action-packed day and I was ready to call it a night, but if he was free, I was definitely free as well.

"I'm just about to wrap things up here," he said. "I could have a quick drink. Seven o'clock? Is that good?"

"Perfect," I said. "Where would you like to meet?"

"Do you know a place called O'Halligan's? North of here?"

"I do indeed," I said. "See you at seven."

Curious choice. And one that would guarantee that I wouldn't run into anyone I knew. The Foster's Landing crowd liked to stay close to home, for the most part, preferring the Dugout or one or other watering holes in the village.

I went back to my apartment and got cleaned up. I wasn't going to tell Cargan about this plan, his internal antennae likely to be raised. Heck, who was I fooling? This was a long shot, the longest shot, maybe. The likelihood that James Casey was going to tell me anything about Pauline or their connection was slim to none. But it was worth a shot.

I dressed in my best "I'm serious about exporting

soda bread" outfit: a white shirt just back from the cleaners, black pants, and a scarf to cover the big stain on the white shirt just back from the cleaners that had not been there when it went to the cleaners. I looked like a part-time Aer Lingus flight attendant and full-time soccer mom but it was better than the alternative: a Shamrock Manor T-shirt and a pair of jeans, the only other two items in my limited wardrobe that were clean. Before I left, I did a little research on Casey Imports and saw that they had a well-done Web site complete with photos of the primary stockholders—James, Pegeen, and of course, Mr. Casey. I searched each person's name separately but there wasn't a lot on any of them besides professional-looking LinkedIn pages and an article about Mr. Casey winning the American Order of Hibernians Hibernian of the Year award from the South Boston chapter of the organization, a photo of him with Pegeen and James flanking him. There wasn't a lot to see here, nothing to suggest that what Mr. Casey had told us, that he imported this, exported that, wasn't the truth.

With nothing to go on, I ran down the steps to the parking area, jumped in my car, and set off for O'Halligan's.

The bar was crowded but I spotted James Casey at one end, sitting on a bar stool and protecting another one for me. I made my way through the crowd and sat down, shaking his hand like a professional with a soda bread business would do. "Thanks for meeting me on such short notice," I said.

"My pleasure," he said. "You've been so kind to our family during this difficult time. I can't thank you enough. Listen, before we get started, have you found my sister's bag?"

"Her bag?" I asked. I hadn't heard a word about it. "I'm sorry. We haven't."

He smiled sadly. "Oh, thanks, then. Seems like it's gone."

I had forgotten, almost, how cute he was. Pretty cute, indeed. "How is your sister doing?"

He flagged down the bartender and looked at me. "Drink?"

"Yes," I said. "A bourbon neat, please."

"Ah, a lady who drinks actual drinks," he said. "That's refreshing."

"I do like a cheap Chardonnay every now and again," I said. "And I'm not above a hearty Italian table wine."

He smiled. "Good to hear."

The bartender slid the drink in front of me. "Your sister?" I asked, taking a sip. "Is she doing okay?" I looked around but there was no sign of Angus Connolly.

"That's hard to say," he said. "She hasn't gone out at all since the wedding. We know it hasn't been long but, still, we're worried."

"Does she work?" I knew she worked and where she worked but wanted to hear his answer.

"She works in Dad's business. Like I do." He sipped his own whiskey.

"Yes. Your dad's business. Import/export?" I asked. "What exactly does that mean?"

"We bring things in and ship things out," he said. "It's pretty simple actually."

"Things like what?" I asked. "And how?"

"Trinkets. Larger items from around the world. Furniture." He took a sip of his drink.

"How do you do that?" I asked. "Planes?"

"We use ships mostly."

"Interesting," I said. "There's still a shipping industry for goods?" In my mind, I thought that everything got to where it needed to be by air; it hadn't occurred to me that the shipping industry was alive and well internationally.

"Oh, yes. That's how we ship most of our items."

"And your sister is in the business, too?"

He nodded. "She is. She's Dad's right-hand man, so to speak." He looked at me intently, trying to discern my purpose in asking a lot of questions about the import/export business. "Thank you for asking after her. But enough about that. Tell me about your business plan."

Business plan? There was no business plan. What there was was the wisp of a fictional idea that if I didn't flesh out quickly would expose me as the biggest liar of all time. "Well . . ." I started.

"Bel?" Behind me a man's voice, one that I knew so well, called my name. So much for not running into someone I knew. I couldn't know this guy any better. Why? He was my brother.

I turned and came face-to-face with Feeney and a young woman who was definitely not his girlfriend Sandree. "Feeney?" I looked at James Casey. "You remember my brother? Feeney?"

Feeney eyed James suspiciously but held out his hand to shake. "Nice to see you again," he said, but it was insincere. He looked at me and I smiled. I had nothing to feel guilty about beyond the fact that I was lying to a nice guy who had chased one of our servers in his car this afternoon. What was Feeney's story exactly? I could tell just by looking at him. He was up to no good. It was a look I knew well, having grown up with a guy who gave hooligans a bad name.

"And who is this lovely lass?" I asked, giving his companion the once-over. She was sixty if she was a day, a good two decades older than my brother, and dressed to the nines in an expensive leather jacket and the kind of jeans that moms with money wore: fitted, boot-cut, dark-washed, and high-waisted. I held out my hand. "Belfast McGrath."

"Patricia Sandford," she said. Her hand felt like a skinny dead fish in my own meatier palm. Her face was stretched tighter than the snare drum that Derry played in the band, her enhanced lips glossed and shiny. A little nip and tuck, for sure, but she looked good.

"And Feeney? How did you and Ms. Sandford meet?" I asked.

He narrowed his eyes. "I could ask you the same thing," he said, realizing, too late, that he knew how I had met James Casey. "Um, what I mean is, why you're here. With him," he said, pointing at my fake future business partner. "And not with Brendan Joyce."

Heck, were we really going to do this here in front of two people who had no business in this? Old sibling baggage is tough to tote around but even tougher to explain to nonfamily-members. "Mr. Casey here is helping me with a business idea that I have."

"And that's what, Bel? Shamrock Manor coasters? Belfast McGrath doohickeys?"

" 'Doohickeys'?" I said. "No, not doohickeys, Feen."

James Casey jumped in. "Soda bread."

Patricia Sandford and Feeney said it in unison. "Soda bread?"

I did some quick thinking, some quick talking. "Yes, Feeney," I said, staring straight into his eyes to let him know that whatever I said, he should go along with. "Remember Great-grandmother Blair's soda bread?"

"I thought you said it was your great-great-grandmother?" James said, exhibiting an incredible memory for ridiculous details.

"Right. Great-great-grandmother Blair," I said.

Feeney played along. It was always good to have a hooligan on your side, someone for whom lying was a daily event, the only thing that could keep him out of trouble where Mom and Dad were concerned. "Of course, Belfast. Great-great-grandmother Blair. A true Irish lass."

That was laying it on a bit thick and I let him know that by grabbing his hand and squeezing it. "The soda bread. The one that Mom makes. Handed down over generations."

"It's a thing of beauty." Mom's soda bread was like eating plasterboard dotted with caraway seeds and currants.

I squeezed his hand harder. "Well, what would you think of us exporting it?"

Patricia Sandford asked the most obvious question. "To where?"

"Canada," I said. "Mexico."

"Mexico?" she asked. "Is there a call for soda bread in Mexico?"

"Yes, large Irish expat population in Mexico City," I said.

Feeney covered his guffaw with a cough. "Coming down with something," he said, pounding his chest with his fist. "Been going around."

James Casey studied me with intensity. "This is becoming much more attractive as a business opportunity, Bel. Mexico City? Really?"

I nodded and swallowed any pride I had left, continuing with the lie. "What do you think, Feeney?"

"It's grand, Bel. Truly grand." In his smile was evidence that if he didn't leave soon, he would completely lose it in front of James Casey and the jig would be up. "Now, we must be going. Pleasure to see you again, Mr. Casey," he said, turning to his date. "Ready, Patricia?"

I watched them weave through the crowd and, when I was sure they were gone, turned back to James. "My brother is a character."

He leaned in close to me. "This isn't about soda bread, is it, Bel?"

I felt a sheen of sweat break out on my upper lip. "Whatever do you mean, James?"

"Soda bread? Great-great-great-grandmother Blair? The large expatriate population in Mexico City?" He came closer to me. "You really didn't have to go to such trouble. I would have met you anyway." He put his hand over mine. "The attraction has been undeniable since we first met."

It has? "Oh, James. You caught me," I said. "But this can never go anywhere. I do have a boyfriend whom I love very much."

He raised an eyebrow. "Do you?"

Before he could get any closer, plant a kiss on my lips, I drew back. "This was a mistake," I said. "I never should have called you. This never happened." I got up off my bar stool and gave him my best look of regret, biting my lip for emphasis. "I'm sorry, James. This was all a terrible, terrible mistake."

He sipped his whiskey, buying some time, thinking

of what to say. "If things change, Bel . . . if your boy-friend and you . . ."

I put a finger to his lips to quiet him. "No more. It's too painful." And before I could say anything else that might make the situation go on longer than necessary, I made haste out of the restaurant and into my car, driv-ing as quickly, but responsibly, as I could to Shamrock Manor. I had wasted an evening and really mucked things up. I couldn't see or talk to James Casey again without him thinking that we were destined to be to-gether and that left me with another wrinkle in a mys-tery that just got more convoluted as time went on.

I fell asleep less than an hour later and dreamt of la-dies with face-lifts eating duck ballotine while prepar-ing soda bread.

# CHAPTER *Twenty-four*

That Saturday, I was in the last stages of defying Mom's orders about hors d'oeuvres, putting the finishing touches on a small red potato with caviar and crème fraîche, when Brendan entered the kitchen, taking one from the tray and popping it into his mouth.

"Who's the lucky couple today?" he asked around a mouthful of caviar.

"Dorothy Murphy and Patrick Stewart," I said, rearranging the tiny appetizers on the tray to cover up the spot left by the one Brendan had eaten.

"The guy from *Star Trek*?" he asked.

"Yes, Brendan, the guy from *Star Trek* is marrying a girl from Foster's Landing," I said, shoving a tray of pigs in a blanket into the oven, slapping his hand as he reached out for another potato.

"Cool," he said. "I've always wanted to meet him and I've got nothing to do today. Can I help in the kitchen?" he asked.

I turned back around and he was right behind me, leaning down and giving me a long kiss. The day would go much better certainly if he was around. "You're not a lot of help, you know," I said. "Your feet are big and you're slow to expedite. What other services do you have to offer?" I crossed my arms, taking him in. We hadn't seen each other the night before, him in the throes of doing midterm grades and me exhausted from the week and feeling a wee bit guilty about my passion play with James Casey the night before.

"Well, I can feel you up between courses, and I pour a nice glass of wine and give a good foot rub when service is over." He smiled. "I have other talents as well but I have a feeling your mother is around here and I wouldn't want her to know what other services I offer."

"You're hired!" I said. "For real though, I do need your help. We're down a server and obviously we can't pull any of the boys off band duty. It's not a huge wedding, but we could use your help. Do you have black pants and a white shirt at home?"

"I do," he said.

"That begs the question, why?" I asked. "All I've ever seen you in is a blue oxford and khakis."

"I'm Irish, Bel. Every good Irishman has a nice black suit in the closet," he said. "You never know when a good funeral is going to present itself."

"Good point," I said. "Now go home and change if you're really serious about this."

"I have to serve food?" he asked.

"We'll make it easy on you. Maybe just bus tables. I'm sure Mom and Dad will throw a twenty your way when the day is done."

"Riches!" he exclaimed.

"You don't have to do this," I said.

He kissed me again. "Anything for you, Bel," he said before popping another potato in his mouth and heading out the door. I heard a respectful and slightly terrified "Hello, Mrs. McGrath" come from the foyer when he ran into Mom who arrived in the kitchen moments later.

"That Joyce boy is certainly sweet on you," she said.

"I hope he is," I said. "We've been dating for a few months now. You know that."

"Is it serious?" Mom asked, her gaze falling to the caviar. She kept her mouth shut and surveyed the rest of the kitchen, knowing resistance was futile when it came to the menu.

I thought about that. Was it? I thought so, our relationship righting itself after that bump in the road, the day Amy's things were discovered. "Ah, we're just having fun, Mom," I said.

"Tick, tick," Mom said, tapping an imaginary watch on her wrist. "You're not getting any younger, Belfast. The time for fun is over."

Did this woman ever hear herself? "Tick, tick"? That veiled reference to my gradually hardening ovaries was about as subtle as the crucifix she had hung over my bed when I first moved back home along with an admonition to always do as "Jesus did." "Great advice, Mom. Thanks." I turned and set the timer on the counter, hoping that when I turned back around, she had disappeared, taking her opinions on relationships and unborn grandchildren along with her.

But no such luck. She was still standing there when I was done, staring at me with concern. "I'm worried about Pauline, Bel. So is your father. We were very close. Loved that girl like a daughter."

"Pauline?" I asked. I wondered why they were so

close, why Mom considered her family. I didn't think Dad could have picked her out of a line up based on his inability to tell the girls apart.

"We feel that way about all of our girls, Belfast. You should know that." She bit her lip. "I'm very, very worried."

"You and me both, Mom." I pulled the tray of pigs in a blanket out of the oven and set them on the counter to cool. "Any idea where she might have gone?"

"Back home?" she asked.

"Doesn't sound like it was the place for her," I said. And she thinks Gerry Mason was poisoned but I'll never tell you that.

"Then I don't know." She tucked an errant blond strand behind her ears. "And I hesitate going to the police . . ."

I held up a hand to stop her from saying the one thing I knew she knew. "I know. We all are. It could be bad for the other girls." I looked her in the eye. "For you. For Dad."

She dropped her voice to an angry whisper. "Don't you think I know that?" She leaned on the counter, coming closer to me. "These girls have limited options over there, Belfast. We give them a well-paying job, a roof over their heads."

"And turn a blind eye to the fact that not one of them has legally made her presence known in the United States."

Mom sighed, the fight gone out of her. "It was easier for your father and me, back then. It was easier to become a citizen, live here legally. It's harder now and I feel for them. Everyone needs a chance."

"But is it really doing them any good, Mom? What about in ten years when they are pushing forty and are still hoisting trays of entrées into the dining room? And ten years past that?" I asked, a mental picture of me, my graying hair pulled up into my head scarf, my joints a bit achier, orthotic insoles in my clogs. I shook my head to dispel the image. Not everyone aged like Mom, which is to say, not at all.

Mom's face indicated that she hadn't thought about the future, only the present and where the girls fit into it.

"Plus, she probably stole our tip," I said. "Forgive me if I don't feel that compassionate toward her."

"If someone steals, it's because they need it more than we do," Mom said, channeling her inner saint.

"Or they are just a lousy person," I said.

Mom stood up straighter, smoothed down the front of her black sheath dress, one of several that she kept in her closet for her hostess duties as queen of the Manor. "Remind me what's on the menu." Clearly, we weren't going to talk about this any longer.

She knew. She always knew. It was an awkward tactic to steer us away from the topic at hand and her role in it. "We'll find her, Mom. Cargan and I have been doing some digging."

"And your 'digging.' What have you found out?" she asked.

"Nothing," I said. I turned and looked at the pot of potatoes on the stove, the water bubbling away. Beyond what I had found out two days prior, that she thought she had seen something sinister at the Manor, I had to think about why I cared so much about her and where she went. I thought back to a talk Cargan and I had had a few months earlier, about how his life hadn't really gone the way he had hoped, how he wanted to meet someone, have a family, maybe distance himself from the Manor. He was attracted to her, that was for sure. Did he love her? I thought maybe he did. That alone made me want to find her, to see if maybe Cargan, unlike the other men with whom she seemed to be involved, could have a life with the mercurial Pauline. Did I want that? I didn't know. But I also knew that he loved her and she was out there, terrified. "Maybe I should talk to Kevin?"

"Let me talk to your father about that first."

Dad wouldn't know what to say, what the right thing to do was. He would bluster and wonder and think and perseverate, but in the end no decision would be made. So I made the decision for him, right then and there, that I would talk to Kevin when the time was right. We had a long history and we were back to being friends, the duck ballotine notwithstanding. He would help me; I was sure of that.

Mom surveyed the kitchen one last time. "Well done, Belfast. Let's have a flawless event," she said.

That was my plan. That was *always* my plan. But here at Shamrock Manor, things had a habit of going awry and without warning. Alone in my kitchen once again, my preferred state of being, I continued prepping for the guests who would arrive in the next several hours, the plan for a "flawless event" at least a little bit in my control.

After Mom left the kitchen, Feeney came in. "Ah, another county heard from," I said. "Who's the chick in the mom jeans, Feen?" I asked, referencing the lady from O'Halligan's.

"You mean Patricia?" he asked, opening the refrigerator and taking out a gallon of juice. He poured himself a glass and drank most of it before answering. "She's a talent manager."

"Of whose talent?" I asked.

"Mine," he said. "She heard me play at a wedding here and thought I was the most talented person in the band."

"She did, did she?" It was an age-old argument among my brothers but at the very least Feeney was the one who wanted the musical career the most. Arney had his law practice, Cargan did his management work here while on leave from the police department, and Derry was a stay-at-home dad whose wife was the breadwinner. No one was interested in making music their full-time job except for Feeney who had never really found a career outside of it to satisfy him. Right now, he was working construction for a local company and I could see that it was taking its toll with its long days and manual labor. He looked exhausted and, most of all, unhappy.

"I know what you're thinking, Bel."

"You do?"

"You think that she's just interested in me sexually . . ."

I put my fingers in my ears and started singing to drown him out. "Please don't ever say anything remotely like that again," I said. "First, I didn't think that, and second, it is gross." I didn't tell him that that's the first thing I thought. She had looked at him like he was a gallon of ice cream at a Weight Watchers' meeting.

"You never believed in me," he said.

"Oh, jeez, Feeney. Do we have to go there right this minute?" I looked at the clock. "With less than an hour to go until the cocktail hour starts?" I went around the counter and gave him a hug. "I've always believed in you," I said. "I think you're terrific. You're a better singer than—"

He cut me off before I could come up with a name. "Justin Timberlake?"

"Well, maybe not him, but definitely Justin Bieber."

"Thanks, Bel," he said. He finished his juice. "Showtime."

Brendan Joyce returned a half hour later, looking spiffy in his black pants and white shirt. "So I'm really going to be a waiter?" he said.

"Yes. A waiter," I said. "Is that beneath you?"

"No, not at all," he said. "Though I'd much rather be in the kitchen with you," he said, coming up behind me and wrapping his long arms around my torso. He burrowed into my neck, pulling away suddenly and knocking into a hanging pot over the counter when Cargan appeared in the kitchen.

"Get a room," my brother said. His violin was in his hand and he was dressed in the standard McGrath Brothers getup: black tuxedo, green cummerbund, and green bow tie. I had recommended they go with a traditional tux—black and white—but had been summarily dismissed.

"We're the McGrath Brothers," Arney had said, as if I had besmirched the good name of Bono and the other boys in U2. "People expect a touch of the old country in our songs, our dress."

Do they expect you to have a near knock-down, drag-out fight after almost every set? I had wanted to ask, but one thing I had learned in the early going here was to keep my mouth shut when I had what seemed like a reasonable question to a crazy statement.

"What's on the musical menu today, Cargan?" Brendan asked. I reached up and undid the hastily done tie that Brendan had knotted around his neck, retying it and drinking in his scent: shaving cream coupled with some kind of shampoo that only a middle-schooler should use. The smell of it made my eyes water. I had seen it in his shower and had recommended he buy something that wasn't called "Jungle Prince." People might get the wrong idea as the odor preceded him and assume a fourteen-year-old was making his way into the room.

"Ah, the usual," Cargan said, plucking a few notes on his violin that sounded like an old Clash song. "A few jigs, a few reels . . ." he said, trailing off. "Hey! You used to step dance, didn't you?"

Brendan blushed a deep red. "I did," he said. "Just a little bit."

"That's not what I remember," Cargan said. "I remember you being an All-Ireland champ."

Brendan blushed a deeper red.

"I'm right, aren't I?" Cargan said. "When we do our reel set, you should dance. The guests will love it." He lifted his face, sniffing the air in the kitchen. "Food smells good but what's that other smell?"

Brendan smiled, proud of himself. "It's my shampoo," he said, looking at me as if he had won some important argument, one in which the outcome really mattered. "Jungle Prince."

Cargan looked at him quizzically. "One of your students give that to you? It's not really a grown-man smell," he said before leaving the kitchen.

"Your family hates me," Brendan said. He straightened his tie, using the stainless countertop as a reflective surface.

"They don't hate you," I said. "They are an unusually tough crowd." In the foyer, I could hear the guests arriving. "Hey, you'd better get going. We have a wedding to serve."

Before he left, he kissed me, leaving me in the kitchen with a little flutter in my stomach and looking forward to the day's end.

I turned my full attention to my one, true love: food. I dove into prepping the entrée for the guests, focusing on the little things that made me happy: the proper cut of the meat, the presentation of the vegetables, the dollop of creamy potatoes on which the beef rested. Brendan whistled appreciatively when he came back into the kitchen and saw the plates in the warmer, asking the girls to help him get the requisite six onto his tray so he could hoist it onto his shoulder and move it out to the dining room where, just moments earlier, I had observed him dancing like no one was watching, as the saying goes, smiling as his tie whipped around furiously as he moved across the floor to the delight of the guests. Part-time server and part-time entertainer. Full-time boyfriend. He was fitting right in with the Mc-Grath clan. He was wrong: my family didn't hate him. Rather, he fit right in, which in and of itself was a scary thought.

I looked out into the dining room and the guests appeared happy, everyone tucking into their beautiful dinners. I turned back around, preparing to start my work on the dessert, and came face-to-face with a handsome, but clearly angry, guy who looked like he had just stepped out of a music video from the nineties, a flannel shirt, jeans, and boots completing the look of a Seattle-area grunge rocker. "Can I help you?" I asked.

"Don't know," he said. "I'm Domnall Kinneally. Have you seen my wife?"

# CHAPTER *Twenty-five*

"Sit down, lad," Dad said.

Domnall Kinneally had been mollified by a plate of beef and mashed potatoes, and while he was angry when he arrived, he seemed a bit more composed now, seated in Dad's office, a glass of Guinness in front of him. It was a half hour after the wedding had ended and I had bid Brendan adieu with the promise of an evening rendezvous. "Thank you, Mr. McGrath."

Dad sat on the desk, one foot planted on the ground, his hands clasped together, his serious pose. "Tell me, son. What is this all about?" He looked at me. "Did you know that the lass was married, Bel?"

"No!" I lied, a little too vociferously. Dad looked at me, unconvinced, but I knew that if Dad knew that she had been married, had been fleeing a bad marriage, he wouldn't have been happy. "No," I said again, taking a little bit of the mustard off my response. Cargan stood behind Dad studying his own shoes with an intensity they didn't require. I finally gave it up, told the truth. "Yes, but only recently. We heard through the grapevine that Pauline might have been married."

"We didn't know, Domnall," Dad said. "Is there a reason you've come all this way?"

Domnall sipped his Guinness. "There is."

We waited. "Well, are you going to tell us?" Dad asked after close to a full minute of silence.

"It's her ma," he said. "She's not well."

Dad gasped. "Oh, goodness," he said, making the sign of the cross on his chest. "God bless. It is the cancer?"

Domnall looked flustered. "No, not the cancer." He looked at Dad quizzically. "She had cancer?"

"Not that I know of," Dad said. "What is it then?"

Domnall clutched his chest. "The heart. It's her heart. It's not working."

"A blockage?" Dad asked.

"Yes, that. A blockage," he said. "No one knows how long she can go on like this." He looked at all of us, his eyes darting around from one to another of my family members. "Blocked."

"So why didn't you call her? E-mail her? Text her? Send a Western Union letter?" Cargan asked, his arms crossed over his chest in a defensive stance. So there it was. He loved her more than just a little bit. He loved her a lot. I could tell and he could tell that I could tell, the flush starting at his collar and going up to his ears. "Why not, then?"

"Done all that," Domnall said.

"Even the Western Union?" Cargan asked.

"Well, not that, obviously, but everything else. Haven't heard a word from her."

"Did you ever think that maybe she just doesn't want to talk to you?" Cargan asked.

"When it's about her ma?" Domnall asked. "She has to talk to me about that."

Dad held up a hand, sensing the mounting tension in the room. He picked up a stapler and turned it over in his hands. "We haven't seen her, son, and we assume that she has ended her employment here."

"There's more than that, Dad," I said. I didn't want to tell him what I had heard, that maybe Domnall wasn't the poor sap he was pretending to be, sitting here and looking bereft.

"Yes, I know, Belfast," Dad said, cutting me off. "But if this young man here," he said, gesturing toward Domnall with the stapler, "hasn't heard from her and neither have we, then it's clear that we have to do what we have to do." He looked down at the floor. "Whatever the consequences."

I kept my mouth shut, not wanting Dad to know I had seen her. If the girls were to be believed and this guy was an abuser, I wasn't letting anyone know that Pauline was still in the country.

Cargan, surprisingly, was the first one to speak. "I'll call Hanson," he said, leaving the room but not before giving Domnall a sinister glance, one that told the poor guy all he needed to know about what Cargan thought of him and his unannounced arrival.

"Another beer, son?" Dad asked, motioning toward the empty glass in the guy's hand.

"No, sir. No, thank you," he said, standing. "You'll let me know if you find her?"

"Where are you staying?" Dad asked, and in my mind, I sent the strongest telepathic message that I could, letting Dad know that under no circumstances should he let this guy stay at the Manor.

And after the telepathic message, I prayed to God that Domnall had a place to stay. This was getting complicated and the last thing we needed was a houseguest who was looking for his estranged wife, someone who had overstayed her welcome in the great old U.S. of A.

"I'm staying with a friend, Mr. McGrath," Domnall said. "It's all good."

It wasn't all good but I kept my mouth shut. Mom wasn't around and I wasn't sure where she was but once she got wind of this situation, she wasn't going to be happy. I asked him who he knew in Foster's Landing and its environs being as he had told us that this was only his second time in the States, the only other time being a class trip to New York City to see the Statue of Liberty and a bunch of other landmarks.

He pulled at the front of his shirt. "Um, just a lad. A bloke. No one you would know."

"Try me," I said, smiling. "I grew up here and, with the exception of about ten people, everyone I knew then is still here."

"Henry Miller," he said.

"Like the author?" I asked.

"Don't know about that, but that's his name."

I smiled again. "You're right, then. I don't know him," I said. "Must be one of the recent transplants from Brooklyn." Or a nonexistent person that you made up on the spot, the name "Henry" displayed on an envelope on the desk, "Miller" being an easy, American-sounding name that could be plucked out of the rarefied air that lived inside Domnall's obviously dusty brain.

Dad gave me a look: *Don't say it.* So I didn't.

As I watched Domnall Kinneally go, taking his sad brand of lies with him, I wondered just what it was that made him feel like he couldn't tell us one true thing about him or his situation. So here we were with Pauline's abusive husband showing up, and her on the lam with ten grand that belonged to the Manor. I wanted to give him some advice: if you were going to lie, at least make the lies plausible. I didn't have time to teach him the finer points of subterfuge. I had a girl to find. Again.

# CHAPTER Twenty-six

After Domnall left, I found Cargan in the kitchen, staring at the walk-in.

He turned and looked at me, his face a mask of sadness. "I think I loved her a little bit, Bel." The appearance of Pauline's real-life, all-flesh husband had brought out a little feeling in Cargan, this the biggest display of emotion I was likely to get.

"I think you did, too."

"She was gorgeous."

"*Is* gorgeous," I said. "She is gorgeous."

He ignored that. "And funny. And loads of fun."

"No one would blame you for falling for the girl, Cargan," I said. I hearkened back to a conversation we had a few months before when he was recovering from a tragic, awful accident, and when he told me that he was lonely. And tired of being alone. "Did you date? Go anywhere with her?"

"Yes, a few times. Not in the Landing, of course," he said. "She kind of kept me at arm's length. Said her life was 'complicated.'"

"She was right," I said. "Maybe it was better this way." He needed to meet an uncomplicated girl, someone who didn't have quite so much of the kind of baggage that Pauline seemed to have. "Did you call Hanson?" I asked.

He shook his head. "Nope. Changed my mind. I don't think Mom and Dad realize just how much trouble they'll be in if the INS gets wind of this. Which they will if the police get involved."

"And what of the fact that Pauline thinks Mason was poisoned? And that Casey was following her? What about all of that?" I studied my brother's face for some sign that we were on the same page, that he was starting to become as terrified as I was. But there was nothing, just his usual placid expression. "I'm worried, Car."

He pulled off his bow tie. "Let's keep this to ourselves for the time being. I have some work to do."

So did I, I thought, but didn't tell him. Although I love playing Holmes to his Sherlock, I was ready to embrace my inner Nancy Drew and do this on my own. Things weren't moving fast enough for me and I felt as if I were running out of time. I texted Brendan. "Exhausted," I wrote. "Rain check?"

His response was a smiley face, the perfect response for a guy who smelled like a ninth-grader. I felt bad lying to him, but the situation here at the Manor, with my family—with my brother in particular—was getting dicey. No more dancing around the issue. There was a missing girl and before he went to the nuclear option, going to the police, we had to try to figure this out on our own. Why was she running? Was she scared? Had she taken our money? Did she know Donnie was looking for her? Or was it something else? The whole thing stunk to high heaven.

Cargan had gone back into the office to talk to Dad;

Mom had joined the conversation and their hushed tones sounded as if a bunch of snakes had gathered for a meeting. I snuck past the office and across the foyer, going into a quick trot to my apartment, racing up the steps while opening my chef's coat and undoing my pants. Once inside, I did a quick cleanup and let my hair loose from the headscarf in which it had been imprisoned during the wedding; I threw on some clean clothes and spritzed myself with some perfume. When I was done, I looked in the mirror, thinking that a shower would make things a hundred times better. But I had a plan and I wanted to get a jump start on its execution. My appearance wouldn't really matter, or so I hoped.

It would have to do.

As I grabbed my purse from the counter in the kitchen, I noticed that several of the drawers were open. I didn't remember not closing everything up; as someone who had worked in kitchens for a long time, I was meticulous about leaving things as pristine as I had found them. I pushed the drawers shut and left the apartment, thinking that I was either losing my mind or someone had been in my place, not the first time that that had happened. My money was on Mom; she had a tendency to poke around when I wasn't home, making sure that I had enough Clorox to wash my whites or Swiffer dusters to . . . well, not dust.

The old Volvo wagon that Dad had procured for me was on its last legs but it was fine for getting around the Landing and doing local errands. The odometer had just hit 310,000 miles and if I were a more creative type when it came to things like advertising, I would contact Volvo and let them shoot a commercial about me, a chef driving around in a really old car that they had painstakingly built in Sweden a couple of decades prior. Heck, maybe even before I was born. Alas, I didn't have time for that and prayed that the car would hold together until I could buy something a little more suited to my personality and taste. I had a little less than a quarter of a tank but that didn't matter; I was only headed into town.

I pulled up in front of the Dugout, hoping that the person I wanted to talk to might have stopped by on his way home from work. There was no love lost between me and Jed Mitchell and I also hoped and prayed that he didn't throw me to the curb the minute he saw my face. When I walked into the bar, almost empty on this Saturday afternoon, late in the day, I was in luck. He was there.

But as I expected, he wasn't happy to see me.

"Where is everyone?" I asked, settling onto the bar stool next to his. He was as handsome as he had been as a teenager, some incredible genes running through the Mitchell family. Amy had been stunning, a long and lithe blonde, the perfect counterpoint to my shorter and chubbier redheaded self. We were Frick and Frack, Laurel and Hardy. Two opposites who had been best friends from the start. Jed's hair was a little darker than it had been when we were in school but he retained the tight runner's body that had propelled him from high school track star to state champion. He put his elbows on the bar and looked away from me, staring straight ahead.

"You're not welcome here, Bel," he said. "I'm sorry, but you're not."

"It's okay, Jed. I understand." The bartender, a young guy with the hearing of a bat, or so it seemed, had started down the length of the bar to take my order but turned suddenly, the jukebox requiring his attention. "What's New Pussycat?" blared over a janky speaker system, Tom Jones a jaunty juxtaposition to the tension between me and my long-lost best friend's brother. "How's your dad? How's Oogie?" I asked.

"He was fine before you got here. Before you screwed everything up," he said.

"I'm sorry, Jed. I had nowhere else to go," I said. Sad, but true. I had had to come home. It wasn't my first choice, but with no job and no fiancé it was my only option.

"He thought she was alive. All these years," Jed said, shaking his head sadly.

"It's not my fault that she was found," I said. "I had nothing to do with that. That was because of the drought."

He snorted derisively, taking a swig of his beer. "Right, Bel. The drought." He turned and looked at me, something in his eyes. It wasn't exactly hate but it was close. "I guess I should thank you for not pressing charges. For letting my old man off the hook for bringing a gun into your apartment. For threatening you."

"For accidentally causing my brother to be shot?" I asked. It was an accident, yes, but one that could have been avoided. Cargan had almost been killed and if anyone here should have been angry it was me. I had seen my brother in so much pain that he would make us all leave the room, hiding until it subsided, the scar on his side a constant reminder that he wasn't supposed to be here except for the grace of God.

He didn't respond. "What do you want, Bel? My sister's gone and my father's in an institution—which everyone kindly calls 'rehab'—for the foreseeable future.

And then it's house arrest. No coming back to the Dug-out for him. What else could you want from me? I've got nothing else to give you."

"Pauline."

He looked into his glass of beer.

"Tell me about Pauline."

He laughed, a cold sound that belied any merriment. "What do you want to know? That she took me for about ten grand?"

Same amount a sour tip. That seemed to be her sum of choice.

"That my marriage is over because of her?" he continued. "That once she got my money, she was gone with the wind, as they say?" He finished his beer, pounded the bar to get the bartender's attention. "What do you want to know?"

"Where she is," I said. When the bartender appeared, I ordered a beer, too. Jed gave me an angry look. "No one's going to tell me where I'm not welcome, Jed. So get used to it." I watched the bartender carefully to make sure that an errant finger or something more disgusting didn't end up in my pint. "Where'd you meet?" I asked.

"Where'd we meet?" he asked. "Where else do I go besides here?"

"How long did you date?"

"Three months," he said. "Three long, tempestuous months."

"Nice SAT word, Jed. What do you mean by 'tempestuous'?"

"It was a crazy ride. One I had never had. So, I stayed with her and threw everything away as a result."

"When did it end?" I asked.

"About a month ago. Found out she was 'dating' Angus Connolly, too," he said, air-quoting the word. "Maybe others."

You couldn't get two more different men than Jed Mitchell and Angus Connolly. And then there was my brother.

"And you haven't seen her since?" I asked.

"Nope," he said. The radio on the bar next to him crackled to life. He picked it up and listened to it. "Another 911 from the nursing home. Now there's a surprise," he said.

Gone was the lighthearted boy I had known in school and in his place was a cheating, jaded local cop who had lost everything because of an indiscretion. He stood. "I've got to go," he said.

"One more thing," I said.

He threw some money on the bar, just a tip; he drank free at his father's place even if his father was no longer the present proprietor. "What?"

"Why did you give her the money?" I asked.

He picked up the radio. "So that she wouldn't tell my wife." He laughed again. "That didn't work out so well now, did it?"

"What do you mean?" I asked.

"She told her anyway. Cassie left me, Bel. Took my kids. Said I'll never see any of them ever again."

I looked down at the bar.

"Do you know what it's like to have nothing, Bel?"

"I do," I said. I had once had it all but it all had been taken from me, the job, the fiancé, the life I loved. I did know.

"I don't think you do. It's the kind of thing that could make you kill someone," he said, giving me one last look before exiting the bar.

# CHAPTER Twenty-seven

Jed's words ringing in my ears, I texted Cargan from a spot on the sidewalk in front of the bar. "Where are you?" I typed.

"In Hell," was the response so I knew he was home and probably watching one of the celebrity dance shows that Mom and Dad found endlessly entertaining.

"Wanna go for a drink?" I texted back. "Angus Connolly's place?"

"Um . . . sure? Do I want to know why?"

"Just meet me at the bottom of the hill."

"But Hillary Duff is just about to dance the *paso doble*."

I stared at my phone and within a few seconds there was a ping announcing a new text. "Just kidding. On my way."

I drove back to the Manor in the gloom of the evening; it would rain soon and there was an eerie glow coming from between the tree branches, branches that were going to lose their leaves soon. Cargan was standing at the bottom of the hill, as instructed, poking at his phone. He jumped into the Volvo, looking into the backseat, which held a mess of reusable grocery bags.

The car sputtered a bit when I put it into drive, something that caused a little twinge of concern in my gut. Old Phoebe wasn't going to last much longer, that was certain.

"I love what you've done with the place," he said, his foot grazing an empty coffee cup on the floor of the passenger side of the car.

"I've been busy," I said, making a sharp left onto the main street.

"What's this all about?" he asked. "Not that I care. If I have to watch one more episode of reality television with Mom and Dad, there's no telling what will happen to me. Next up was some group of housewives who are young but who have had so much plastic surgery that they look like old women trying to look young. I was thrilled to get your text."

I recounted my conversation with Jed Mitchell, and while I could tell he was curious about the conversation, I could also tell that he wasn't happy that I had struck out on my own.

"Bel . . ." he cautioned.

"Oh, stop," I said. "I've known Jed almost as long as I've known you. Nothing is going to come of this. I just wanted to find out what his relationship was with Pauline."

"He sounds pretty angry."

"At who?" I asked. He seemed pretty angry in general so it was hard to tell.

"Pauline," he said, picking up a paper bag and tossing it into the backseat. "You."

"Seems like he's lost it all, Cargan. That's not a happy place to be."

Connolly's place was jumping when we arrived and

the bar was three deep with thirsty patrons. We walked in and took a look around, wondering how Angus packed this place so tight given the food's nasty reputation. A sign over the bar that touted dollar beers gave us our answer.

"Car, I need the ladies' room," I said. "Order me a Pinot Grigio."

"But that's more than a dollar," my brother said, dead serious.

I pressed a five into his hand. "You always were a cheap bastard," I said, wending my way through the crowd and finding the small corridor that led to the rest-rooms. For a large place, the accommodations were scanty, just one toilet marked "Men" and another marked "Lasses." The Lasses, as always, was occupied and after standing there for a few minutes, the inhabitant show-ing no signs of vacating the premises, I tested the handle on the door to the men's room and, finding it open, went inside. Having grown up in a predominantly male household, I'm hard to shock in the lack-of-cleanliness department but this was one truly disgusting facility, the trash can overflowing, the urinal—pronounced "your-eye-nail" if you're my dad—looking as if it had been installed before the last century. I held my nose and did my business, realizing that there were no clean paper towels on which to wipe my washed hands, so instead, I ran them down the front of my jeans, hoping that the bar was so crowded that no one would notice two large, wet handprints on my pants.

I opened the door and came face-to-face with Angus Connolly whose good cheer from our previous visit seemed to have evaporated. I thought that the level of anger that showed on his face was a little out of proportion to my crime, being a female in a male-designated bathroom, but he was apparently pretty peeved.

"Couldn't get into the ladies," I said by way of explanation, motioning toward the still-occupied lavatory.

"You're not Canadian, are you?" he asked, getting close to my face. "And that guy you were with, he's not Canadian either, is he?"

And not a mute, I thought, but I kept that to myself. Some things were better left unsaid, no pun intended. I wasn't sure how to respond so I just stood there, a mute myself.

"Why did you make up that story?" he asked. "I know who you are. You're Belfast McGrath. You went to school with my brother Jamie."

"How did you put all that together?" I asked.

"Never mind that," he said. "Why did you lie to me?"

"Information. I am trying to find Pauline."

"That wench worked for your parents."

"She's not a wench but, yes, she worked for my parents. And now she's missing." And may have witnessed a murder. And taken ten thousand dollars that didn't belong to her along with the ten grand she extorted from Jed. I tried not to appear intimidated, but I was. He was bigger than I was and three sheets to the wind, as Dad would say, the smell of alcohol coming off him in stale waves, the kind that led me to believe that the drinking had started earlier and would continue well into the evening. This was professional drinking, not the stuff of amateurs. "And she could be in danger. Are you sure you haven't seen her? Heard from her?"

"No. Haven't seen her. Haven't heard from her. And don't want to. She made a lot of trouble for me and my family," he said, grabbing my arm. He pulled me down the hallway and into the dining room. "If I do see her again, I'll . . ."

I wrested myself from his grip. "You'll what?" I said. He was the second person in as many hours who seemed to want Pauline gone. Or worse. I looked around the bar hoping to catch sight of my brother, but his back was turned to me, his attention on a baseball game on the giant flat-screen television over one end of the bar.

"What do you want me to say?" he asked. "That I'd kill her?" He smiled his snaggle-toothed smile. "I'm too smart for that." He pushed me forward, through the throng of people drinking at the bar. "Let's go. You're not welcome here."

"Why?" I asked. "What have I done?"

"Not sure. I just don't like the looks of you," he said. "Now where's your mute brother?" he asked, grabbing my arm again. "Canadian, my ass."

I squirmed beneath his viselike grip and let out a little howl as his fingers wrapped tighter around my upper arm, the skin beneath them becoming chafed and raw. I wriggled loose and started for the end of the bar where I had last seen my brother, but before I could get to him, I heard the crack of bone as someone's fist made contact with Angus Connolly's nose, the spray of blood prolific and widespread, customers ducking for cover, their hands protecting their drinks as several of them hit the deck.

Cargan finally turned around to see what the commotion was and, seeing me, standing in the middle of the melee, my one hand gripping my sore upper arm, put his drink down and hurried toward me. Angus Connolly was out cold on the bar floor, his nose broken, his shirt covered in viscous slime, the person who hit him seeming to have disappeared into thin air. It had all happened so fast that I had no idea who it was, my only memory being a fist whizzing by my face and landing square in the middle of the bar owner's mug.

Around us, different scuffles were breaking out, someone taking offense to Angus's injury, someone else defending the guy who had the killer uppercut that had bloodied Angus and everyone around him. A chair was lifted overhead and I ducked for cover, wincing as it flew overhead and crashed into an empty table in the dining room. Somewhere in the distance, a woman screamed and curse words and invective flew so freely that I felt as if I were in the middle of a war zone. Glass shattered and droplets of beer soaked my shirt.

Cargan reached me and touched my arm in the same place where Angus had held it, the pain now a throbbing reminder of my perp walk from the bathroom to the front of the restaurant. "Let's go," he said, propelling me forward through the gaping, drunken revelers, and toward the front door.

Covered in Angus Connolly's blood, I didn't seem like an innocent bystander, something that was evident by the look on Kevin Hanson's face, the cop car out front indicating that some quick-thinking patron had had the wherewithal to call the police before things got further out of hand. He had just entered through the front door, and, taking stock of the situation, looked at me and shook his head sadly.

"What's the Foster's Landing PD doing here?" I asked.

"Budget cuts," Cargan said. "Towns are combining forces." He stopped a few feet from Kevin and his cop friends. "And let's face it: not enough going on in the

Landing to keep these guys busy." He looked at me. "Until you came back."

"Want to tell me what's going on here, Bel?" Kevin asked, two uniformed cops running to the aid of Angus Connolly, who was slowly coming back to life.

He sat up and pointed a finger at me, still groggy. "She's not Canadian!" he said.

I looked at Kevin. "Guilty as charged."

# CHAPTER *Twenty-eight*

Cargan's arms were crossed over his chest, his face a mask of consternation. "If you say one word to Mom and Dad about this, I will kill you," he said.

"What did I do?" I hissed back. "It's not my fault that a brawl broke out. I was just minding my own business, using the restroom—"

"Men's room," Cargan said. "You were using the men's room."

"And that's an excuse to get manhandled by Angus Connolly?" I asked. "I was minding my own business," I repeated.

"But you weren't, Bel," Cargan said. "You were minding everyone's business but your own." He sunk lower in his plastic chair, avoiding eye contact with anyone else in the police station. "It's time to let this go," he said. "It's time to let Kevin and the professionals handle this. It's too much for us."

"But the girls, Cargan," I said. "And Mom and Dad. They will get into a lot of trouble if the authorities find out that they've been harboring illegals."

"They're not harboring them, they're *hiring* them," he said.

"Oh, yes. That makes it much better," I said. I dropped my voice to a whisper. "I don't see Mom being very happy about being a new cast member on *Orange Is the New Black*. And Dad won't do very well in the pen. You know he can't fall asleep unless Mom is in the bed next to him. I don't think some big inmate will serve the same purpose."

Cargan looked at me, incredulous. "Have you always had this vivid an imagination?"

I shrugged. "Maybe. But I don't think I'm too far off." I walked up to the front desk where Francie McGee was logging hours as the police department's secretary and town gossip hound. "Francie, why are we still here?" I asked. As far as I could tell, Cargan and I had had little to do with the bedlam that had ensued after some thug had broken Angus Connolly's—nose in a ham-fisted attempt at protecting me, I had come to find out later. Seeing me manhandled by Angus had given some anonymous guy the idea that I was in peril, and that, plus about five or six whiskeys, had propelled him into action. Someone heard this unknown protector exclaim, "That's no way to treat a woman!", as if we were all in some 1950s noir film, before all hell broke loose.

And who said chivalry was dead?

Francie looked at me. "Detective Hanson still wants a word with you? Remember?" she asked, not asking "are you deaf?" but insinuating it with her tone. "So sit tight, sugarplum. I'm sure he'll be with you when he gets a free moment."

"Sugarplum?" I asked. When she didn't respond, I huffed away, sitting down in the seat next to Cargan.

The people involved in the melee had ended up in the cells in the basement of the police station so I looked on the bright side that Cargan and I were allowed to mingle with the other people in the station. It was getting late, and although Mom and Dad didn't keep strict tabs on where we were at all times, they had a sixth sense for stuff like this, when things had gone wrong. I prayed that they were fast asleep in bed, their reality shows having come to an end, and not wondering where their grown son and daughter might be and why.

I looked at Cargan. "I'm hungry."

"You're always hungry."

"So are you."

"If we get out of here in time, we can go to the diner. You're paying."

"Deal," I said. "Though I don't know why I have to pay. It's not my fault."

"And you always need to get the last word in."

"Do not," I uttered under my breath. We sat in silence, watching people come and go. It was shocking to me how many people were registering complaints being it was getting late on a Saturday night, but it was also a full moon. That had to account for the number of disgruntled Foster's Landing villagers who were in the station that night. Mrs. O'Leary said someone had trampled her azalea bush and she wanted the full cooperation of the FLPD in finding the culprit. A kid came in saying he lost an iPhone model that when he described it and what it did, made mine look like a hunk of papyrus on which I tapped out crude, rudimentary cave paintings to express myself and contact family and friends. Still another person came in with photos, expressing his displeasure at the shape and size of the new bike racks that sat in front of the local sandwich shop, saying they looked vaguely phallic. I tilted my head, trying to get a good look at the enlarged photos he was showing Francie McGee.

Guy had a point.

The door to Lieutenant D'Amato's office had been closed when we arrived and I assumed he had gone home for the evening, his tour of fighting the crime in our little burg done for the day. Behind that door, however, voices were raised and weeping could be heard, making it clear that whoever was in that room had just received what sounded like the worst news ever. Muffled sounds of comfort came drifting out through the over-the-door transom followed by more sobbing. I looked at Cargan. "Sounds bad," I said.

He stared straight ahead and didn't answer but the color leaving his cheeks was an indication that he was hearing exactly what I was.

The door opened a few minutes later and a distressed Lieutenant D'Amato emerged, looking back at the other people in the office, the look on his face suggesting that he wanted them gone as quickly as possible. I was shocked to see Pegeen Casey and her ever-present brother, James, exit the office, Pegeen weaving between the desks, her face tearstained, mascara running in rivulets and dropping onto her very expensive white silk blouse. James was cradling his right hand, which was wrapped in an Ace bandage.

Pegeen spotted me just before she reached the half-wall that partitioned off the waiting area from the squad area. She went through the swinging door and stood in front of me.

She started slowly, her voice soft. "I had my doubts about Shamrock Manor, Bel. Really I did." James came up behind her and put a protective hand on her arm, which prompted me to touch the area where Angus Connolly had gripped me earlier. "But my father was convinced that with you at the helm, it would be new, exciting."

"And cheap," Cargan said in the softest whisper possible so that only I could hear him.

"And it was. It was beautiful, the river in the background, the lawn manicured and tidy. Our photos," she said, swallowing a sob, "well, those we have, are beautiful."

Her voice started to get louder, more shrill. Francie McGee's eyes grew wide and the lieutenant strode across the squad area, flustered.

"But how was I to know that a world-famous chef," she said, pointing at me, "who won the Culinary School Award of Excellence—"

"Oh, I didn't win, but it was an honor to be nominated—"

She put her hand up and closed her eyes. "Stop."

I shut my mouth. She seemed pretty serious about whatever it was she had to say.

"How was I to know that this award-nominated chef would poison my husband?" she asked.

I stood. "Poison him?"

"Yes, Bel," she said, the pain of Gerard's fate emanating from her in prickly waves. "You poisoned my husband. With your beets. You and your goddamned beets."

# CHAPTER *Twenty-nine*

Cargan had forgotten how mad he was at me after Pegeen had accused me of murder, and later, in my apartment, a beer in his hand and a glass of wine in mine, we sat side by side with my computer and googled "beet allergy." I had texted Brendan and he had come right over, too, interested in this turn of events. I had kept a lot of what was going on from him, afraid that if he knew what really went on at Shamrock Manor—how crazy my family and the cast of characters who worked for them really were—he'd run screaming for the hills, figuring that although I had cooked some of the best meals he had ever had, I just wasn't worth it.

I pushed those thoughts down and filled him in. If his face was any indication, I was worth it and he was enjoying every second of this macabre tale.

"Says it mostly affects domesticated animals," Cargan said.

"Well, a new groom could fall into that category, I guess," I said.

He gave me a disappointed look. "Is this really the time for your comedic stylings, Bel?"

Brendan snorted loudly. "I thought it was funny."

"You would," Cargan said. Brendan had fallen into the role of fifth brother if Cargan's treatment of him was any indication.

I went quiet. Down the hall, I heard footsteps on the stairs that led to the landing outside my back door and a soft rap on the metal surrounding the screen. I got up, knowing who it was before I even turned the corner. "Hey, Kevin," I said, letting him in.

"Hi, Bel," he said. In the living room, he looked at Cargan and Brendan. "Who knew that you could be poisoned from eating beets?" he asked. "That would have come in handy when I was little and forced to eat borscht."

Kevin's father was as Irish as Paddy's pig, as Mom would say, but his mother was a Riefenstahl by birth and prone to making food that my family considered exotic and fairly unpalatable. But I had been a huge fan of her rouladen, that is, before a hypnotist took away any delight I had in eating onions. You couldn't get more onion-laden than rouladen.

"This is all our mother needs to hear," Caragan said. "She hasn't been a fan of Bel's beet-heavy menu."

Brendan looked at me. "What's not to love about beets?"

"Right?" I asked. "It's not beet-heavy. Jeez, you two." I looked at Kevin. "Tell me that it wasn't my beets that poisoned him?"

Kevin shrugged. Well, that was reassuring. "There was something just strange about this whole thing. Healthy guy, sudden catastrophic illness."

"Seemingly healthy people get sick all the time, Hanson," Cargan said. "There's stroke, heart attack, aneurysm. Undiagnosed cancer."

"That's a thing?" I asked, thinking about the constant crick in my neck, the pain I always had in my knee.

Brendan nodded. "Yep, my uncle Nolan got diagnosed on a Friday and was dead by Monday."

"Thanks, Mrs. Joyce," I said.

Brendan cocked his head questioningly.

"You sound like our mothers," I said.

Cargan ignored me. "There are a host of things you can die from, things that can poison you. But a beet allergy isn't high on the list."

"That's just one thing the ME threw out there," Kevin said. "Could be anything."

"So why did Pegeen attach to that one in particular?" I asked.

Kevin shrugged again. "No clue. I think it was the first thing the ME said and the one thing she heard. A food allergy. He said you could have an event like Gerry did from an undiagnosed food allergy and Pegeen hit on that. He listed some foods and beets happened to be one of them. He even said it was a long shot but Pegeen said that Gerry never liked beets."

"That is ridiculous," I said, but the accusation was out there now and couldn't be taken back. "Where do we go from here?"

"Well, I'm not sure," Kevin said. "We'll keep investigating." He anticipated my question before it came out of my mouth. "Cremated. No chance of exhuming the body and investigating that way. Nothing was saved. The ME doesn't routinely test for poisoning so deemed this a catastrophic heart attack based on other evidence or perhaps this undiagnosed food allergy."

"So in addition to a guy being murdered here over the

summer, I now have to live with the idea out there that Bel McGrath served a guy a plate of beets that may have killed him?" I asked. "Great. That's just great." I looked at three men standing in my apartment. "Get out. I need to be alone with my thoughts."

I walked Brendan down the hall. "Sorry about all of this. I just needed to hear that it wasn't me."

He kissed the top of my head. "It's not you. That's the craziest story I've ever heard," he said, shaking his head. "Beets? No one has ever died from eating beets."

"If you listen to my mother, they have."

"Well, she's wrong," he said. "I think your beets are delicious." He opened the door and started down the stairs. "Let me know what happens, okay?"

"I will," I said, watching as he drove off down the driveway of the Manor.

I turned and Cargan and Kevin were still in the living room. "Get going," I said. "It's late and I'm tired."

Cargan started for the door, but Kevin stayed rooted in place, standing in the middle of my tiny living room and looking around. When Cargan was gone finally, he looked at me. "Three weeks," he said.

I straightened some magazines on my coffee table, putting *Newsweek* on top of the *US Weekly*s, the *People* magazines that went back several months. The copy of *O, The Oprah Magazine* that Mom thought had a great article about depression and how to snap out of it by re-designing your wardrobe, a not-so-subtle hint that she wanted me to redesign my wardrobe, not being terribly concerned about the state of my mental health. "Three weeks until what?" I asked.

"The wedding, Bel. My wedding."

"Oh, right!" I said. "Your wedding. We have work to do." Especially if Dad was going to make me prepare duck ballotine for a hundred and fifty.

"Yeah, like I have to lose ten pounds before then," he said, smiling.

"No you don't. You look great," I said, punching him in the arm.

"You know what I want, right?" he said.

"Yeah. We went over the menu. It's all on my prep sheet," I said, sitting down on the couch and putting my feet up on the coffee table.

"No. Not that," he said, taking a seat in the chair across from the couch, and dropping his hands between his knees, his posture one of defeat, despair.

I hesitated to ask him what he really wanted, a stolen kiss that we had shared a few months back one that I remembered, as hard as I tried to push it deep down within me and forget it. I was happy now with a very uncomplicated man, one who liked me, warts and all, and wanted nothing more than to spend time with me, eat with me, drink a little wine with me. Love me. I didn't want Kevin Hanson anymore, as attractive as that possibility had once been, and hoped that he felt the same way.

I had seen a change in Kevin lately, one that I liked. He seemed stronger and more confident, more capable. I didn't know why that was, but wondered if Mary Ann had something to do with that. It was there, though, and I liked it.

I waited for what seemed like an eternity for him to reveal what it was that he wanted and when he finally started talking, I realized we wanted the same thing because what that represented was a continued hope.

"I just want it not to be her. Amy. I hope it's someone else," he said.

But in our hearts, we knew that that couldn't be true, that it had to be her, and once again, bonded in that shared fear, we stood and embraced, this time letting the kiss go on longer than it had before, skirting danger, but coming so close to the edge.

# CHAPTER Thirty

I wondered if there would ever be a day that I would wake up guilt-free. For years, it was all about Amy and what I had said, and then, how I had thrown my career away for a guy, my former fiancé, who I now knew was beneath me, who didn't deserve me. And now, it was Kevin.

I rolled over and pulled the pillow onto my head. I couldn't stay here all day but I didn't have to get up yet and I had a lot of thinking to do. More than thinking about kissing Kevin the night before and feeling the years melt away, the butterflies I always felt when I saw him in the halls of the school or running toward me down at the river, his hair still wet from a recent swim, making me acknowledge in my heart that no one had ever made me feel that way. Not one, single other person. Not Ben, maybe Brendan, in time. So far, not any guy I had ever met and thought that love might be part of the equation.

And now he was getting married, the years between us having created a chasm in which two lives had developed independent of one another despite the fact that they never should have parted.

I had a boss who once told me, when things were crazy and I couldn't see the forest for the trees: focus on the business problem. Was it that we hadn't ordered enough oysters? Or that we had run out of a regular client's favorite wine? Nothing personal, no one to blame. Just business. I rolled over and picked up my phone, clearing my throat of the uncried tears that had lodged there while I tried to sleep.

"Kevin? It's me," I said. "I need to talk to you about something."

I wasn't sure where he was but wherever it was, it was quiet. He was home. But he wasn't alone. "I don't want to go over that," he said cryptically.

"Not that. It's something else. Something more important. Something I can only tell you," I said. He remained silent. "We have to pretend that this never happened."

"What do you need to talk to me about?" he asked, his voice taking a more professional tone, deepening.

"Pauline." I hesitated. "But all off the record."

"Why do I feel like I don't want to hear what you're going to say?"

"Ah, you know me well, Hanson," I said.

"I'll meet you by the picnic table in an hour," he said. Before he hung up, his voice dropped to a whisper. "I love her, you know. I really, really do."

I hung up. I did know.

Most people would need to know which picnic table, but the one that he referenced needed no further description. I knew exactly where he wanted us to meet.

I got up and showered, washing away the remnants of the shame I felt or trying to, at least. It was a kiss, nothing else. Just a little kiss. I knew in my heart that I was justifying my role in all of this, the thought of the beautiful Mary Ann D'Amato and how hurt she would be if she knew what we had done washing down the drain like the suds from my shampoo. Brendan was one thing but Mary Ann was another. She had dated Kevin for years, waiting for him to propose like a dutiful, albeit kind of too dutiful, girlfriend—far longer than I would have waited—and now had her guy. Her wedding would be beautiful, just like she was. I would make sure of that.

I drove over to the edge of the water, where the water used to lap up against the rocks, but no more. The drought had taken its toll and water was in scarce supply in the tiny river. Kevin was already waiting for me, two sandwiches wrapped in tinfoil in front of him on the scarred, pocked wood of the table.

"Sausage, egg, and cheese," he said, handing me one.

"Extra grease from the grill?" I asked, the smell of it making my mouth water.

"Just the way you like it. I told Tony at the deli it was for you. Said he hadn't seen you since you got home."

I patted my midsection. "My cooking alone makes for some tough days trying to stay healthy," I said. "Seeing Tony would push me over the edge and right into a quadruple bypass."

We ate in silence for a few minutes. "So, what's going on, Bel? What's happening?"

"Remember Pauline? The other waitress at the Manor?" I asked.

"Yeah," he said. "I wanted to question her after the wedding but she was gone. You know, after you poisoned the groom," he said. Seeing my face, he recanted. "Just kidding! Did she ever come back?"

"No," I said. "Well, not exactly. But I did see her Thursday."

"And? Did you tell her I wanted to talk to her?"

I shook my head. "Didn't have a chance. But she did say something interesting. Weird."

"What?" Kevin asked.

"She, too, thinks Gerry Mason was poisoned and not by me or my beets. Not that she said, anyway."

Kevin tried to play the professional but wasn't successful; his eyes grew wide. "What do you mean?"

I told him everything, start to finish, ending with the chase yesterday. "And the car chasing her belongs to James Casey."

"Do I want to know how you know that?" he said. I had told him that I never did see the driver's face.

"You do not," I said, knowing full well that he had figured out that I must have enlisted Cargan's help in solving that mystery. "Here's the thing, Kevin. Pauline was here illegally."

"And the other girls?"

"Them, too," I said. "You see why I need your full confidence on this."

He rubbed his hands over his face. "Is there any chance your parents didn't know?"

"Not a one."

He grimaced, putting his sandwich down, his appetite gone.

"So there it is. I need your help and we can't say a word. Ridiculous, right?"

He leaned in, preparing to tell me something I already

knew. "Your parents are in a whole lot of trouble if anyone finds out about this," he said.

"Don't you think I know that?" I said. "So will you help me?"

His sigh was inscrutable; I couldn't tell if it was resignation or something else. "Yes. Of course I'll help you."

"Thanks, Kev," I said.

"Isn't Cargan's help enough?" he asked.

"Would be," I said, "if he hadn't fallen in love with her. He's not, as one would say, objective in this whole thing. And we need real professionals here. Not professionals on a mental-health break from the police department."

"Cargan is a great cop, Bel. A great cop." He thought for a moment, looking up at the blue sky. "But I could see how that might change things a bit."

"I know that, Kevin, but we need someone on the inside, someone who can really help us."

His face told me everything: he didn't want to be involved but he knew he had to help me. "I don't know what I can do that will help you if I can't tell anyone anything, but I'll do my best."

I touched his hand and he flinched as if my fingers were on fire. "Thank you."

"I have to admit, Bel: it's been strange since you came back to town," he said.

"It has been," I said.

We got up and walked toward our cars. He opened the door to his personal vehicle, an SUV of some kind that traversed the rocks on the parking area with ease. "I'll call you if I find out anything."

"And, Kevin?"

"What, Bel?"

"Tell Mary Ann that I would be happy to make duck ballotine for the wedding."

# CHAPTER *Thirty-one*

I regretted it the minute it was out of my mouth but there you had it. I was going to make what was considered one of the most complicated dishes in the culinary world for one hundred and fifty people and I had no one to blame but myself. I thought about that as I drove through town, my concerned reverie interrupted by the sight of a guy walking down the main drag in the village, a guy I hadn't thought about all day and with good reason: I had a lot on my plate of both the personal and professional variety. I pulled the car over, put a couple of coins in the meter. I already had a ticket for speeding and not having a license; the last thing I needed was another run-in with the "law," Jane McDermott, the longtime parking enforcer, having a tangential relationship to actual law enforcement. She did take her uniform and her job very seriously, regardless. It also helped that she wore an invisibility cloak; that was the only explanation I could come up with for the fact that one minute she wasn't there and the next, she was.

"Domnall!" I called as I ran down the street.

The guy turned and looked at me, breaking into a run that, to my mind, was completely unnecessary and beyond my current athletic abilities. "I just want a word!" I yelled as I dodged the other people on the street, running straight into a jogging stroller that held not one, not two, but three babies. The mother, far too fit for having just birthed three children, her yoga pants hugging a very shapely behind, a shirt that said NAMASTE accentuating her perky breasts, gave me a hard "hey!" as I charged past. I turned and looked and the babies seemed fine so I kept going, running after a guy who had remarkable speed. The one thing he didn't have going for him, however, was knowledge of the little streets of Foster's Landing and how if you cut down the one on my left, you would come out exactly where I could tell he was heading, the street that ran alongside Oaktree Lane.

I cut through the parking lot of the Episcopal church and then down a small alley and waited until he was just rounding the corner before jumping out, scaring the hell out of him, and giving me just enough time to grab his jacket collar and bring him to the ground. "You're pissing me off, Domnall," I said. "Why were you running?"

"You were chasing me!" he said from his place on the ground. He grabbed his left elbow and rubbed it vigorously. "Skinned my elbow. What are you, crazy?"

"Crazy?" I asked, getting up. "I called your name and you took off. Who's the crazy one?"

He rolled over and got to his knees, finally hoisting himself up. For a young guy, he wasn't particularly limber and I felt bad for knocking him to the pavement. I held out my hand to steady him. He bent over and coughed loudly into a handkerchief that he took from his pocket.

"Are you okay?" I asked. He was tall and thin, thin

in the way of someone who never had much meat on his bones to begin with, one of those fast-metabolism people whose inner workings were a mystery to someone like me who looked at food and gained weight.

"Yes," he said. "Just a touch of pneumonia."

"A touch of pneumonia?" I said. "And you flew here from Ireland?" I took a good look at him. "You don't look good. Your skin is the color of cement."

"Ireland?" he asked. "Yeah, Ireland." He straightened his shirt. "I'm fine. Have you heard from her?"

My face told the whole story. I wasn't the best liar in town and clearly didn't have a great poker face. I didn't have a tell like Mom who always licked her lips when she was lying, but in this instance, it was written all over my face.

"You have, haven't you?" He had another coughing fit, which gave me the opportunity to change the subject.

"Listen, I'm taking you back to the Manor. You're not well. Where are you really staying?" I asked.

He mentioned a motel out on the edge of town; it was a seedy place and I never could figure out how it survived financially. Most likely a "hot sheets" place that charged by the hour, it had been there for as long as I could remember yet always looked vaguely uninhabited, even though we all knew people must have been in there at various points in its history.

"What happened to Henry Miller and his lodging?" I asked, knowing full well that there was no Henry Miller now or ever. "You can't stay at that motel," I said, taking his arm. "You're coming home with me."

I guess I was more like Dad than I wanted to admit, bringing home strays. I just hoped Domnall didn't turn out to be like the feral cat that Dad had arrived at the Manor with one day, the one that bit me before proceeding to tear all of the drapes in the bridal suite and then catapulting itself out of an open window, never to be seen again.

Domnall was silent the whole way to the Manor, but as we drove up the driveway, he turned to me. "Is she safe?"

"I wish I could tell you, Domnall," I said.

"Please call me Donnie. My friends do."

"Okay, Donnie. I don't know if she's safe. Seems like she might be in a spot of trouble." I pulled onto the parking pad outside of Dad's studio.

"She's always in a spot of trouble. That's the way she is," he said. "I thought it was exciting at first but it's not exciting. It's fecking exhausting."

"What kind of trouble?" I asked.

"Well, you know. This and that," he said. From the tone of his voice, I could tell that he didn't want to besmirch her reputation to me and part of me was glad about that, even though I was curious.

"So you're really still married?" I asked.

He held up his left hand, wincing from the pain in his elbow. A gold band glittered on his hand, the hand of a guy who labored. "We're still really married. And I still really love her."

"She's been here a long time," I said.

"And we've been married a long time. She was always supposed to come home after the summer season, but she never did. Kept sending money, but never came back." He couldn't look at me, so he looked out the window. "I sound like an eejit."

"And her ma isn't sick?"

"I think it's pretty clear that her ma isn't the sick one."

"Then what?" I asked but his face closed down; I wasn't getting anything else for the time being. I thought food might be the thing that softened him, made him tell me what was really going on.

I led him into the Manor and straight to the kitchen. I didn't ask him when he had last eaten; it was obvious he was hungry by the way he stole a look into the refrigerator when I opened the door. I pulled out some eggs and cheese and a loaf of multigrain bread and took a few minutes to make an omelet and some toast. I pushed a plate of butter across the counter to him. "Dad gets the butter from an Irish distributor. It will taste just like you're home," I said.

I put the kettle on and made us both a cup of tea while he ate. When I turned around, two steaming mugs of tea in my hands, his head was on the counter and his thin back rose and fell as muffled sobs filled the room. He raised his head and ran his hands over his face. "Thank you for your kindness," he said. "I'm sorry I ran. I'm sorry I lied to you."

"What did you lie about?" I asked, putting my tea down. Suddenly, I wasn't so thirsty.

"About it all." He pulled the ring off and put it on his plate. "It's not her ma. And we are married. We do love each other. And she was supposed to come home. This time for sure."

"Really? She was going home?" I asked. I don't know why he believed her this time if she had failed him in the past.

"End of August, she told me."

And now it was October.

"Why now, Donnie? Why would you believe her this time?"

He looked up at me and I knew the answer before he said it.

"Because I'm dying."

# CHAPTER *Thirty-two*

Mary Ann D'Amato asked me to come into the foyer for a private chat but since the ceiling is so high and the sound reverberates, I took her up to the bridal suite instead. A plush Persian rug coupled with heavy drapery and a thick door made it the perfect place to have a conversation that no one else could hear.

She was a medical professional but it was clear that what Donnie had told her had unsettled her. "It's lung cancer, Bel. He's awfully young for it but he did grow up in a home with two smokers and has smoked himself since he was a teen."

"So everything he told you checks out?" I asked. There had been so many lies perpetrated that I wasn't sure what—or who—to believe anymore. But lying about having cancer would have been stooping pretty low. I wasn't sure even Donnie was capable of that, so when he told me his situation I was inclined to believe him. Mary Ann was insurance that my instincts were correct.

Mary Ann nodded, her face sad. "It does, Bel. And from the sounds of it," she said, pointing to the stethoscope around her neck, a medical bag in her hands, "it's pretty serious."

I could tell by the look on her face that she was very worried. "Are you sure?"

"I mean, he recited some treatments, medical terminology." She sighed. "If he's not sick, he's an incredible liar."

"Why is he here?" I asked.

"I stuck to the medicine of it, Bel. I didn't ask any other questions and he didn't volunteer any additional information."

Standing with Mary Ann in the bridal suite, I almost forgot that I should feel uncomfortable around her, and it was only when the sun hit the room in a certain way, casting a glow around her head that glinted off the steel of the stethoscope, that I did feel the shame of what had happened between me and Kevin. This woman was truly an angel and not deserving of what had transpired between me and her fiancé. Although it would have made me feel better to confess everything to her, assuage my guilty conscience, I did nothing but thank her for coming to the Manor as we walked onto the second-story landing.

"I really appreciate it, Mary Ann," I said.

"It's not a problem, Bel. I'll help in any way I can," she said. She leaned in and gave me a hug. "You're family." As we walked back out, she said, "He should rest. He's going to stay here in the Manor for a while?" she asked.

"That's the plan," I said.

I walked her through the foyer and closed the heavy door behind her. I went into the kitchen and regarded

Donnie, still sitting at the counter. I leaned against the sink and crossed my arms over my chest. "So, tell me everything," I said. "Everything. Tell me what's going on because if you don't, we can't help you."

He had finally stopped crying and was coming back to life after a meal and some attention. "Your friend is really pretty."

"I know," I said. "Inside and out."

"She says she's marrying your high-school sweetheart." He looked down at the counter, at his empty plate of food. "That must be hard."

"She said that?" I asked.

"She said you guys dated. Were serious."

I opened the refrigerator and pulled out a leftover piece of the McCarthy wedding cake, this one a luscious chocolate with a raspberry filling, a piece that had escaped Cargan's roving eye and that remained untouched. I put it on a plate and gave it to Donnie. "It would be hard if we were still in high school but we're not. We're older now . . ."

"Middle-aged," he said.

"Well, I wouldn't say that."

"You are," he said. "What are you? Forty? Forty-five?"

"Not even close!" I poured him a glass of milk to wash down the cake and set it down with a thud and a glare, making clear that the discussion of my age was off the table. "Anyway, she's a lovely woman and always has been." I watched him eat for a few minutes. "But back to the matter at hand. Why are you here? You're very sick and traveling can't be easy. Why did you come here?"

"We had a plan, me and Pauline," he said. "When we

found out about . . ." He paused and looked up at the ceiling, not able to say the words. "About this, she promised to help me. To get the money I needed for treatment. To get me to . . ."—he paused as if trying to remember where he was—"the States."

"You were running pretty will for a guy with cancer," I said.

"Well, that run nearly killed me," he said.

"How was she going to get the money?" I asked.

He shrugged. "You've got me. She transferred ten grand in dollars to me a few weeks ago and said more was on the way."

Even I, with my limited experience in the medical world, knew that ten thousand dollars wasn't going to come close to helping this very ill man whose face, at this very moment, looked like it belonged to a much older person. I had seen Cargan's hospital bills after his recent stay there and they were well beyond ten thousand and he had good insurance that would cover most of the cost. "Did she say where she was getting the money?" I asked again.

"No. But more was on the way. That's all I knew."

The Manor was quiet, uncharacteristically. I brought Donnie up to a room on the second floor and set him up. I handed him the remote controls to the television.

"About nine hundred channels but there'll be nothing to watch. I guarantee you," I said. "Make yourself at home. This room is en suite, so the bathroom is next to that closet there."

I found Dad in his studio, working on an installation. "Hi, Dad."

"Belfast!" he said, happy to see me. I hoped he was still happy when I told him we had a boarder. "What brings you here? Shouldn't you be trussing up ducks for the D'Amato/Hanson wedding?"

"Very funny," I said. "Listen, Dad. I have something I need to talk to you about."

He was bent over a large piece of wood on an even larger table and measured a corner. "What's that?"

"The plot has thickened a little bit where Donnie Kinneally is concerned."

"How so, Belfast?" he asked.

I explained briefly what I now knew to be true. Dad blessed himself, kissing his thumb at the end of the gesture. "God bless the lad. Terrible thing, the cancer."

"Yes, it is," I said. "But here's the thing. You know that old motel out on the edge of town?"

"Not fit for man or beast!"

"Right. Donnie was staying there."

Dad looked up from the piece of wood. "He can't stay there."

It had to be Dad's decision even though it was already in progress.

"How long?" Dad asked.

"How long what?"

"How long will he be staying?"

"Don't know, Dad. But he can't stay at that motel."

Dad pulled a thick pencil out from behind his ear and marked the wood. "Put him in the room next to the bridal suite. It's got its own facilities. I believe you and your fancy brother call it an 'en suite.' Make the lad at home."

Before Dad could pull out the power drill that was next to his right hand—or change his mind on the subject of Donnie Kinneally—I walked around the table and put my arms around him in a proper hug. "Thanks, Dad," I said into his barrel chest.

He pulled away, flustered. "Well, good, then, and all right, and it's fine," he said. We weren't prone to any kind of public displays of affection in the family. Or private ones, for that matter. But Dad was a good egg and he needed to hear that from time to time even if it made him uncomfortable.

Tonight should have been our family Sunday dinner, but for some reason it hadn't materialized, the e-mail sent by Mom for the command performance not having gone out as usual. She was still in a stew about Helen but it didn't matter to me. That meant I had a free night. Did I really care why Mom didn't plan dinner this weekend? Not in the least. We were all working like dogs at the Manor and certainly had our fair share of togetherness. It's not like we didn't see each other all the time and without fail. Maybe Mom had finally come to the conclusion that it might not be the worst idea to take a break from one another every now and again. It could actually help our relationships and the boys' in particular. That was a group who spent way too much time together.

I left the studio and wandered around the grounds of the Manor for a while, at loose ends. What did I know? I reviewed everything in my mind. We had a girl who was married but not living with her dying husband, and not really respecting her vows. She had disappeared, seemingly without a trace, only to reappear and tell me that the poor sot who had died with his pants around his ankles at his own wedding, ostensibly of a heart attack, had been poisoned. She had been involved with a guy in town and one right outside of town, how deeply, it was hard to say. She had taken money from one and had made things difficult for the other with regard to the Health Department. To what end? Blackmail?

Thinking about all of that helped me decide just what I was going to do that evening. I got in the Volvo and headed to O'Halligan's.

Angus Connolly was at the end of the bar closest to the door when I arrived, his eyes blackened, if I had to guess, hidden behind large sunglasses that looked more than a little feminine. I suppose it's hard to find big, oval shades to cover your war wounds if you're a dude, so Angus was rocking ladies' sunglasses. I resisted the urge to laugh and put on my most sober face, the one that would tell him that I meant no harm and just wanted to set the record straight about what had happened the night before and the nights previous when I had crossed the threshold of his watering hole.

I put up my hands to show I meant no harm. "Mr. Connolly, I'm sorry."

"You should be!" he said. "And you are no longer welcome here. Don't make me get a restraining order."

"A restraining order? For using the men's room?" I asked.

"You know what you did," he said. "Canadian, my ass."

I sat down on the bar stool next to him but didn't go so far as to order a drink. I was on borrowed time; I knew that. "Listen, I'm sorry I lied and I'm sorry that I used your men's room."

"And what else?" he asked.

I was at a loss and looked at him blankly.

"The fight!" he said. "You're sorry about the fight you started!"

"I didn't start a fight," I said. "A fight started around me but I didn't start a fight." I looked at my reflection in his sunglasses. "There's a difference."

He sighed. "What do you want? Why do you keep coming here?"

"Pauline."

"What about her?"

"Did she blackmail you? Try to get money from you?"

"I already told you all that."

"But the Health Department stuff. Did she try to extort money from you?" I couldn't tell if the punch to the nose had addled his brain or he just didn't want to tell me. I waited. What he didn't know was that I was the family staring champion, having once stared down Derry until he almost cried when defeated.

"Oh, fine!" He put his drink down on the bar with such force that the sound of it got the attention of the entire bar. "Yes. She got money from me."

"How much?" I asked.

"Twenty-five grand."

Holy crap. That was a lot of dough. Between that and the money she got from Jed Mitchell, she was amassing quite a lot of wealth. Sadly, if what she was doing was what I thought she was doing—saving money for Donnie's treatment—she was way short. Thinking about her bedroom and its beautiful appointments as well as her luxury car, I wondered if she had done the unthinkable and used the money on herself. She had lied; the kid wasn't abusive, just sick. In my mind, Pauline went from a minor nuisance to Public Enemy Number One.

"Lot of money, huh?" he said.

"To what end? To keep the Health Department away?"

I said. "Seems like a lot of money for something that you could probably have made go away by just cleaning your kitchen, huh?" There was something else; there had to be.

He looked away. "Mind your business. Go to Canada. Just get out of here and stay out of here."

The waitress who looked like Pauline drifted by, giving me the stink eye.

"Her?" I asked. "Is she the issue?"

He leaned in close and I got a whiff of whiskey-tainted breath. "Get. Out."

I had my answer. A dirty kitchen coupled with an angry waitress. Still didn't seem like something that required a twenty-five-thousand-dollar pay off but what did I know? I slid off the stool and started for the door.

"Hey!" Angus said.

I turned.

"If you find her . . ."

I waited.

He waved his hand dismissively. "Ah, it's nothing. I've forgotten about her already."

He could say it as many times as he wanted but that didn't make it true.

# CHAPTER *Thirty-three*

On my way through the village, I passed an ambulance, lights blazing, siren blasting. Although it was coming from the direction of the Manor, I didn't give it much thought; there was an assisted-living facility—sorry: fifty-five and better!—a few blocks away from my home and seeing an ambulance go by was an unfortunate common occurrence. I pulled into my usual parking spot at the Manor and spied members of my family standing on the front porch, one and all looking concerned.

As I got closer, I could see that Dad, more than Cargan, more than Mom, was bereft. Cargan looked concerned and Mom looked nonplussed, as if what had just happened had interfered with her Pilates class and been a giant inconvenience but nothing more. When I reached the porch, however, I could see that she was crying and that what I took for annoyance was a grim set of her mouth that was stopping the floodgates.

Dad shook his head. "Poor lad," he said.

"Who?" I asked.

"Donnie. He had come downstairs for a glass of water

and collapsed. He's a very sick boy, Belfast," Dad said. "Sicker than we thought."

"Someone should be with him at the hospital," I said.

"I'm following the bus," Cargan said.

"Bus?" Dad, Mom, and I asked in unison.

"Sorry. Ambulance." He held out his hand and Dad handed him the keys to the Manor van, the one the boys used for those odd times they played off the premises. "Old habits die hard. That's what we called it at work."

"I'll go with you," I said.

I hadn't been in the van in a long time but it smelled exactly the way I remembered: like boys and leather and cold cuts. It was a replacement Vanagon, the one we had had as children having died a spectacular death on the side of the Taconic State Parkway on the way to a *feis,* an Irish music and dance competition in upstate New York. I remember standing by the side of the road, everyone holding their instruments as cars whizzed past us, their drivers probably wondering what they were doing, a troupe of little boys, all clad in black-and-white, holding a violin, a guitar, drumsticks, and a keyboard. And why there was one little girl leaning into the engine of the van with one very red-faced man who had no idea what he was looking at.

"I think it's clear, Car. We've got to step this up a little bit. We've got to find Pauline. This whole situation is getting completely out of hand," I said, holding on as we bounced along the gravel drive.

"*Getting* out of hand?" he said. "It's been out of hand for days, Bel. Was ending up in the police station any indication that we were beyond *getting* out of hand? Was bringing a dying man into the Manor a clue that things were beyond *getting* out of hand?"

"Hey," I said. "That's enough of that. We're in this together, right?" I looked straight ahead, noting that he was going down a street that led away from the hospital. "Where are we going?"

"I have a lead. I think I know where Pauline is."

We headed out of town toward a little city north of us called Chesterton, one that was once down-at-the-heels but was now home to a burgeoning number of hipsters. Row after row of beautiful brownstones, some still abandoned, others with FOR SALE signs, and still others carefully and beautifully restored, sat on narrow cobblestoned streets. It was a town in the process of coming back to life and I took note of a coffee shop here and a farm-to-table restaurant there. Maybe this was where I would end up when I finally put down real roots, roots that didn't have members of my family dragging them down.

"Why are we here?" I asked. "And how did you find her?"

"Well, I haven't found her yet," he said.

We pulled up in front of one of the brownstones on a tree-lined street; with the leaves changing from green to a burnished, earthy hue, it made me feel as if we were walking into a painting. Gorgeous hues, the sun almost set, it lulled me into a false sense of security, a feeling that we had come a-calling, not preparing me for what would happen next.

Cargan knocked on the door in a way that suggested he meant business. None of this light tap to let the inhabitants of the house know we were there, but more of a loud bang, the way I suspected he had knocked on more than one suspect's door when he was working. When he didn't get a response, he left the porch and went around back, me following like that annoying little sister who isn't supposed to be on your playdate but who your mother says has to come along.

The back yard was appointed with an aboveground pool and a cement-block porch that came off the kitchen. Cargan banged on the door again and, not getting an answer, tried the doorknob, which turned easily in his hand.

"How did you find her?" I whispered as we stepped into the kitchen, the feeling of being where I wasn't supposed to and definitely where I wanted to be causing contradictory emotions inside. The adrenaline rush, however, was all mine and all positive. This was what his job had felt like and this was why he loved it. Why he had stepped away was another story entirely.

"It's a long story," he said, but I had a feeling it wasn't. He was that good.

We made our way through the kitchen and started into the dining room, beautifully appointed with an antique dining-room set, rich mahogany carefully tended throughout the years, not a mark on any of the pieces. From the corner of my eye, I spotted a blur, got a glimpse of a dark ponytail, and heard a door slam.

It was Pauline and she was on the run.

Cargan moved faster than I had ever seen him move, even years before when he had run track for two weeks because Mom made him. He was out the front door and onto the sidewalk before I could even find the where-withal to move, rooted in place in the dining room, admiring the vast collection of original pieces of Waterford that resided on the glass shelves in the china cabinet. When I finally realized what was going on, I took off after him, spotting him just about caught up to Pauline, an impressive runner in her own right, and grabbing the back of her billowy blouse.

When I finally reached them, out of breath and ready to pass out, I noticed that neither of them were winded or had even broken a sweat. That was the fastest two hundred meters I had ever seen and I haven't missed one Summer Olympics.

Cargan had a light hold on Pauline's arm. "Where you going, Pauline?" he asked as casually as if he were asking her what she had had for breakfast.

"None of your business, sweetheart," she said.

"Is this about Gerry Mason?" I asked.

"Who?" she asked.

"Gerry. Gerard Mason. The groom you say was poisoned and not by me."

At that, her face paled and she tried to wrest free from Cargan's grip. "It's about a lot of things," she said.

"Yeah, you've left a trail of broken hearts," I said, assiduously avoiding my brother's gaze, "as well as a number of pissed-off ones, behind you in Foster's Landing."

"I've got nothing to say about that," she said. "Now, please. Let me go. I have to get out of here."

"Alleging a deliberate poisoning is a very serious thing, Pauline," Cargan said. "I think we should talk to the authorities about that."

If by "authorities" he meant Kevin Hanson, well, that was a bit of a stretch of a description.

"How was he poisoned? Who did it?" Cargan asked. "What happened?"

"Let's go in the house," she said, looking around nervously. "I don't want anyone to overhear us."

In the house, we sat in what was once the parlor but

was now a cozy living room. "Whose house is this, Pauline?" I asked.

"What's it to you?" she asked.

"It's everything to me because you've made all of our lives a living hell since you split the Landing. So I feel like we should be asking the questions now and you should be answering."

She tried to stay strong, to keep up the brittle façade that she had perfected, but it all became too much for her and she sank onto a plush ottoman, hanging her head. "Where do you want me to start?" she asked.

"Why don't you start with why you abandoned your poor husband, the one with lung cancer, in Ireland, promising him that you'd come home, but never returning?" I asked, my righteous-indignation meter registering off the charts.

She looked up. "What?"

"The husband. Domnall Kinneally. The one with terminal lung cancer."

She laughed for the first time since the last time I had seen her at the Manor. "Donnie Kinneally?"

"Yes," I said, a weird prickly feeling starting in my spine and working its way up to the back of my neck. "Your husband."

She looked me dead in the eye. "Not my husband and no lung cancer. Jeez, Bel, I thought you were smarter than that."

# CHAPTER *Thirty-four*

Pauline had no interest in seeing her ex-husband, the one who didn't abuse her (as she had told Eileen and Colleen) and the one who didn't have lung cancer. We got confirmation on the latter when we arrived at the hospital and a stone-faced Mary Ann D'Amato greeted us in the hallway of the medical center, Donnie's room a few doors down.

Before we left the house in which she was holed up, Pauline grabbed a very expensive bag, one that I recognized from my days on the NYC food scene—it had been on the arm of more than one well-heeled female client—and I resisted the urge to ask her *(a)* how much it cost, and *(b)* if she had felt any remorse buying it with the Manor tip money.

At the hospital, Mary Ann started talking as soon as we came through the double doors. "He said that he was diagnosed three weeks ago and that it was a Stage Four diagnosis." She crossed her arms over her chest. "So, he has the lingo down. He had the names of treatments." She shook her head, confounded by the deception. "Remember when I said that he was either sick or a really good liar? It's the latter."

I didn't want to tell her that anyone who had seen one episode of *Grey's Anatomy* could have looked up the diagnosis, learned the lingo.

Mary Ann looked at Pauline and held out her hand. "Mary Ann D'Amato."

"Pauline Darvey." She gave Mary Ann the once-over, clearly unaccustomed to not being the most beautiful person in the room.

"Your husband either was lied to or openly lied to me—"

Pauline held up a hand. "Not my husband, sister. Ex-husband."

Mary Ann was unruffled. "Your ex-husband."

I stepped out of the way of a gurney being wheeled toward me. "So what *does* he have?"

"Pneumonia," Mary Ann said. "A pretty serious case. Exacerbated by overexertion."

My mind flashed on our trek through Foster's Landing on foot, me bringing him to the ground, his coughing. "I see," I said, buying time and hoping no one would ask me how I had contributed to that overexertion. "Can we see him?" I asked.

"He was sleeping a few minutes ago but he's not in danger," Mary Ann said. "I would keep my distance from him because while he's not contagious, any germs brought in from the outside could be harmful to him."

Cargan spoke for the first time since we left what turned out to be Pauline's aunt's house in Chesterton. He had let me ask all of the questions, many still unanswered, as he drove the old van down the windy streets of the old city. "Let's go see him."

In the room, Donnie awoke with a start, his eyes falling on Pauline and staying there. Everyone stood around awkwardly until I spoke. "I feel like you two should start your own school. It would be called the 'Lying Academy.' Free tuition. Just tell us your best lie, the one that hurts the most people, and you're in!" I said, clapping my hands together.

If I didn't know now that Donnie wasn't as sick as he said, I would still think he was close to death. His eyes were sunken, the skin beneath them bruised and black, his lips chapped. "I'm sorry, Miss McGrath. I'm very, very sorry." He coughed into his hand. "I'm in a bit of trouble."

"I'll say," I said, going to the window and hoisting myself onto the wide sill.

"My wife here," he started before being interrupted by Pauline.

"Ex-wife."

He looked at her. "You know we're still married. You know that the divorce was never finalized."

She looked away, not making eye contact with any of us.

"And you were divorcing why?" I asked. "Because you abused her?"

His eyes filled with tears. "Is that what you told them? That I was abusive to you?"

Boy, this was not a woman I wanted to get to know any better and I was happy that she was no longer in our employ at the Manor. She was flint and steel, hard as a rock. "Well, you were. You were verbally abusive."

"I was not!" he protested, which brought on another bout of coughing.

"You called me a 'fat cow' once!"

"And should I tell them about you?" he asked, pushing the button on the side of the bed that would raise him up, giving him a better view of his wife and the ability to aim his protests directly at her. "Should I tell them about the affairs and the lies and the cleaning out of our joint bank account? Should I tell them that?" he asked.

"I think you just did," Cargan said unnecessarily.

"Why this whole thing?" I asked. "Why were you amassing all of this money?" I asked Pauline.

She stared at Donnie in the bed. "Should I tell them or do you want to?"

It didn't take him long to decide, the words coming out in a rush. "Gambling debts. It's a disease. I have a disease."

"Well, at least you have one disease that we can verify easily," I said. "How much?"

"I owe a ton to a shark. Twenty grand."

By my estimation, that was way less than Pauline had accrued over the last few weeks with her lying and thieving. She had already given him ten, according to Domnall.

I looked at Pauline. "And why are you involved?"

"Asshole here threatened to turn me in to the authorities for living here illegally." She turned her attention to Donnie. "Any other bright ideas, Einstein?"

"No. No other bright ideas," he said.

"Why didn't you send him all of the money?" I asked. I held out my hand. "And I'd love it if we could get back our ten thousand dollars, please."

She looked at me, confused.

"The tip?" I said. "We'd love to get our stolen money back."

Pauline was deciding how much she wanted to tell

me, how much she wanted Cargan and Donnie to hear, whether or not she would give the money back, so she didn't address the missing tip. "I was going to send him the money but then I had to get gone. And quick."

"Why?" Donnie asked.

She looked at me pointedly. The poisoning of Gerard Mason. "None of your beeswax."

I had lost patience and interest in this tale of marital deceit, gambling, faked illness, and possible murder. "Here's what we're going to do. You," I said, pointing at Donnie, "are going to stay here until you get better and then off with you back to the old country. And you," I said, taking hold of Pauline's arm, "are going with me to the police station to tell them everything you know about Gerard Mason, poisoning, and blackmail. With any luck, the worst that will happen to you is that you'll be shipped off with Donnie here and then the two of you can finalize your divorce and live unhappily ever after. In Ireland. Sound good?"

"I think that sounds like a great idea," a voice behind me said.

We all turned and found Kevin in the doorway, Mary Ann behind him. "Pauline Darvey. You are coming into the station with me for questioning in the death of Gerard Mason."

# CHAPTER *Thirty-five*

We know exactly two lawyers. One is Philip Grant who represented Cargan when some circumstances conspired against him and landed him at the police station, and the other is Arney McGrath, my brother and well-known Foster's Landing divorce attorney. As soon as Kevin expressed his interest in bringing her to the station, she clammed up with the exception of one sentence: "I want Arney McGrath to meet me there."

I wanted to tell her that she had a better chance of getting good help from fictional lawyer Matlock on her side, but I did as she wished and called Arney who sounded as if he had been sleeping.

"What, Bel? It's nine-thirty."

Yep, he'd been sleeping.

"We've got a situation and we need your help."

"You do realize that the only time you talk to me is when you need help?" he asked. I heard the muffled sounds of another person, his wife presumably, asking why someone was calling at such an ungodly hour. "Oh, your sister . . ." I heard clearly, the disdain dripping from my charming sister-in-law's lips. The only time they called me was when they needed a babysitter so in my mind we were even.

I explained what was happening, and even if Arney is the laziest lawyer in town, he's also been known to enjoy a bit of gossip, to trade in the odd rumor or two. This was too good to pass up, his curiosity piqued by the details I provided. "So are you in or are you out?"

"I'm in," he said, though I could hear resignation in his voice. He wanted to be out but this one was interesting in both the worst and best ways possible. He seemed to be missing the main point in that Mom and Dad were implicated, and if poisoning had been on the menu that day at the wedding, I was in some kind of trouble as well.

It was all a little too close for comfort on many levels. I had lost my last job, the one at a fancy New York City eatery, because of an overlooked fish bone nearly choking a patron—an ex-president nonetheless—and now this, a possible poisoning, if Pegeen Casey was to be believed and her story had any credence whatsoever. Maybe it hadn't been the beets but maybe it had been something else, a previously undiscovered allergy being exacerbated by something in one of my dishes. It was possible. It was legitimately likely. And it was the worst thing I could hear, if it turned out to be true.

Off we went again to the station after saying our good-byes to Donnie. In the hallway of the hospital, Mary Ann looked at me sadly. "I'm sorry, Bel. I had to tell Kevin. He's been worrying over this case for weeks. And once you told him about the missing girl . . ."

"He told you about that?" I asked.

She nodded. "He did. There are no secrets between us."

Um, yeah. There was at least one. Maybe two. I didn't have the heart to tell her that, though.

Arney hadn't exactly dressed himself for the matters at hand, showing up at the police station in a wrinkled polo shirt and khaki pants with a button fly that had been buttoned incorrectly. I pointed at his crotch. "You may want to take a moment there, brother."

He looked down and excused himself, handing me his briefcase before going off to the men's room. Pauline had been led into a conference room, and through a crack in the door, I could see her long legs extended beneath a table, crossed delicately at the ankle. She had an unlit cigarette in one hand and a cup of tea in the other and looked decidedly unconcerned by what was transpiring, even though just hours earlier, she had been high-strung and agitated.

I wondered what had happened to change her mood or if she was just that good of an actress.

"We don't need to stay here," Cargan said. "I don't know about you, but I'm exhausted."

"Yeah, we've certainly had our fair share of mental gymnastics today," I said. "I've never heard so many lies and lies on top of those lies in my entire life. Bunch of lying liars."

Cargan held the door to the station open for me and we went into the parking lot. "Lying about cancer," he said, shaking his head. "That takes the cake."

That was the lie that seemed to bother him the most.

"My partner on the job. Mickey Genovese. Died at forty-one of colon cancer. Left behind two little kids and a wife." He shook his head. "You can't lie about having cancer. It's just not right."

"Donnie doesn't strike me as the sharpest tool in the shed," I said.

"That's just wrong," he said. "Wrong."

"He and Pauline seem made for each other." In the Vanagon, I turned to my brother. "Do you think Gerry Mason was poisoned?"

"I don't know, Bel. We are doing our best and will come up with an answer."

I wasn't sure it was possible but I decided to go with it, for the sake of my own peace of mind.

Cargan parked the Vanagon in its usual spot and we headed toward our respective abodes, his in the Manor proper and mine in the apartment above Dad's studio. "Will you let Mom and Dad know that things are not quite as dire as we thought?" I asked.

"Sure," he said. "See you in the morning."

I went up to my apartment and poured myself a healthy glass of Cabernet, something I figured I deserved after a day that felt like three rolled into one. Brendan and I texted back and forth and I blamed a long day prepping in the kitchen to my absence from his life, something he seemed to accept, a lovely red heart coming back with the words "sleep well" accompanying it. I carried the wine to my bedroom, put it on my nightstand, and lay on top of the covers, never taking a sip before I fell asleep.

I awoke to the sound of knocking at the back door to the apartment and roused myself—not an easy task—and found Pauline standing there, a cross look on her face, her posture tense. "I have nowhere else to go," she said.

"What about your apartment?" I asked, "How did you

get here? "That nice cop? Hanson?" she said. "He drove me to get my car." rubbing sleep from my eyes.

"That would be the first place they would look," she said, as if I knew what that meant.

"Who?" I asked. "Who is looking for you?"

"The people who poisoned Gerry Mason," she said.

"Oh, God, Pauline," I said. "I'm so sick of this story-line. Did you tell Kevin what you supposedly saw? Does he believe you?"

"I told them everything I told you."

"And?" I asked. I really wanted to go to sleep and this was cutting into my slumber time.

"And I think they believe me," she said.

"Why?"

"Because they have another witness."

# CHAPTER *Thirty-six*

I wanted to get to the bottom of this once and for all. The lies, the secrets, everything else. Was he murdered or not? "Spill it, Pauline. This is getting ridiculous. Do you know how hard I've been looking for you?"

"Why, Bel? Why are you looking for me?" she asked.

"A few things," I said. I held up my hand and ticked off my responses. "First, I wanted to find you to see if you were being held in a detention center, hoping that if you were, I could get you out. When that turned out to be not where you were, I wanted to find you so we could get our freaking money back. And then there was the 'abusive' husband. I was afraid for you, Pauline."

"Afraid and mad about the tip." The purse that she had had with her earlier sat on the coffee table, a reminder of her larceny.

Well, yes, there was that.

"But really, I wanted to find you because people just don't disappear," I said.

"Yeah, Bel, they do," she said.

She was right. Amy Mitchell had just disappeared.

"What did you tell the police?" I asked.

"Do you remember the mushrooms on the plate?" As

she asked this, she looked around my apartment; apparently, it wasn't up to her exacting standards.

"Is that a haiku?" I asked. "What in God's name are you talking about?"

She rolled her eyes at me, impatient that I couldn't follow along. "The mushrooms on the plate," she said.

"You can say it as slowly as you want, Pauline, but I still don't know what you're talking about." I poured her a glass of wine; maybe if we were both half in the bag, everything would make more sense.

"The day of the wedding, I came into the kitchen and you were scraping plates. You wondered where the mushrooms came from. We thought some rogue vegan had brought their own food to the event. Remember?" she asked, taking a long sip of the wine. "This is pretty good," she said.

"Life's too short to drink bad wine," I said. I thought back to the wedding and, indeed, I did remember the mushrooms on the plate. "So what do mushrooms have to do with murder?"

"I was on my way to the ladies' room and I saw Gerry go in there."

"Now why would Gerry Mason go into the ladies' room?" I asked.

"Men's room was full up and he wasn't feeling well. I helped him into the ladies' room and then left." There was a lot of that going around, full-up lavatories and cross-gender usage.

I wasn't following. "So the groom uses ladies' room because men's room is full." I didn't tell her that my experience with that just recently had resulted, after a series of unfortunate events, in a barroom brawl breaking out. "The men's room is never full."

"It was that day," Pauline said.

"I don't see where this is going."

She pulled a sheaf of papers out of the back pocket of her jeans. "Here. It's all there. Poisoning by mushrooms. Can cause instant death."

"I didn't serve mushrooms that day," I said. "How did they get on his plate?"

"That creepy brother. James. The one who seems like he's in love with his sister." I hadn't gotten that impression from him, thinking that he might have had a crush on me, but she seemed convinced. She finished her wine in one dramatic arch of her neck, the burgundy liquid drained in seconds. "I came out of the bathroom and he was standing there, staring at me as if he had something on his mind. I asked him what I could help him with and he just stared, like he was in a trance. Didn't say a word."

"You told the police all of this?" I asked. I wasn't sure I was buying what she was selling. Seemed like there was more to the story.

"Yeah," she said. "There's one more thing. I heard Gerry say one thing."

I waited. I'm not a fan of the big reveal, preferring to get my information in real time.

"He said: 'They finally got me.'"

Now it was my turn to roll my eyes. Something about her delivery, the excessive drama of it all, the storytelling technique, made me suspicious of the whole thing. Pauline had proven herself already not to be a reliable narrator and this tale was just adding credence to that fact.

"And who is this other witness?" I asked.

"They won't say," she said. "They just said that

someone else has come forward with information about Gerry Mason's death."

I left that for later. "And you ran why?"

"Because they knew! They knew that I knew!" she said. "And I knew that they knew that I knew!"

Oh, jeez. That was hard to follow. "About the mushrooms," I said. "How did you know that part exactly?"

"I didn't. I guessed. I looked it up online." She pointed to the papers that she had been carrying around and I looked at them. Yes, there were mushrooms that could poison you in a short period of time, leaving you gasping for breath and then, ultimately, dead. It was all there in black-and-white but my money was still on the rogue vegan bringing her own food to the wedding. Seemed like a lot of trouble to go through, carrying mushrooms around on a wedding day and then making sure they got onto one specific plate.

"That's a ridiculous theory, Pauline," I said, flinging the papers onto my coffee table.

"Got a better one?" she asked, defiant.

"What did you tell the police?" I asked.

"Everything I told you," she said. "All of it. The rehearsal dinner, the wedding . . ."

"The rehearsal dinner?" I asked, stopping her in her tracks. "What do you know about that?"

"It was at Connolly's place. Weirdly enough, three nights before the wedding, not the night before," she said. "I was still working there at the time. Moonlighting. It was my last night."

Interesting. A place I thought no one would know, would ever go to if they were Foster's Landing folks, was becoming ground zero. "So, you're going to be deported?" I asked.

She looked up at the ceiling. "Don't know. If what I think is true, and that James Casey killed his brother-in-law, well, I guess I have to stick around for a while. Until they prove it. Until a trial."

I thought back to the day when I followed her in her car. "James Casey was following you the other day after I gave you your check."

"Of course he was!" she said. "He's been looking for me. Are you an eejit, Bel?"

"That's no way to talk to the only person who is going to give you a couch to sleep on," I said. "Were you black-mailing him?"

"No," she said.

"So he's the only one that you're not trying to get money from?" I asked. "We've got Jed Mitchell, Angus Connolly, and who knows who else."

"Those guys knew what they were getting themselves into with me. A good time. Nothing else," she said.

"And blackmail. Don't forget that."

"Who cares, Bel? They're not nice guys."

We could debate that point all day long so I changed the subject. "So you were moonlighting at Connolly's place but decided blackmail was a quicker way to get funds?" I asked.

Her look was inscrutable but I took it as a "yes."

"And why are you so devoted to helping Donnie get rid of his debt?" There didn't seem to be any love lost between the two of them but what did I know? Maybe there was some leftover affection from a marriage that didn't seem to ever have a chance in hell of surviving, if what I had learned about Pauline over the last few days was any indication of her character.

"I've known the lad all my life," she said. "He thinks

we're soul mates, but we're not. More like brother and sister."

"Then why did you marry him?"

As I waited for an answer, I saw something I never thought I'd witness: Pauline began to cry. I poured her the last of the wine, hoping I'd get the remaining answers to the questions I had to ask.

"A baby," she said. "There was a baby."

"You left a baby in Ireland?" I gasped. "All this time?"

"No!" she said, shooting me daggers. "It died. A stillborn. After that, nothing was the same between us. He was gambling and I was sadder than I'd ever been. I left and never looked back." She softened her gaze, knowing that the story had a lot of holes but that she wasn't willing to fill them in. "Until now. Until he called me and told me that he was into Mugsy Calhoun for a couple of thousand large."

"Mugsy Calhoun?" I asked. "You're kidding me, right?"

The look on her face told me that she thought she had said too much, that she wished she could take it all back, but she just shook her head. "Nope. Scariest loan shark in Ballyminster. Wears a guy's pinkie around his neck just to let everyone know what a badass he is."

"A pinkie?" I said, my voice going to a register I didn't even know I had. "Okay, Pauline, between this and poison mushrooms, this has gone beyond preposterous."

She shrugged. "It's just what I heard."

"From Donnie?" I asked.

"From Donnie."

It was late and my head was spinning. I went to the closet in the hallway and pulled down a set of sheets, a pillow, and a blanket; I tossed them to Pauline. "It's been a long day. I hope you'll understand if I try to get some sleep?"

She made the couch up in silence; she was plumping the pillow as I went into my bedroom. On my night-stand, my phone was lit up, a text from Brendan Joyce having just been received, and it was different than the earlier ones, leading me to believe that he was starting to wonder why we weren't spending as much time together as we had previously.

"Are you avoiding me?" it said.

I held the phone in my hand. I'm going to avoid every-one, I wanted to type, but instead, I sent him a heart emoji, something he'd never know didn't have a lot of sincerity behind it. Before I got into bed, I stuck my head out into the hallway and called to Pauline in the living room. "Pauline?"

"Yes, Bel?" she said, her voice sounding weary.

"What was on the menu at the rehearsal dinner?" I asked.

"Chicken. A Marsala, maybe?" she said.

# CHAPTER *Thirty-seven*

I don't know why I made it my responsibility to see how Donnie Kinneally was doing, but when Pauline awoke, after scrubbing my tub clean with some kind of cleanser that Mom had left for me and that I had never used, and taking a long, hot bath with some scented bath beads left over from the seventies, or so they smelled, she asked me if I would go to the hospital and check in on her ex-husband. The bath had clearly rejuvenated her but she still didn't want to be seen in public.

"I have work to do," I said, knowing that as the words came out of my mouth, I would indeed go to the hospital because in spite of everything, Donnie, to me, was a bit of a sad case and my heart wasn't that hard. Being into someone for tens of thousands of dollars, a guy who wore a man's pinkie around his neck no less, must have been terrifying. I drove down to the medical center and, dutiful as always, stopped at the front desk where a woman named Cassandra gave me a visitor's pass and instructed me not to pass it on to anyone else and to abide by the half-hour visitation rule that had been indicated on Donnie's chart.

I headed up to the fourth floor and Donnie's room; a

new staff had assembled at the nurse's station and I nodded at them as I walked past, thinking that I would find a sleeping Donnie Kinneally in room 332, more color in his cheeks thanks to whatever antibiotics and magical juice were flowing through the IV into his veins.

Instead, I came upon an orderly stripping an empty bed of its soiled sheets.

I knocked lightly on the door. "Excuse me? Is Mr. Kinneally here?" I asked. Mary Ann had done us a solid, as Cargan would say, and gotten Donnie a private room so there was no roommate I could ask regarding his whereabouts.

The orderly stuck to his task and pushed all of the sheets into a large bin that he wheeled past me. "He's gone," he said, making his way down the hallway.

"Gone?" I asked. A sick feeling took hold of my stomach, my head getting light-headed at the thought.

"Yeah, gone," he said, making his way toward the elevator.

"What time?" I asked. I didn't think that we still lived in a world where people died of pneumonia, but apparently, I was wrong about that. Dead wrong, as it were.

"Dunno," he said, pushing the cart into the open elevator door. "If you hurry, you can probably still catch him." The doors closed and I was left standing in the hallway, the sound of footfalls on the polished hallway floors the only sound after the orderly and his cart of dirty laundry departed.

Catch him? He wasn't dead, just gone. I eschewed the elevator and headed down the stairs, swinging myself around the landings and hoping I wouldn't end up in this very hospital's ER with an injury as I busted out the ground floor's door and into the lobby. Cassandra issued a stern warning as I raced through the lobby and out into the parking lot, just in time to see a more robust-looking Donnie Kinneally talking to a guy who could only be described as rakish, a fedora sitting atop a craggily handsome face. I flashed on the fedora and the same guy dancing with Pegeen Casey at her wedding. But before I could register what was happening now, Donnie was in the car, a black Town Car, a grimace on his face as he caught sight of me running toward him.

"Wait!" I called, but it was no use, the car driving away at a leisurely pace, one that allowed me to find the Volvo in the parking lot and bring it to a noisy start—I had to remember to get Dad to look at the muffler—and begin my tail of the fedora-wearing man and his passenger.

We wound through the streets of the lower county, finally getting onto the highway, the driver of the car in front of me never going over the speed limit, coming to a complete stop at every stop sign, yielding responsibly when asked to yield to other drivers. It was the most reasonable chase I had ever been on, despite the fact that I had only been on one other chase. But I had watched enough cop shows and movies to think that every one resembled the famous scene in *The French Connection* where cars darted in and out of traffic, avoiding young mothers pushing baby carriages and old people using walkers. This was like a Sunday drive—a strange one, but a nice one nonetheless. At one point, Donnie turned around from his position in the backseat and gave me a wave, one that said "Nice to see you, Bel. Odd that we're taking the same route, isn't it?"

Odd, yes. And even odder when I realized where we were going.

As we drove up the driveway to the Manor, the Town Car coming to a stop in front of my apartment, I wondered if the man wearing the fedora was interested in booking a wedding.

When I saw his gun, trained on Donnie, the young guy walking in a straight line to the steps to my apartment, his mouth set in a grim frown, I realized that that probably wasn't the intention of his visit. As I threw the car into reverse, putting pedal to metal, the Volvo breathed its last gasp, sounding eerily similar to Gerard Mason as he took his last gasp on his ill-fated wedding day.

The guy in the fedora waved at me to get out of the car and I didn't see that I had a choice. The ubiquitous lawn service, who interrupted every Monday morning of my time here at the Manor with their lawnmowers and leaf blowers, were nowhere to be seen, nor were any of the members of my intrusive family. Kind of like cops—there was never one around when you needed one. I thought for a moment about what I would do but it was clear that I had no choice. I got out of the car and started for the duo standing at the bottom of the stairs to my apartment, my legs feeling as if they were filled with lead.

"What's going on?" I asked, a stupid question and one that I wasn't sure I wanted the answer to.

The man in the fedora smiled. "Just a spot of trouble," he said, and in those few words, I heard the lilt of Ballyminster, this brogue sounding identical to Mom's and Dad's. "Nothing that a quick chat can't fix."

Donnie and I headed up the stairs to the apartment, taking our time, the man in the fedora behind us. At the top of the stairs Pauline's stricken face appeared in the window of the bathroom, her head going out of sight so quickly that I felt as if I may have imagined seeing her. I opened the screen door and went into the apartment, making as much noise as I could to let her know that we were past the bathroom and into the living room, hoping that my telepathic communication to her to flee was received. I also hoped that she would be as quiet as she could be as she exited the bathroom and went for help, but I had seen this woman in action and there was nothing quiet about her. I also wasn't sure that she would have our best interests at heart, her own safety paramount.

She was neither quiet nor interested in our safety as she busted through the bathroom door, hitting the screen door and heading down the back stairs. On the kitchen counter, I spied her car keys, wondering just how far she would get on foot.

Fedora man looked at us and calmly said, "Stay here."

No chance, Dapper Dan. As soon as he was out the door, I slammed the back door shut, locked it, and yelled to Donnie, "Call 911!"

When I got no response, my heart racing from the panic, I raced down the short hallway to the living room where I found my partner-in-crime, as it were, passed out cold on the couch.

# CHAPTER *Thirty-eight*

Kevin looked at Donnie Kinneally, now revived and drinking a cup of tea in my living room. "You'll have to do better than 'I dunno.'" He was clearly out of patience with the guy and who could blame him. Since Donnie had come back to life, all he had said was "I dunno" in response to every question he had been asked, even the easy ones like "What day is it?" Kevin looked at me, exasperated, while Cargan stood in the kitchen, his arms crossed, his face displaying the same placid look that it always had.

I took a stab at the fedora-wearing man's identity. "Was that Mugsy Calhoun?" I asked. I hadn't detected a pinkie necklace around his neck but everything else about him screamed gangster.

Donnie's face went white at the mention, which led me to believe the answer was "yes."

Kevin looked at me. "What's a Mugsy Calhoun?"

"Irish gangster," I said, as if that were the most normal thing about the whole conversation.

"You're making that up," Kevin said.

Cargan spoke up, a dozen feet away from the questioning going on in the living room. "Sadly, she's not.

Mugsy Calhoun is a notorious gangster in Ballyminster. Has started plying his trade in Boston recently. In my previous line of work, we were very aware of his activity."

"Why?" Kevin asked. "What does a gangster in Ireland have to do with things here in the U.S.?"

"Oh, you'd be surprised," Cargan said.

"Well, surprise me, then," Kevin said, rapidly losing patience with Cargan's "less is more" approach to conversation.

"There's drugs, for one. He's got a container ship that makes its way back and forth across the Atlantic quite regularly to deliver 'shipments.' "

I flashed on the words "import/export" in my brain, my meeting with James Casey and his contention that most of what his company shipped was done by sea.

"If you know this, how come you haven't caught him yet?" Kevin asked.

Donnie looked from Kevin to me to Cargan. "Aren't you a banquet manager?" he asked my brother.

Cargan looked him dead in the eye and told him the truth. "Yes, I'm a banquet manager." He left out the part where he had been one of the best undercover cops the NYPD had ever had and was now on medical leave for PTSD. "Working on it, Hanson." He gave Kevin a hard stare. "Working on it."

Kevin considered Donnie Kinneally, the look on his face telling me that he couldn't figure out what was weirder about this conversation, Donnie Kinneally's denial of knowing anything or Cargan's assertion that one Mugsy Calhoun was in our midst. The way things had gone since I arrived home several months earlier, all of it made sense to me. Black was white at Shamrock Manor and up was down. Once you set foot on the grounds of the Manor, you had to suspend all disbelief. It was Crazy Town.

Kevin put his hands on his hips, surveyed the living room as if my coffee table held the key to understanding all of this. "Where are you staying, Mr. Kinneally? And if you say 'I dunno,' I will resort to police brutality."

Donnie pointed out the window to the Manor in the distance. "There."

"Okay," Kevin said. "Remain 'there' until further notice." He looked at Cargan. "You and I need to talk."

Kevin and Cargan went outside and I sat down on the couch next to Donnie. "How are you feeling?"

He shrugged. "I dunno."

"On a scale of one to ten, ten being the worst one could feel, how do you feel?" I asked.

"Fourteen."

"Okay, then," I said. "Go on back to the Manor and get some rest. I'll bring you some food later. Unless you're hungry now?"

He shook his head. "No. Not hungry." He stood. "Really worried about Pauline, though. If he finds her, he'll kill her."

"Why? Aren't you the one who owes him money?" I asked.

He fell back into the couch and held a pillow to his face. "Yes. It's all my fault," he said, his voice muffled behind my pillow. "He knows she's got the money to pay my debt and he really wants to be repaid."

"Really? The amount you owe doesn't sound like it would be worth the trouble on this guy's part." There was more to the story—there always was with Donnie and Pauline, I had come to learn. "Well, I can't imagine how far she'll get on foot," I said.

"You don't know her. She's fast. She'll get as far as she needs to," he said. "At least I hope so."

I sent him on his way. Guy was sick and needed his rest and I needed to be left alone to look into things on my own terms. I pulled my computer out from under my bed and made myself comfortable while I poked around. I had a hundred things to do at the Manor, but finding out if the guy I had seen was actually Mugsy Calhoun or some other nefarious type was at the top of my to-do list.

As I scrolled through the information about Calhoun—all news to me—I thought back to a conversation Cargan and I had once had about criminals. We had been watching a *Law and Order: SVU* marathon one dreary Sunday afternoon prior to our family Sunday dinner, a command performance, and I had mused that in real life, criminals seemed to make mistake after mistake after mistake and that it didn't take the keen eye of Detectives Benson or Stabler to figure out what had happened, what had been perpetrated, and by whom. I had remembered a case where a guy had kidnapped a woman and then proceeded to use her credit card all over town, something that had led to his capture and arrest. I had asked Cargan why the guy would have done that.

"Because, Bel," Cargan had said, "criminals are stupid."

I thought of that as I looked at the various Web accounts of Mugsy Calhoun, a guy who had grown up in South Boston, not Ballyminster, and who still resided there after having lived in Ireland for a long time, according to the latest account of his exploits. To my mind, he had been hiding there most likely. He was a Southie, through and through, and while extortion, blackmail, and drug running were part of his past and present, so was philanthropy, apparently, something that made the South Bostoners who remained, despite rapid expansion and downtown growth of buildings and businesses, devoted to the guy, more so than they should have been. He was a guy who engendered a lot of loyalty and trust from the neighborhood types and was wily enough to escape the police. He lived in the shadows yet out in the open. He spent time in Ballyminster but more of it in Boston now. And he had a devoted crew, one of whom, if the photo in the news story that I was currently reading was recent and accurate, included Domnall Kinneally, otherwise known as "Donnie the Gazelle" for his ability to outrun anyone in a foot race.

Before I was finished with Donnie—aka the Gazelle—and Mugsy, I went to the online yellow pages and put in the address where we had found Pauline previously. Although I shouldn't have been surprised, I was. The name Connolly appeared, the phone number belonging to one of Angus's brothers, one of the juvenile delinquents with whom I had grown up. I wondered if Cargan had known about the home's owner.

I slammed my computer shut and raced down the stairs of the apartment, thinking about Donnie's nickname. It was a terrible one but clearly apt because when I threw open the door to the suite in which I had situated the louse, the bed was made and everything was neat and tidy, despite being completely empty of any signs of life, particularly those of Donnie the Gazelle.

# CHAPTER *Thirty-nine*

I took the Vanagon, telling Dad about the dead Volvo and lying that I needed to make a run to Restaurant Depot for supplies.

"Ah, Jaysus, Bel," he had protested as he handed over the keys. "That car ran just fine until you got your mitts on it."

"It's not my fault, Dad!" I said, sounding like a twelve-year-old. "That car's got so many miles on it that you should see if Volvo wants to do a commercial with you in it! The muffler was gone and now it won't start. How is that my fault?" I was yelling at him, the stress of all of this getting to me, something that he was unaccustomed to, and when I saw his face, I dropped my voice to a whisper. "It's not my fault." I couldn't count how many times I had uttered that sentence in my life. A thousand? Two? Whatever. The Volvo could wait. I hadn't stopped thinking about how two people could disappear into thin air and wondered, if I were them, where I would go? I left Dad in his studio, working on a new installation, the keys to the car in my hand. I got into the van and drove down the Manor driveway with no clear plan or destination. In the rearview mirror, I spotted Cargan and Kevin walking the grounds of the Manor, two men with a shared occupation in deep conversation. What it was about, I had no idea, but I knew that I didn't want to involve either one of them in what I planned to do.

Thoughts of chicken Marsala and beet poisoning filled my brain and I took the Vanagon on a familiar journey to O'Halligan's to see Angus Connolly. He was at his usual place at the bar when I arrived, a smile plastered on his face as he listened to the tale being spun by a very drunk patron seated next to him. The smile faded when he saw me. The bruises around his eyes were still prevalent though a little less multihued than they were when I saw him last. "You," he said. "How many times do I have to tell you that you're not welcome here?"

"Blah, blah, blah," I said. "I get it. Now, answer me one thing: have you seen Pauline?" I asked. It was a long shot but one worth taking. She had few allies, and even though she had bilked Angus out of money and he was angry at her, clearly she had few options. And obviously, she was quite the sweet-talker, getting guys to do what she wanted whenever she wanted them to.

"I have not seen her," he said. "Are you an idiot? I don't want to see her and I hope I never lay eyes on her face again."

"But you put her up. In your brother's house north of here. Why did you do that?" I asked.

He pointed at the door. "Out."

I sat down at the bar. "I'm not leaving until I get some answers."

"You will if I call the police. None of this is your business," he said.

"It is my business and I want answers," I said. I was tired of people not talking, or talking and telling me lies. It was all completely frustrating, and now that I was in it, a mobster ending up at my house, now that a mobster knew where I and my family lived, it was definitely my business.

When this was over, I was definitely talking to Mom and Dad about their hiring practices, their lack of interviewing skills.

Angus Connolly leaned in close. "I have a soft spot for the girl. What can I say?"

"Enough to protect her? To give her a safe place to land?" I asked.

"Yep. All of that. I didn't want you to find her first so I lied to you. I thought I could get my money back. Quid pro quo, as it were. But the girl's got a heart of stone." He turned and looked at the bartender. "If you see this woman in here again, remember that she's not welcome." He looked back at me. "Now, out." He pointed at the front door, where Cargan and Kevin were entering, their thoughts coinciding with mine and bringing them here to O'Halligan's for a wee chat with the business owner.

I knew my time with Angus was short and that it would probably turn out that I'd never speak to him again, so I asked the one question that I had on my mind. "What did you serve at the Casey/Mason rehearsal dinner?" I asked.

He looked at me, confused, not really knowing why I would ask and figuring, I guessed, that he didn't have to lie. It was an easy question, one that didn't require a half-truth. "Salmon. Chicken français. A beef dish."

"Mushrooms in any of it?" I asked.

He looked at me quizzically. "Not a one. Hate mushrooms. Always have. You won't find them on the menu at O'Halligan's."

# CHAPTER *Forty*

She would have to come back for her car. I figured that was a given. Cargan was a whiz at electronics; I had learned that a few months earlier when I discovered that he had bugged the whole Manor and had spent many a night in the basement, listening in on the goings-on upstairs, hoping to figure out how deep one of our father's friends was in gunrunning for the IRA. An alarm triggered by the opening of a car door was child's play to him and the system would be rigged in no time flat.

After I left O'Halligan's, I stopped in at the Manor and went to the lost-and-found box where a necklace that sure looked like it held a human pinkie on it was sitting, right where I had left it. The pinkie was rubber, as it turned out, but it confirmed for me that Mugsy Calhoun had been at Pegeen and Gerry's wedding and had a relationship with someone in the family, maybe even Pegeen herself.

The next night, after configuring an alarm system, Cargan stood back and admired his invisible handiwork. "Works like a charm," he said to himself even though we hadn't tested it. He was that sure.

"Will you hear it in the Manor?" I asked.

"Won't need to," he said. "I'm staying with you."

Pauline's car was parked where she left two nights earlier, right below the window in my living room. If the alarm went off—*when* the alarm went off—I would hear it, and if Cargan was staying with me, he would, too.

"So you knew that the house up north belonged to one of the Connollys?" I asked once we were back in the apartment and I had started making macaroni and cheese, one of Cargan's favorite meals.

"Had a lead," he said. "Figured I would check it out." He watched me whisk some flour and butter together to make a roux. "You've got to stay away from Angus Connolly."

"Why?" I asked. The answer was obvious—it was none of my business and entirely police business—but I figured it was worth the ask.

"This is getting dangerous, Bel," he said. "Mugsy Calhoun is no one to be trifled with."

"Why hadn't any of us heard of him?" I asked. "Usually you hear mobsters' names bandied about. Funny that we have never heard of him."

"You'd be surprised what you don't know. Who lives beneath the surface. He's not exactly on the Most Wanted list but he does his fair share of damage in Boston."

"And Ballyminster?" I asked.

"By extension, yes. Ballyminster," Cargan said. "Runs the drug trade pretty well, from what I understand."

I thought about my parents' hometown, the rolling hills, the bucolic setting high on a hill, the tiny village with its tidy little storefronts boasting the one thing they sold: beef. Chicken. Bread. Pastry. The fact that there was a dark underbelly that provided a foundation for what lived aboveground was sobering and sad.

"And Angus Connolly?" I asked, peeking into the refrigerator for some cheddar. I figured if I kept the conversation casual, continued with the food prep, Cargan would be more likely to spill, to not realize what we were really talking about.

"Collateral damage," Cargan said. "Like me. Got caught in her web."

"You're smarter than that, Car," I said. "Much smarter."

He chuckled. "You'd think so, wouldn't you?"

"At least she didn't try to blackmail you, too," I said.

"Nothing to blackmail. I get up, I play soccer, I go to work, I watch television. Got no money to speak of. No secrets."

The secrets were out in the open now so he was right: he had nothing to hide, nothing to protect. Except us, Mom and Dad and the other brothers. Me. We both knew it and left it unsaid.

"So what do we do now?" I asked, pouring milk into my roux. I wasn't sure the Cordon Bleu would approve of how I made mac and cheese but it was how I had always made it and always would.

"*We* do nothing. *I* do something. You stay put," he said. He got up and looked out the living room window. "Getting dark."

I knew what that meant. If she was coming back, she was coming back after dark. So there was nothing to do but make dinner, have a glass of wine, and wait.

"Haven't seen too much of Joyce around here lately," Cargan said, not taking his eyes off the front window, even though there was nothing to see.

I was in the kitchen putting together a salad. "We're both busy. Superbusy."

"You need to spend some time with him. He's nice." He turned back from the window and sat down at the kitchen counter. "You guys were inseparable over the summer. What happened?"

"Too soon," I said, but it was a lie. "It was too soon for me to jump into a relationship again." It hadn't been too soon in the beginning; it had been just the right time to make me forget that I had once loved a guy who was all wrong for me. But something had changed, and my brother, previously thought to be a few cards shy of a full deck, was perceptive enough to pick up on it.

"He was there that night."

I didn't have to ask which night. "That night" was frozen in my mind as the night that everything changed. "He was? I don't remember."

"He was. I remember now. The party on the island. He was there, if only for a little while."

"What made you remember that?" I finally turned around, ready to meet my brother's eye.

"His braces. I saw a commercial the other night about braces, how they are different now, clear and invisible, and I got to thinking about braces. And Amy. That night on the island."

My brother's mind was a thing to behold. I remembered Brendan's braces all too well, had noticed when I first met him again how great his teeth had turned out after years and years of wearing braces, but only Cargan would make the connection between now and then. "Yes, he wore braces for a long time."

"He was there," he repeated. "And by the look on your face, I can tell you had no idea."

"No, but it explains a lot," I said. "The day they found Amy's stuff in the river, we were there, having a picnic. And he left me there. Ran away from the scene."

"Why? Did he ever say?" Cargan asked.

"He said that it made him upset. That it reminded him of too many things, of how things changed after Amy disappeared."

"You believe him?"

I thought about that. I wanted to believe him but did I really? It was hard to say. It was the first time I lied to my brother when I said, "I do believe him. I do." I was putting Brendan off, though, and if I were being completely honest with myself, it was because of that day by the river. The Pauline situation had been a mysterious distraction that had kept me busy and not thinking about Brendan's desertion and what that had meant to me.

And it was the first time my brother didn't believe the lie, but he sipped his wine quietly and for the next hour we sat in companionable silence, waiting for the blare of an alarm that seemed a long time coming.

The bottle of wine finished, I went into the cabinet and pulled out a Rioja that I had bought a week earlier. "Rioja?" I asked.

"Sure," Cargan said, holding out his glass.

I poured him a healthy slug. "I don't think Pauline's coming back, Car."

"Just wait," he said. "She'll be back."

Another hour passed and another glass of wine was consumed. I yawned, trying to give my brother the hint that this was a lost cause, that Pauline was in the weeds, never to be seen again. I picked up my glass when the yawn yielded no movement on his part and was on my way to the kitchen when the alarm finally sounded. The glass fell to the floor and shattered in what seemed like a million pieces. Although we had both been waiting for it, it was still a shock to hear it, bleating in the otherwise quiet night, likely waking up Mom and Dad, early-to-bed types who didn't like to be disturbed once the clock hit nine. Cargan was off the couch in a shot, moving fast through the apartment, glass crunching under his tennis shoes, the same style he had worn since high school. Stan Smiths. Classics. He was out the door and down the apartment steps before I could even think to move, the glass all around me, my bare feet, the thought of stepping on a piece of glass paralyzing me. I picked my way over the floor and around the little shards that were everywhere and raced into my bedroom, pulling on a pair of clogs and racing down the stairs after Cargan but he was already in the Vanagon in hot pursuit of Pauline.

The Vanagon versus the BMW? No contest.

I stood at the bottom of the stairs and looked around. The Manor was dark, a light on in an upper bedroom, the only light being cast from the two massive electrified lanterns on either side of the massive oak doors that fronted the place. Odd. The car alarm hadn't awoken anyone, or if it had, they were unconcerned. My family defied logic.

The sounds of the two cars far in the distance, I turned around, ready to reenter the apartment to clean up the glass and sit and wait for Cargan. Behind me, I heard the crunch of leaves, the sound of footfalls. I turned, and despite the lack of good light, the shadows that played across the lawn and the driveway, it was hard not to know who was approaching me.

Mugsy Calhoun cut a fine figure in his suit and fedora.

# CHAPTER *Forty-one*

"Can I clean up this glass while we talk?" I asked, not having moved from the hallway since we arrived back in the apartment.

Mugsy smiled at me. "I don't think that's a good idea. Despite the fact that I have a concealed weapon that I am more than prepared to use on you at any time, a broom would make a very handy weapon." He looked around the apartment. "Have a seat."

I crunched over broken glass and went to the chair next to the couch, which afforded me a perfect view of the screen door and, hopefully, any help that might arrive. The darkened Manor was not heartening in that regard. "What do you want?" I asked.

He sat on the couch, his hands clasped together and hanging down between his legs. It was a relaxed posture but nothing about this meeting was relaxed. "Well, why don't you start with telling me where Pauline Darvey is?"

"I would but I don't know," I said. "She was here but now she's gone again."

"That's kind of her M.O."

"Why are you looking for her?" I asked. Outside, it was still dark and quiet. Not a sign of life.

"She has something that belongs to me," he said.

"Drugs?" I asked.

His smile turned into full-blown laughter. "No. Not drugs. It's something much more mundane. Simple." He settled down again. "And money. She owes me money."

"I thought Donnie owed you money?" I asked.

"Him, too," he said. "If she wants him to live, she'll come up with the money."

"You're going to kill Donnie over twenty grand?" I asked. "That seems like chump change to a guy like you." I figured if I kept him talking, he wouldn't kill me as quickly and maybe Cargan would come back in time.

He laughed again. "Twenty grand. That's cute."

I thought about Pauline's empty locker in the basement of the Manor. She hadn't even returned her apron. I had nothing related to the girl or her life so I couldn't imagine what Mugsy Calhoun wanted with me and told him so. "Why don't you enlighten me?"

"In due time," he said. "Now, if you don't mind, my colleague and I will take a quick look around and see if it's already here."

"Colleague?" I asked. I hadn't seen anyone else but I wasn't surprised, either, when Domnall Kinneally's face, a sheepish look on it, appeared at the back door. "Now, you. You I want to kill," I said. Since the guy had arrived in town, we'd had nothing but trouble. "I thought you guys were on the outs with each other."

"He owes me money. I have jobs to do. It works out perfectly," Calhoun said, looking at his colleague.

Donnie grimaced. "Sorry, Bel. Some old business that needs attending to," Donnie said. He went to work in my bedroom while I sat with Mugsy Calhoun, going through every inch of the room, the sound of drawers opening and closing, clothes and shoes being flung around willy-nilly.

"Hey!" I called in to him. "That's my stuff!" I thought back to discovering the open kitchen drawers. "You were already in here," I said to Donnie who had finished in the bedroom and was now in the kitchen. "God, I was so stupid. I wanted to help you."

"Sorry again, Bel," Donnie said while tossing a colander into the sink.

I looked at Mugsy. "And what kind of mother names their kid 'Mugsy'?" I said.

For the first time since he'd arrived in my apartment, I saw Mugsy Calhoun have a flash of anger, real and terrifying. "A proper Irish ma, not that it's any of your business," he said.

Great. Now I had insulted the mother. Good going, Bel.

"Sorry," I said.

"It's short for Martin." He looked away as he gifted me with that little tidbit.

I trained my eyes on the back door, hearing footsteps on the outside stairs. Mom and Dad appeared, one looking sleepier than the next, Mom in a silk bathrobe with kitten heels—her preferred nighttime look, I had come to find out over the summer—and Dad in boxer shorts and a long T-shirt. Dad pounded on the back door. "Jaysus, Bel! What's going on? We heard a car alarm and then someone took off in the Vanagon."

I tried to give them a look to tell them to hit the road and head back to the Manor but Donnie Kinneally left the kitchen and opened the back door, greeting them as if they were long-lost friends. "Mr. and Mrs. McGrath! How nice to see you."

Mom and Dad spoke at the same time.

"Donnie," Mom said. "Shouldn't you be in bed?"

While Dad asked, "Aren't you supposed to be in the hospital?"

"Feeling much better," he said, and motioned toward the living room. "Why don't you join Bel and my friend Mr. Calhoun in the parlor?"

Mom and Dad walked in. Mom crossed her arms. "I didn't realize you were entertaining, Belfast. I would have dressed accordingly." Mom looked at the broken glass on the floor and then back at me.

"I'm not entertaining, Mom," I said. "Mr. Calhoun here has a gun in his pocket and Mr. Kinneally is looking for something that Pauline had in her possession that is"—I leaned in toward the bedroom and yelled—"definitely not here!"

Calhoun stood up and offered a hand to Dad, who refused it, putting his hands behind his back. "Mr. Mc-Grath, it's a pleasure."

Mom narrowed her eyes. "You were at the Casey wedding," she said.

"For a moment," Calhoun said. "I wanted to pay my respects to the bride and groom but business intervened."

I hooked a thumb in his direction. "He's a mobster."

Mom gasped while Calhoun refuted that notion. "I'm in the import/export business."

"Oh, just like Mr. Casey," Dad said, as if it were the most natural thing in the world, two guys just happening to be in the "import/export" business.

"And what does this have to do with us?" Mom asked.

Calhoun decided how much he would tell us. "I'm

looking for the girl. She has something that belongs to me."

"And what is that?" Mom asked, trying desperately to maintain a steely posture but wilting a little bit at the thought of the gun in the guy's pocket, her eyes trained on his hands.

"Just a key. Nothing more."

Kinneally came out of the bedroom, his work there complete. He went back to his work in the kitchen, tossing pots and pans onto the floor, a stick of Irish butter into the sink on top of the colander. Seriously, I was going to kill this guy the first chance I got. That was expensive butter.

Dad looked at me just before he fell to the floor, managing to find a place that wasn't covered in broken glass, his body convulsing on my could-have-been-cleaner area rug. He clutched his chest. "Help me!" he screamed, his voice high-pitched and strangled.

I jumped up and went to his side, bending over to see if I should perform CPR. I didn't care if Mugsy Calhoun shot me; my only concern was my stricken father. Back in my restaurant days, I had taken a course on first aid and a variety of lifesaving techniques, never in my wildest dreams imagining that I would have to perform one of them on my father. I ripped open the neck of his T-shirt, thinking that the neck looked a little tight, and studied his face, only to be shocked at what he did, what I saw.

The old guy winked at me.

"Oh, Dad," I said, continuing the drama. "Hang on!" I thumped his chest and counted out loud, turning around to see that Kinneally and Calhoun were standing together in deep conversation, deciding whether or not to let my father die, talking about whether or not he had anything to do with anything. I poured on the drama for effect, hoping I wasn't overdoing it. "Don't you die on me!"

Kinneally was talking of my parents' hospitality in a bid to get us true, professional medical attention, but Calhoun was a viper, and didn't care. Neither noticed that while they decided the fate of my father, who they didn't realize was quicker and smarter and more clever than they would ever be, Mom, ever vigilant, held a massive Lenox vase over her head that I didn't even know I had, her arms cut and muscled from years of doing and teaching Pilates. She brought the vase crashing down on Calhoun's head, much to the surprise of Kinneally, who started for the door. Shards of porcelain flew around the apartment as did a bunch of bills, fifties and hundreds mostly, the currency landing on every surface of the room. Donnie looked at me, wide-eyed, and started to run after the bills in the air, but seeing that I had other ideas, that I was about to take flight and bring him down, he changed his mind.

Gazelle, my ass.

I got up and started after him, remembering the tackles that my brother Derry had taught me what seemed like a thousand years ago. I lunged at the guy's back and wrapped my arms around his knees, bringing him down like a sack of potatoes, my heft covering his thin frame and trapping him on the hallway floor.

Dad pulled me off and grabbed Kinneally by the hair, bringing him up and throwing him against the wall. "We took you in. And this is how you repay us?"

Mom was on the phone to the Foster's Landing Police Department by the time Dad returned Donnie to the couch. Calhoun was making noise on the floor, still not completely cogent, as Dad searched his pockets, coming up with a very scary-looking knife and a very tiny gun that I knew could have killed me with one shot despite its toylike size. Dad hauled him to his feet as well, tossing him onto the couch beside Donnie, the two of them looking not quite as scary as before, bruised and battered from a manhandling from my father.

Dad held the gun like a pro and I didn't want to think why that might be. I think Dad had a few secrets of his own, secrets that I hoped never to learn. He pulled up a kitchen chair, straight-backed, and sat there, the gun pointed at the two louses on the couch, and asked them the question that I had been thinking but would never have gotten an answer to had my parents not arrived when they did. Gone was my dad the overreactor, the blusterer, the one everyone tried to keep things from because he was so emotional. In his place was a confident, wily guy who looked a lot imposing, sitting there in his boxer shorts and ripped T-shirt, a gun in his meaty paws.

He studied Donnie and Calhoun intently. "So, tell us. What the hell is going on here?"

# CHAPTER Forty-two

I was starting to consider the Foster's Landing Police Department's station house my second home. For the second time in a week, I sat in a chair in the waiting area hoping that I could find out what was going on firsthand from someone whose only thought was to tell lie after lie after lie. It was the next morning and I knew Kevin had pulled a long night dealing with Donnie and Mugsy, but he looked as handsome as ever when he exited the conference room and strode across the room toward me, a smile on his face. He pulled me into the hallway, away from the prying eyes of Francie McGee and the rest of the people who had arrived for the eight-to-four shift. I had told Kevin and Lieutenant D'Amato that the money wasn't mine, that I didn't even know I had a vase in the apartment, never mind a vase filled with what turned out to be twenty-five hundred dollars.

He dropped his voice to an excited whisper. "That guy is a genuine gangster!" he said.

He was a little more enthusiastic about that than I would have liked or thought. "You like that?"

"Well, I never thought I'd have a gangster to question

here in the Landing. It's kind of strange," he said, "but good strange!"

It was then that I noticed that he was overcaffeinated and underrested. The events of the last few weeks, coupled with the all-nighter, had made him a little cuckoo. "I think you need some rest, Kevin," I said, putting a hand on his arm.

"Who needs rest?" he said, looking more than a little crazy. "I've got work to do!"

"Did you find out anything?" I asked. Cargan had come back empty-handed shortly after our run-in with Mugsy and Donnie, Pauline once again in the wind.

"Oh, not too much but we're going to keep them here until we find out something." He looked at me. "Did you know Calhoun was at the Casey wedding?"

"Yes, I remembered," I said. "Do you think that's significant?"

"It's gotta be, right?" he said. "I'll let you know if I find out anything."

"Are you still thinking that Gerry Mason was poisoned?" I asked. Pauline had told him what she had told me; I made sure of that by repeating her assertions about poisonous mushrooms.

"Yeah, she told us that, Bel," he said. "I don't know that we'll ever know."

As I walked back to the Manor, I thought about everything I had seen and been told over the last few weeks. Pauline hadn't told me one true thing about herself; why would I believe that she was right about Gerry Mason having been poisoned? We were back at square one. A poisoned groom, a girl who was going to get my parents into a heap of trouble if she surfaced and if the real authorities—not Kevin—found out about my parents' hiring practices at the Manor. Gangsters and guys with gambling debts and pneumonia. Lots of stories, lots of situations. Every detail led to a dead end. What a waste of a couple of weeks. As I walked along, I decided that I didn't care where Pauline had gone. I would help Colleen and Eileen get legal, keep my parents out of trouble, and right the ship that was Shamrock Manor. We were almost there, Calhoun and Kinneally in police custody; the rest would fall into place eventually.

I trudged up the hill to the Manor, wondering how I would pull together a down payment for a new car. It was time to start acting like an adult, get a proper savings account and start putting money away for my future. I couldn't stay here forever. The situation was fine for right now but long-term? That wasn't going to work. I had to think of a plan. Life outside of the Manor should be my goal, as hurt and wounded as I felt when I had returned home, feelings that were definitely abating but that would take some time to go away for good.

My phone pinged in my pocket and I saw that Brendan had texted. "A drink later?" he asked.

"Most definitely," I texted back, thinking that getting our relationship on the right track would be the first thing I would do to start my new life here once again. He had apologized and explained what had happened that day and I had no reason not to believe him. I would ask him why he had never told me he had been on the island that night with me, Amy, Kevin—everyone—and get a truthful answer, I was sure. We would clear the slate and pick up where we had left off, moving forward instead of looking backward.

It all made perfect sense, the world I had constructed

in my ambulatory daydreams. I was so lost in thought, thinking of all the answers I could get and the questions I would never know the answers to that I almost didn't see the black BMW speeding toward me, coming from the Manor and going down the steep hill at a speed that Dad wouldn't consider safe, the driver ignoring the signs the man had posted saying TAKE IT SLOW! painted in his scrawl.

It was Pauline. She slowed down and finally stopped when she saw me, rolling down the window. "Can't thank you enough, Bel!" she said, a smile on her face.

"For what?" I asked. Cargan's phrase "criminals are stupid" floated through my brain.

"For getting those two eejits out of the way," she said, holding her arm stiffly out of the window. "Don't come any closer."

I stopped in the middle of the road and looked at her, her face full of glee. "Donnie and Calhoun?" I asked.

I thought back to the night before. "They came to my home. They wanted to hurt me. Said they were looking for something. Know anything about that, Pauline?" I asked.

"Oh, I know all about it, Bel." She warned me again to stay where I was, noticing that I was drifting closer to the car.

"And what was it?" I asked. "Please, God, tell me that you didn't put drugs in my apartment."

She laughed, throwing her head back, her graceful neck white and smooth. It was a neck I wanted to choke at that very moment. "No, not drugs. It was the money, Bel. I needed a safe place to keep it and your place seemed as good a place as any."

"When?" I asked.

"When what?" she asked.

The low hum of the car's engine was the only sound out on the road. "When did you put it there?" I asked.

"Been putting it there for weeks," she said. "In that old cookie jar on top of the cabinets."

"What cookie jar?" I asked. "I didn't even know I had a cookie jar. As a matter of fact, I didn't know I had a vase until last night."

"I put that there," Pauline said. "It was my mum's. Saw that it was broken. What happened?"

"Wouldn't you like to know?" I asked. "You already know that Donnie and Calhoun are in jail so you probably can figure out the rest.

"And incidentally, how did you smuggle a giant vase into my apartment?" I asked. "Without me noticing?"

"Ah, Bel. Poor sweet Bel. You hardly notice anything," she said.

"That's not true," I said. "I notice a lot." Maybe she was right. Maybe everything that had happened right under my nose was my own fault for not noticing.

"Heck, I'm only down twenty-five hundred. That was just the money I couldn't fit behind your toilet."

"My toilet?" I asked. "You hid money behind my toilet? Mugsy Calhoun's money?"

"It was all my money," she said. "I earned that money. It was all mine."

"Earned" wasn't really the right word. "Donnie's gambling debts?"

"Well, yes, there were those. Eejit was blackmailing me. Told me he'd call the cops and tell them I was illegal, get me deported, unless I coughed up the money he owed Mugsy. But I knew if he found me, they'd kill me."

"Kill you?" I asked. None of this was making sense, not one single, solitary detail of her ridiculous story.

"Mugsy told him he'd let him off the hook if he found me and brought me back. And we both knew what would happen." She turned and looked out the front window of the car. "He told me that later." Clearly, she was disappointed in Donnie's behavior if not his lack of intellectual prowess.

Criminals *are* stupid. Cargan was right. Again.

"And why is Mugsy after you? Why does he want you back so badly?"

"Ah, Bel. There's the story right there. I broke his heart. And he wants it fixed."

I didn't even know what that meant but having had a broken heart myself at different points in my life, I thought about how I had wanted it fixed, how I had gone about fixing it. Eating too much, sometimes drinking too much. Finally, coming back to my family, to my childhood home. "That's why you needed to leave. Why you wanted to 'get gone,' as you say," I said. I looked around. Still no one in sight. "So you blackmailed everyone around you to get a little nest egg so you could start a new life somewhere. Correct?" I asked. The sun was beating down on my head and I was tired but I think I was starting to put the pieces together.

Pauline shrugged.

"He said you have a key," I said.

"I do," she said. "And it's in a safe place. You've got one, too."

"I do? Where is it? What's it to?" I asked.

"Enough, Bel." She looked straight ahead. "It's insurance. It lets you know that I trusted you and that you'll protect me if anything happens to me."

I started to move closer to the car.

"Close enough. And now," she said, putting the car into drive, "I am going to 'get gone.'"

"Wait," I said, putting my hands on the car door. "Did you take our tip? The ten grand?"

"Bel, I'm sorry. Your parents were wonderful to me. Your family has been terrific as well. But a girl's gotta do what a girl's gotta do."

So there it was. "I knew it," I said. "Listen, you'll never outrun Mugsy Calhoun, Pauline," I said. "Guys like that have their tentacles reaching out everywhere." I had seen *The Godfather,* Parts I, II, and III. Mobsters were wily. And well connected.

She gunned the engine. "Wanna bet?" she asked, rolling up the window and speeding down the hill, leaving me standing on the side of the road wondering how much of her story I could believe. Where she would go. If I would ever see her again.

Later, in my apartment, I started to clean up the mess from the night before. Glass had reached every corner of the apartment, leaving scary shards on almost every surface. The cookie jar where Pauline had hidden her largesse, the cookie jar I never knew I had, sat on the counter, the top off, the googly eyes of the cat on the front of the jar focused on me as I cleaned the apartment up as best I could, dumping glass into the trash can, wiping down every surface, spraying air freshener to get the smell of Mugsy Calhoun, an imaginary smell no doubt, out of my apartment. When I was done, I collapsed on the couch, thoughts of looking into documenting the girls, getting them the necessary paperwork to stay in the country, the only thing on my mind. But I was too tired to get up and get my computer, preferring to put my feet up on the coffee table and close my eyes for a moment's rest.

I awoke to knocking at the back door, the sound of it mixing with the dream that I was having. In it, I was down by the river's edge, the day lovely and quiet. The river was full, water lapping up over the edge of my toes, and a blue heron ducked in and out of the dappled, sunlit waves, pulling up a fish here, a pile of leaves there. In the dream, I was tapping my foot to an unheard tune and realized, as I dug out of the deep slumber that I had been in, that someone was at the back door.

I struggled to my feet, my head foggy and my limbs reluctant to move, but I made it to the back door to find a person I had hoped never to see again.

Duffy Dreyer asked if she could come in, and while the last thing I wanted was to talk to a reporter again, my ingrained polite side intervened and I held open the door for her. "I hope I'm not disturbing you," she said, the two of us standing in my narrow hallway. I pulled the bathroom door closed, the sight of it, messy and in need of a good cleaning, distracting me from the woman standing in front of me looking somber and sad.

"What can I do for you, Duffy?" I asked.

"Have you talked to Detective Hanson?" she asked. "Lieutenant D'Amato?"

"Yes, I just saw Kevin. Not the lieutenant, though. Why?" I asked.

Behind her, I saw Brendan Joyce appear in the screen, and as she spoke, I held his gaze, looking for a sign from him that told me that what she was saying wasn't true, that the mystery of Amy, part of my story and a thread in the fabric of the Foster's Landing tapestry, wasn't still a mystery that had to be solved.

He looked at me and I at him and I wanted to ask him here, in front of this reporter, why he had never told me he had been there that night, but all I could do was stand there and try to process the words that were coming out of her mouth.

"It's not her that they found."

Brendan's face crumbled.

"It's not Amy."

# CHAPTER *Forty-three*

After it sank in, after I fully understood what she was trying to tell me, I told Duffy Dreyer, who had a mole in the medical examiner's office, to please leave me alone. Brendan wanted to stay and help me deal with this news, but I wanted to be by myself. The hurt showed on his face, but there was nothing he could do or say—something I said to him outright, causing more hurt—that could help me. I needed to be alone to think about what this discovery actually meant and how it would change the way I looked at that part of my life, if at all. Maybe it wouldn't. Maybe it would keep things exactly as they were, with everyone wondering just what had happened to Amy Mitchell and me feeling the continued sting of our last moments together, me telling her she'd be sorry for betraying me.

I never felt that way, really, that she'd be sorry. I knew we would make up and spend our last summer together before college doing the things we'd always done. We'd kayak and hang out with my brother and all of our friends, party at Eden Island. We'd eat the crappy hot dogs that her father served at his crappy bar and laugh and dream and talk about what we would do when we grew up.

I was grown up now and had followed my dream. I wondered what she would have done, had she lived. Because in my heart of hearts, she was dead and always had been from that last moment on.

I called Kevin. "Who is it?" I asked. "If it's not Amy, who is it?"

He sighed. "Who told you? I wanted to tell you myself."

"It doesn't matter. Who is it?"

"We don't know," he said. "We're searching missing-persons files from years back and hoping to hit on something. So far, nothing." His shoulders, tense before, relaxed. He was defeated. "We may never know."

"So how do you know it's not Amy?" I asked.

"DNA. Things her father gave us when she disappeared."

I let that sink in. If it wasn't Amy, it was someone else, someone whose family had been searching and wondering for all this time. Or maybe not. Maybe it was a person who had slipped through the cracks, hadn't had the love that Amy had had growing up, the love that made people keep searching for her even after it was clear that we would never find her.

I had had no comment for Duffy Dreyer before she left, closing the door behind her and Brendan after they exited, locking it and leaning against it for a long, long time, finally sinking to the floor and sitting there, thinking about what would have been, had Amy still been here. Finally, after about fifteen minutes, I got up and went into the bathroom to inspect it, wondering if Pauline had truly taken everything that belonged to her, the thought of her in there, taping money to the back of my toilet and the stash going unnoticed by me, making me see red. I had come back home to wipe the slate clean, not get involved in anything else. I straddled the toilet and looked over to the backside of the commode, seeing wilted tape hanging down, the sight of something else, something that didn't belong there, catching my eye. I bent over awkwardly, not able to gain purchase on what appeared to be a tiny manila envelope, sealed shut and affixed with tape to the back of the tank.

I finally pulled it off and opened it up, dumping a tiny key into my palm.

I held it up to the light and saw that it had "FLM" stamped on the front; I had no idea what that meant besides the fact that FL for Foster's Landing—was a likely guess. What the key couldn't tell me was how long it had been there, what it opened, why it was taped to the back of my toilet. I put the toilet seat down and sat, turning the key over in my hand and thinking about what secret it held, what door it opened.

I thought about the events of the last few weeks and decided to start at the beginning, wandering over to the Manor, thankfully quiet, and heading down to the basement, where I attempted to insert the key into every locker and coming up empty. I stood in the basement for a few more minutes and went through every day since the Casey wedding, since Pauline had disappeared, thinking that having two things taped to the back of my toilet by two different people was probably unlikely. Or at least I hoped it was—when it hit me.

The kayak racks, the lockers down at the put-in.

I raced upstairs and, not seeing Mom and Dad, lent myself the keys to the Vanagon and headed down toward the water, a two-mile trek that would have taken far too long on foot.

I parked the Vanagon and gave thanks for the drought that had rendered the river unable to host kayakers. It dawned on me as I was walking toward the kayak holders and lockers: Foster's Landing Municipal. I prayed that I was at the right spot, otherwise I would be tracking down every Landing-issued key and its appropriate lock for the near future.

There were three dozen kayak holders and as many lockers. Fortunately, I was alone and only a few of the slots available were empty. Most held kayaks and, even better, the numbers on the kayak holders matched those on the lockers. I picked the ten lockers that didn't have occupied kayak holders and got to work.

It was on my eighth try that the key slid into the lock and turned, opening up the locker and exposing its contents.

It was an envelope, this one larger than the one that had been taped to the back of my toilet. And on it were written two words in bold, black marker.

**INSURANCE POLICY**

# CHAPTER *Forty-four*

I read the contents of the envelope in the Vanagon and did a quick search to get an address for Casey Import/Export. Pauline wasn't the most honest woman on the planet, but she was shrewd and had prepared well, given what I read in the documents that were in the envelope. She explained in the first document that what I was reading was a photocopy of the original she had kept for herself, that she had stolen Pegeen's purse and its nefarious contents—mushrooms—from the wedding just because she liked the bag and knew it held a lot of money. How she didn't tell anyone she had proof because she thought she could score big on this one but had underestimated just how deep this all went.

I called Kevin's cell but it went straight to voice mail so I left a brief but accurate message about what I had found and what my plans were. My family had been dragged into this and before this went any further with law enforcement, I was going to make sure they were dragged out of it.

Casey Import/Export was not far from O'Halligan's, and although that didn't really matter, it made some kind of sense as to why James Casey had suggested the place when we met to talk about my fake soda bread idea. The company was housed in a one-story building that also had offices for a pediatrician and an orthodontist. I walked down the hallway and found the office easily, thinking that it was awfully small for a business that seemed to do exceptionally well, if what I learned through my online digging was true. There was a well-dressed receptionist sitting at the front desk. "May I help you?" she asked.

"Hi, sorry to drop in like this but I'm here to see James Casey," I said. He had chased Pauline that day and now I knew why.

"Do you have an appointment?" she asked, clearly not knowing what "drop in" meant.

"I do not," I said.

From behind me, a man's voice said "Bel?" and I turned to see James striding toward me looking as delicious as ever. I had to remind myself that his endeavors weren't on the up and up and that he had had a hand in his brother-in-law's death, if Pauline was to be believed.

"Hi, James," I said. "Is there somewhere we could talk?"

He led me to a conference room at the end of the hall, one that had floor-to-ceiling windows; it wasn't a place to talk in private, even though no one would be able to hear what we were saying. He took a spot at the head of the long table, obviously accustomed to sitting there. "What can I do for you?" he asked, smiling. "This isn't about soda bread, is it?"

"No," I said, holding the envelope out in front of me. "It's about what you import. What you export. And how none of it is legal."

He pursed his lips, folded his hands in his lap. "Legal? All of what we do is legal."

"You're in cahoots with Mugsy Calhoun. You launder money for him. He and your father grew up together in South Boston."

"Mugsy Calhoun?" James asked, and if I didn't consider him such a good actor, I would have thought he had never heard of the guy. "Who is he?"

"Just a gangster out of South Boston. An old friend of your dad's. He was at the wedding. Danced with your sister." I put the envelope under my arm. "It's all here. Documents that link Casey Import/Export to the Calhoun trafficking. Gerry found out, right? Is that why he was poisoned?"

James continued to look at me as if I had told him the most preposterous story he had ever heard. He stood up. "I think this conversation is over, Bel. I found your quaint story about exporting soda breads sort of humorous, but this flight of fancy is just a little too over the top for my tastes."

From the other end of the hallway, I saw Pegeen. Our eyes met and she held my gaze for a few seconds; I could almost see the wheels turning in her head. I looked back at James. "How could you? Gerry seemed like a really nice guy."

"He was a nice guy. I loved him like a brother," James said.

"But?" I asked.

"But nothing," James said. "I was devastated by his death. At his own wedding, no less."

Pegeen headed down the hallway toward us, nimble in her four-inch designer pumps, her Chanel suit something that I didn't think came in my size. She entered the conference room and closed the door. I noticed a thin sheen of sweat on her upper lip.

"Bel? What can we do for you? I can assure you that despite the events of that day, we have settled the bill with your father for the wedding." She dabbed her eyes with a wadded-up tissue that she held in her hand. "My husband is dead, thanks to you."

"That's not why I'm here, Pegeen," I said. "Pauline Darvey has left our employ but she has also left me some pretty damning documents, documents to suggest that what you import might not be of the legal sort."

James sighed. "I'm sorry, Pegeen. I've tried to disabuse Ms. McGrath of this notion but she seems pretty convinced."

"And what documents would those be?" she asked. "May I see them?"

I held the envelope under my arm. "No, you can't see them. But suffice it to say that Pauline Darvey's relationship with Mugsy Calhoun has yielded some interesting information. Your money. Where it went. Offshore account numbers. It's all here." I looked from James to Pegeen. "That's a lot of money."

"We don't know what you're talking about, Bel," James said.

"I saw you, James. I was the one following you that day when you chased Pauline."

Now it was his turn to look confused. "Followed Pauline? Is she the waitress from the wedding?"

"Yes," I said. "There is also damning information about you, Pegeen. How you may have poisoned your own husband? Ring a bell?"

He looked at Pegeen. "I think you should go, Bel.

These documents that you claim to have can't implicate Casey Import/Export in anything. We are a very legal, by-the-book company. There must be some mistake." His face registered disappointment. "After all I've done for you, Bel."

"Done for me?" I asked.

"Yes. That night at O'Halligans. I stepped in and saved you from being manhandled by that brute." He held up his hand, one knuckle still swollen. "Now, please leave. I can see that I was wrong about you and your intentions." He shook his head sadly. "Fake soda bread . . ."

Next to me, Pegeen let out a little sound not unlike the one her husband had made before he died, and when I turned toward her, I saw the cause of her distress as Kevin and Jed Mitchell, paired together for this investigation, striding down the carpeted hallway toward the conference room. At that moment, it all became clear.

"It was you," I said, looking at her in disbelief. "You were following Pauline. It was you all along."

She grabbed the envelope from under my arm and started out of the room, away from Kevin and Jed. I wondered why Jed, someone who was connected directly to Pauline, would be allowed to work on this case, but it was likely that no one knew of the connection but me, Pauline, and Jed's wife. I didn't know if he was invested in finding her like Pegeen obviously had been.

James saw Kevin and stood up straighter. "What's going on?"

He didn't know. He never had. I'm not sure now he couldn't have known, but it was written all over his sad, handsome face. James had been as much of a pawn in this as Gerry had been, and why he had been standing outside of the men's room door, as Pauline proclaimed, was a question that would go unanswered. I followed Pegeen into the hallway. "You didn't have to kill him, you know," I said. There was a bank of cubicles next to the hallway in which I stood and several faces popped up behind the half-walls.

Pegeen turned and hissed at me. "I didn't kill him. He was poisoned. By you," she said pointing a manicured finger at me. "Your beets."

"Not my beets," I said, walking right up to her and pulling the envelope out from her hands. "But your mushrooms." Pauline had been right: Gerry had eaten chicken Marsala at O'Halligan's but Angus Connolly's chef hadn't prepared it. It was chicken all right, but Pegeen had supplied the mushrooms, just as she had at the wedding. "It took a little longer to kill him than you thought, didn't it?" I asked.

She cracked but she didn't mean to. "I didn't even think there was going to be a goddamned wedding."

"Pegeen! Language!" James said.

She clammed up until Kevin slapped a pair of heavy handcuffs on her wrist. "He was a nice guy," she said, tears falling from her eyes. "But he just couldn't leave well enough alone."

"What does that mean?" I asked. She hadn't confessed to anything but she wasn't protesting her innocence, either.

"It means that it never would have lasted," she said as Jed Mitchell led her out of the office.

# CHAPTER *Forty-five*

I was happy for Kevin and Mary Ann that the day of their wedding, Halloween, dawned as one of the nicest fall days we had had in a long while. It had rained all week, drought be damned, and the river now looked full and robust flowing behind the Manor with a great current, carrying away the bad memories of the last several weeks, at least for me.

Mom, Dad, and I were getting into the Vanagon after the ceremony at the local church, my parents commenting on every aspect of the nuptial Mass we had just attended. In my hand, my phone vibrated, indicating that I had a text from an unfamiliar number. I opened the text and saw a photo. It was a woman, blond with a little spray of freckles across her pert, sunburned nose, holding a drink with an umbrella in it, a wide expanse of ocean behind her.

It took me a minute to realize that it was Pauline.

I guess she had gotten to where she wanted to go. I just hoped that now with Mugsy and Donnie in jail, Pegeen Casey on her way, she would be safe.

Cargan suspected that there never was another witness to what had transpired at the wedding and Kevin had confirmed that. Kevin had pulled the oldest trick in the book by saying there was someone else when there really wasn't. I wished Pauline, with the brains of a Mensa member, had used those smarts for good, not evil. She could have run the world.

The other girls, Colleen and Eileen, were content to stay at the Manor. Arney, in a lull at work because divorces in Foster's handing had hit an all-time low, was working hard on their paper work. With any luck, they would be legal soon and we could all exhale. I was proud of my brother; it was a side of the law he really didn't know but out of loyalty to the girls—to his family—he was figuring it out.

And as for Kevin? As promised, he never said a word.

That afternoon, Mom was critiquing every aspect of the wedding, from the flowers to the bridesmaids' dresses. She finally got to the bride herself. "I'm not a fan of the mermaid dress but, don't you know, Mary Ann has made me a convert," Mom said, getting into the front seat of the Vanagon, Dad at the wheel. In the kitchen back at the Manor, May Sanchez, Pauline's old neighbor, was doing final prep so that I could just walk right in and get to work after returning from the nuptial Mass. I couldn't do it all that day and I knew it. I had dropped by May's house a week earlier to ask if she wanted a job at the Manor. I knew she could cook—I had tasted the dinner she had made that night and it was enough to convince me to hire her on the spot.

Since we had started working together, I realized that I now had a bona fide female friend, one who shared my interest in the culinary arts and one with a wicked sense of humor. This was going to work out really well, if our first week together was any indication. Her execution on one of the many duck ballotines was flawless; I had only had to show her once how to prepare the bird for cooking. I felt as if we had been poaching ducks for days and, in actuality, we had.

"That is one gorgeous gal, that Mary Ann," Dad said, firing up the Volkswagen's engine and taking us back to the Manor.

They were right; everything about Mary Ann D'Amato was perfection. Her dress, a fitted strapless number over which she wore a decorous bolero jacket for Mass, flared out to perfection around mid-calf. Her hair cascaded down her back in perfect waves yet looked as if she hadn't spent more than a moment combing her tresses. Her makeup was understated and dewy, her lips a shimmery pink, her fingernails done in a sedated French manicure.

"Kevin, on the other hand, looked like he was going to his death," Dad said, coaxing the Vanagon up the steep hill toward the Manor. "I've never seen a boy look so scared in all my life. And I've seen a lot of grooms."

"Is the Joyce boy coming to the reception?" Mom asked.

"His name is Brendan and yes, he's coming to the reception," I said. "I don't know why you insist on calling him 'the Joyce boy.'"

"Yes, he's a man now, Oona," my dad said, pointing out the obvious.

"Well, of course he is. I'm not intimating that you're dating an actual boy. And it's just an expression, Belfast," Mom said, turning around and giving me a look.

Back at the Manor, everyone was doing what they were supposed to, the girls putting the finishing touches on the dining room, May executing the hors d'oeuvres in expert fashion, the boys tuning their instruments. Cargan, in particular, was in fine form, busting out a reel that propelled Mom and Dad onto the dance floor, the two of them high-kicking and stepping as if they were two much younger people. Out of nowhere, Brendan Joyce appeared and joined them on the dance floor, grabbing my mother by the waist and swinging her around until her feet gave way and she was off the ground, my much taller boyfriend hoisting her in the air. Cargan finished the reel with a flourish, taking a good look at his bow, strings hanging off disconsolately, before leaving the stage to repair them.

Brendan came into the kitchen, flushed and out of breath.

"I think you almost killed my mother," I said. "But in the best way possible. I think going out to one of Cargan's reels is her true wish in life."

"Man, your brother is quite the fiddler," Brendan said. "Amazing."

"He is that," I said, tossing him an apron. "You're on cocktail-hour duty. The wedding guests should be here any minute."

A few minutes later, I could hear my father glad-handing the bride's father, telling Lieutenant D'Amato that he had never seen a more beautiful bride. From the dining room, I heard the muted strains of instrumental music, less Irish this time, more conventional and suited for a multiethnic guest list. Cargan came into the kitchen and handed me a wallet.

"Your boyfriend lost his wallet while dancing," he said. "I'll stick it up here until later." He placed the wallet on the stainless steel shelf above the sink.

"Thanks, Car," I said. "You sound especially good today."

He held up his bow. "Recently restrung. And restrung again. Helps a lot."

But that wasn't it; it was my brother's talent.

The cocktail hour under way, I stripped off my chef's coat and entered the dining room so that I could toast the bride and groom. Kevin looked better than he had at the church, the color returning to his cheeks. I gave him a hug, feeling a little of the old familiar even after all these years. His chest, his arms, his neck all felt the same but I didn't allow myself to go there in my mind; rather, I broke the hug quickly, my face turning red at the thought that I was hugging my former love, now a man married to someone else.

"Place looks great, Bel," he said, looking around. "I don't know what you've done but this isn't the Manor of our junior prom."

"We've been trying since I got home," I said. "I've been breaking their old habits, one by one, and making them see things in a whole new way." It was the only way in the competitive wedding-hall game, and while my parents, and Cargan to a certain extent, were reluctant to change, they were starting to embrace the idea that change might be good. "You're a married man, Kevin," I said, as much to him as to myself.

He held up his left hand, displayed the ring on his finger. "Amazing, right? Loo says she's finally made an honest man out of me."

"Loo, also known as your new father-in-law," I said. An arm encircled my waist and I looked up at Brendan Joyce, more flushed than he should have been for passing a tray of mini roast-beef sandwiches.

"Congrats, man," he said to Kevin. "Bel, can I take a break? I would love to have a pint with the groom," he said.

"Yes, you can take a break," I said. "Tell May to keep the minisandwiches coming when you get back to the kitchen. Seems like they are a big hit."

Kevin took the last one from Brendan's tray and popped it into his mouth. "These are great, Bel. Where did you get the idea for mini roast-beef sandwiches? They taste like they've been marinated in butter."

"Buttermilk," I said, smiling. "And, you'd be surprised where I get my ideas," I said, looking at Colleen as she walked by.

Before I went back to the kitchen, Kevin leaned in close. "Ever hear from Pauline Darvey?"

I thought of the photo on my phone. "Not a word," I said, starting for the one place where I felt most at home: the kitchen. She was gone and she wasn't coming back, and even though she had caused a heap of trouble for a lot of people, in my opinion, she needed to stay gone. Maybe I would come to regret that decision, but as I entered the kitchen, deleting the photo as I went back through the swinging doors, I didn't think I would.

The dinner was one of my best, if I do say so myself. The effort had been worth it, even if Lieutenant D'Amato had asked if he could have chicken instead, the ministrations to the duck not a skill that impressed him. I prepared a couple of cutlets and sent them out to him, and watched his face light up when he saw two pounded-out breasts on his plate with a side of carrots, just as he had requested.

When it was over, and Mary Ann and Kevin had said good-bye to their guests, I stood in the foyer near the oust of Bobby Sands and waved to the couple as they exited through the big doors of the Manor and out to their car. *Their* car. *Their* house. *Their* wedding.

*Their* life.

I kept whatever it was that I felt off my face, plastering a smile there and bidding them farewell and a safe journey to their honeymoon destination in Aruba. Behind me, my brother's voice whispered in my ear, his tone caring and knowing at the same time.

"You'll be fine, sister."

I leaned back into him, let his hand rest on my shoulder. "I know I will, brother."

When the last guest had left, I went into the kitchen to survey the damage, but May and Fernando had cleaned up almost everything while Colleen and Eileen worked on stacking the dishwasher. It had been a long day and everyone looked exhausted. "Go on," I said, ushering them out of the kitchen. "Everyone take off. Dad will work out the details on the tip later and make sure everyone gets their cut. Does that work?"

I had my answer when everyone scurried out of the room and away from the Manor. We were all shot, it seemed.

Brendan came in and wrapped his arms around me as I washed my hands at the sink. "What's our plan?" he asked.

"Our plan is that we go to our respective apartments, get cleaned up, hopefully get our second wind, and then meet at the Grand Mill for a drink or three." I looked up at him. "Work for you?"

"Sleepover?" he asked, putting his hands together in prayer.

"Oh, definitely," I said, hoping that a night with this

patient, loving, and devoted guy would wipe away the feeling that I had just lost the last best friend I had in the world to someone else.

"I'm off, then!" he said, and after giving me one last kiss, one that held the promise of what was to come later, he left the kitchen. I heard the front doors of the Manor slam shut, Mom's and Dad's hushed tones in the office next door the only other sounds.

I pulled off my apron and let my hair loose from the clip holding it up and did one last sweep of the kitchen, my eyes landing on the shelf above the sink, Brendan's wallet sitting there. We had all worked at a fever pitch that day and I had forgotten to tell him that his wallet had fallen out of his pocket. I took it down, the wallet opening in my hands, a few coins dropping out onto the tiled floor, a dollar that hadn't been in the bill compartment fluttering into the sink. I tried to catch anything else that might fall out, the wallet and its contents representing its owner well; it had the look of the sometimes scatterbrained Brendan, a guy with a huge heart but not devoted to an attention to detail.

Before I closed the wallet, I caught sight of the photo section, the one that held a few photos of Brendan's family. There was his mother, standing on the Cliffs of Moher, windblown but smiling; there was another one of his sister, Francine, a nice girl from what I remember of her growing up here in the Landing. His father, a carbon copy of his son. And one last photo, one that I didn't expect.

It was Amy's graduation photo, tucked into the last plastic sleeve, a heart drawn in the corner of it.